Snow and Straw

Also by Tracy Daugherty

148 Charles Street
The Land and the Days: A Memoir of Family, Friendship, and Grief
High Skies
Dante and the Early Astronomer
Leaving the Gay Place: Billy Lee Brammer and the Great Society
Let Us Build Us a City
American Originals
The Last Love Song: A Biography of Joan Didion
The Empire of the Dead
Just One Catch: A Biography of Joseph Heller
One Day the Wind Changed
Hiding Man: A Biography of Donald Barthelme
Late in the Standoff
Axeman's Jazz
Five Shades of Shadow
It Takes a Worried Man
The Boy Orator
The Woman in the Oil Field
What Falls Away
Desire Provoked

SNOW AND STRAW

THREE NOVELLAS
ON THE
LIFE OF POETRY

TRACY DAUGHERTY

Broadstone

Copyright © 2021 by Tracy Daugherty

Library of Congress Control Number 2021949263

ISBN 978-1-937968-97-7

Design & Typesetting by Larry W. Moore.

So Much Straw first appeared in *Ploughshares*.
Portions of *Akhmatova's Notebook* first appeared,
in slightly different form, in *Southwest Review*.
The author is grateful to the editors for permission to reprint.

Broadstone Books
An Imprint of
Broadstone Media LLC
418 Ann Street
Frankfort, KY 40601-1929
BroadstoneBooks.com

CONTENTS

So Much Straw / 3

The Education of Jack Elliot Myers / 45

Akhmatova's Notebook / 117

Notes / 191

8

What dies before me is myself alone:
What lives again? Only a man of straw—
Yet straw can feed a fire to melt down stone.

—Theodore Roethke,
"Straw for the Fire (1953-1962)"

SO MUCH STRAW

The end of my labors has come. Such things have been revealed to me that all I have written seems as so much straw.
Now I await the end of my life.

—Thomas Aquinas

1.

How did I come to God? As you see me. In these dark Kentucky woods. The hermitage—really no more than a square wooden hut with a desk, a single bed, and a hot plate (you seem surprised) . . . this quiet retreat has been my cherished home these last four years, even as I have remained largely away from it, in my house in Fort Worth with my children and my wife. Only once a month, for a week at a time, have I taken advantage of the monks' hospitality and brought my typewriter to the pine forest, but my craving for solitude and communion with the Divine have kept my mind here even when I was away, and have sustained me throughout each of the last four years in that noisy old cattle town where my mother and father raised me.

"Government big enough to give you everything is big enough to take it away": these were the first words I ever learned to read as a child. It's something Thomas Jefferson said. I tell you this to demonstrate the contrast between the spirit of Fort Worth and the contemplative atmosphere here, on the grounds of Gethsemani—at Vespers, say, when faint echoes from the monastery bells drift up through the fog and the trees. The Jefferson quote was printed at the top of the prescription pads used by my childhood doctor. He was an early supporter of the John Birch Society. Apparently, he wanted even his young patients to know that American citizens should not be tyrannized by centralized government. This stray fact about the mild zealot charged with protecting my health, along with the knowledge that the man who delivered me at birth was the brother of a well-known bootlegger who had become one of the most successful businessmen in our community, tell you most of what you need to know about my earliest spiritual indoctrination.

When I was growing up, the local Chamber of Commerce liked to boast: "Fort Worth Is Where the West Begins!" In those days of fierce white pride and explicit racial segregation, it was closer to the mark to admit, "Fort Worth Is Where the South Continues."

These details explain why, on my initial evening as a resident here four years ago, in early August 1969—my first return visit since Tom's passing—I was unaware until late into the night that dozens of red ticks had attached themselves to my lower legs and were busy draining me of blood. The contrast between my usual orientation and the quiet of the hermitage . . . the murmuring birds outside my window, the trees, tender, rooted shapes assembling themselves in the mist . . . these gentle surroundings unclenched my mind, my troubled spirit, and

3

made me almost forget my damaged body. The last contact I'd had with the outside world before entering the monastery that night was to listen to a radio broadcast in the taxi that drove me to the gate— the latest body counts from Vietnam. Naturally, the news reminded me powerfully of the sainted man whose hut I had come to occupy. I remembered that, after his terrible death, his body had been returned to the U. S. in a jet carrying dead soldiers from Saigon. Later, many of his followers found this circumstance gruesome, but I suspect Tom would have appreciated the bitter irony. No one ever said a monk can't develop a grim sense of humor. Keeps matters in perspective, I imagine he would have said.

The radio's war talk also put me in mind of my former doctor's mistrust of American leadership—a sentiment I now shared with him, and so had Tom—but the moment I settled my wheelchair and my typewriter in the hermitage, Fort Worth, Washington, D. C., Southeast Asia—they all scattered into the distance like starlight gleaming through the treetops while the bells of Compline sounded. Instead of Thomas Jefferson, I heard the words of my dear old friend Thomas Merton: "We pray best when we are no longer aware we are praying," he used to counsel me. I wheeled slowly around his hut, touching his bed, his books.

From one of the fragile volumes slid a torn slip of notepaper, its corners just beginning to yellow. I recognized Tom's handwriting. In apparent haste, one day or night, he had scribbled, from the wisdom of Herakleitos: "True peace is the hidden attunement of opposite tensions." And from Auguste Comte: "The Living Are Forever and Increasingly Ruled by the Dead." Was this a glimpse of his mind, his heart, in the days before he left here for his fatal trip to Bangkok?

A fragrance of beeswax candles clung to the hermitage's cloth curtains—from Tom's many nights of silent prayer and contemplation, I assumed. Through the black woods I saw the muted glow of the vigil lamp in the chapel down by the monastery compound. I fixed myself a simple supper of rye bread, pineapple, and cheese. Locusts jazzed in the bushes just outside the door as I ate, and then fell quiet as thunder rolled through the forest. Swiftly, stealthily, the elements of a storm had collected in the now-purple sky, blotting out the stars. I changed into my pajamas, just the bottoms, took my medications, the blue-white pills and the jumbo red ones. I plugged in my electric typewriter. I knew the abbot had acceded to Tom's request to wire the hut shortly before Tom left for Thailand. The whir of my machine's motor sounded ungodly in the silent intervals between thunderclaps. Already, I was adjusting to—tilting towards—stillness and absence. I was vaguely aware that my legs itched. I placed a blank sheet of paper in the typewriter. No words trembled on my lips or at the tips of my fingers. No melodies swelled in my head and yet in my very lack-of-thought I felt I was singing a series of psalms. The Psalm of the Murmuring Birds. The Psalm of the Gentle Black Trees. The Psalm of the Porch and the Rocking Chair. The Psalm of the Stars. The Psalm of the Rain Beginning to Fall. The Psalm of the Streaked Lightning . . .

And then, as though I were standing across the room from myself, I heard myself scream. The typewriter blazed in my hands and a massive jolt toppled me from my wheelchair. Minutes later, when I realized I'd fallen unconscious and was just now struggling back to blurry awareness, I heard the wind in the trees, the rain pelting the humid windows, the typewriter buzzing, the clock ticking above the bed, and I smelled the shame of my soiled pajama pants.

So. As you see, God came to me.

It was not the first time.

2.

The first time I saw God, He came hurtling at me from a star-pocked and coral-powdered night sky above a deserted ghost island. Morotai was the island's name and I was there, alone, because I had quite literally drawn a short straw. "You'll have your gasoline ready to burn the place up," the section captain had instructed me. "And you'll have your jeep outside to make a run for it. If they follow orders, they'll hit the tower first and you'll have some warning."

The year was 1945: my third deployment as a member of the 424th Bomb Squadron's radar section in the Pacific. I was twenty-five years old. I sat in the radar tent with the captain and my buddies Fendler and Mills, breathing coral dust from the bottoms of our boots, blinded by spears of sunlight through rot-holes in the tent's gently flapping canvas top. Fendler and Mills stood stiffly, sweating, each holding in their dirty hands long paper straws. A cut-off stub lay in my palm. Chance had chosen me for the assignment. "Intelligence has intercepted Japanese communications," the captain explained to us. "We know that two suicide units landed in the bay on the far side of the island yesterday evening. We expect an invasion sometime tonight. They plan to take the airstrip, kill the tower operators, and then proceed to the radar tent, presumably to steal our technical data before it can be destroyed. We've got no back-up, no time to mount a defense. This afternoon, we're evacuating all units—except for you, Griffin." He placed his hand on my shoulder. Did he pity me? "If, for some reason, the invasion is called off or delayed, and there's time for a team of us to return and gather the data, we'll await your communication. If the enemy proceeds as we believe he will, we've no choice but to destroy everything. It's essential that you carry out that task." "Yes, sir," I said. Fendler and Mills looked at me like two mourners glancing into a friend's open casket.

"I'll be in continuous contact with you by field telephone from headquarters," the captain said. "Don't set off the gasoline until you're absolutely sure they've hit the tower or until you get an order from me. Is that clear?"

"Yes, sir, but—couldn't I just grenade the place?"

"Too risky. Some papers might not burn. You're going to have to be thorough—every file's got to go."

For the rest of the day, as rumors spread through camp that the Japanese were 47,000-men strong across the bay, propeller backwash from the departing B-24s chalked the palm fronds white with coral dust

I placed my duffel full of clothes and a few days' rations in the back of the jeep. I shaved and washed my face, using my helmet as a sink—as though preparing for a special date.

"Man, wouldn't an ice cold beer taste good right about now?" Mills asked me. He cleaned out his side of the tent and packed his stuff. I nodded. From my small radio, on a bamboo stand beside my cot, Tokyo Rose squawked, "I really feel sad about all my boyfriends on Morotai. I like you boys. I'm thinking about you today while you eat that tasteless dehydrated food. I could just cry when I think this is going to be your last meal on earth."

"Turn that damned thing off," Mills said. "Griff," he said. "You ever think about God? Like—like on Judgment Day?"

Under the circumstances, the question struck me as obnoxious. I didn't answer.

"Honestly, I think if God was sitting under that tree over there, and some good-looking woman was standing across from Him, half-naked, maybe, in the chinaberry bush . . . or hell, even a *lousy*-looking broad . . . I'd run to her, and so would every other healthy man in this shithole. Unless he felt he was in danger, and then, and *only* then, would he approach the Old Fellow and say, 'Beggin' pardon, Sir . . . '"

Fendler rushed in to say goodbye, spiffy in his khakis, smelling of lavender talc. He was already imagining R & R somewhere, though the officers had promised no leave. "Say your prayers, fellows, and I'll see you on the other side," he said. He shook our hands. "Griff, don't try to win any goddamn medals out there tonight."

By 4:00, I was alone in the camp. I arranged square metal drums from the shower stalls in front of the radar tent, as a protective fence. I set all the data files in the center of the floor, to make it easier to douse them with a five-gallon gas drum. Thunder grumbled in the distance. Lightning seared green clouds behind the palm fronds. By the ocean's edge, wet sand glowed blue, like freshly-fallen snow.

I had forgotten to pack my musical scores and my books, *Rhythmique Gregorienne*, Dom Mocquereau's *Gregorian Chant*. The books' pages curled, stiff as parchment—all that tropical heat. I stacked the items on my cot, to remind myself to stuff them into my duffel. I turned my radio on and sat still gripping my carbine. The Beethoven String Quartet Opus 132 swelled in the speaker—Beethoven's sublime musical dialogue with Heaven. Do you know it? Lydian harmonies . . . well, they calmed me. It was like receiving a warm massage. Everything around me in the tent—the books, my boots, a coffee thermos, one of Mills's crumpled old cigarette packs—snapped into astonishing clarity as if, until touched by the music (like a sudden infusion of blood), they had remained partially immaterial, neither part of this world nor out of it. The one discordant object in the tent was my gun. It lay across my lap like trauma twisted into steel. I imagined an Imperial soldier thrusting his shoulders through the canvas doorway. Could he really kill me while the opus played? Could I possibly act against him? I knew the answer. I knew I was being naïve. And yet the music continued to hold me in some sacred space beyond the tangible moment.

I remembered, as a child, hearing our ragged local symphony practice Beethoven in the basement of St. John's Episcopal Church in Fort Worth. I credit the music with showing me the possibility of alternative worlds, beyond stern doctors prescribing sour medicines and lecturing me about civil liberties (whatever those were), beyond bootleggers-turned-oilmen preaching the gospel of supply and demand, legalities be damned: if you did something good with your money, like putting your brother through medical school, then who the hell cared where it came from?

The music in the church basement invigorated me intellectually as well as emotionally—the complex structures of its movements, the themes weaving in and out, disappearing then reappearing in fresh variants. On my tenth birthday, I believed I could actually feel my brain expand, like the purple irises in my mother's garden swelling forth, in the spring, from within their thin green shoots.

In the afternoons, after school, I'd dial through stations on the old Crosley radio in the storage room of my father's wholesale grocery, hoping to discover more Beethoven, only to find fiddles and plodding banjos; drag-racing ads out of Oklahoma City; announcements for county parades sponsored by the Chamber of Commerce and the Ku Klux Klan (above-board and highly visible back then). I returned to the church for my musical nourishment. I donned the red cassock and the white surplice of an altar boy and enthusiastically joined the congregation each Sunday, singing the processional hymns, "Stand Up for Jesus . . . "

The priest recognized my precocious understanding of the music. He did not have to work much to persuade my mother to furnish me with further musical education. She was a piano tutor, giving lessons to all the Southern Baptist children in our neighborhood. Every day she sat me at the keyboard but it was soon apparent that my skills as a composer—my intuitive feel for structure—were far greater than my playing abilities. The priest insisted that my grasp of structural development would be enhanced by a fuller grounding in Western history. "The superb richness of Romantic melodies, the reasons for their evolution, will open for you if you realize the significance of Goethe, Schelling, and Novalis," he said. "An awareness of the politics behind the French Revolution will enable you to appreciate more deeply the passions behind Beethoven's the Eroica . . ."

Everything he was saying . . . I suppose, after all these years, his words led me to this moment. I've landed where I belong. He was pressing on me the same broad knowledge Tom sought through his solitary studies here in the hermitage.

In any case, to say the least, the Fort Worth public school system did not offer the depth of education I craved. No Latin or Greek. No Aquinas, no Augustine. The curriculum struck me as being on a par with, or maybe a bit below, the stock-car ads bellowing late at night on the scratchy AM radio. The priest recommended a program of study in France, at the Lycée Descartes in Tours. His sweet soul loved saving underdogs, evident in the church's food drives, the used clothes give-aways. He relished the thought of sending a West Texas boy to Europe! He helped me apply for a full scholarship, and draft a letter offering to do maintenance work or to sweep the headmaster's floors for room and board. It took six months, but finally I received my acceptance letter from the school. My ambition burdened my parents. Horribly. My father had always assumed I would go into the oil business—"The only business there is," he said, echoing most older Texans I knew; I guess they'd forgot about bootlegging, or maybe it was all part of the same wheeling and dealing. My mother feared France was "immoral." As a good Episcopalian, she felt deeply suspicious of Catholicism. But the priest convinced her this was a unique and splendid opportunity perfectly aligned with my unusual sensibilities. "You cannot deprive him," he said. The family could only afford a one-way ticket on an ocean liner.

So, in the fall of 1935, at the age of fifteen, I found myself sleeping in doorways in Saint Nazaire and Tours—I had arrived several weeks early for the school term. I carried a French-English dictionary along with a small bag of clothes. Slowly, I began to teach myself the language. I was amazed at the ease with which dark-skinned men and women walked the towns' cobbled streets and stood laughing in the plazas, openly. Like most white, middle-class Fort Worth boys, I had been taught to act distantly polite toward black folks, but I believed they could only be laborers or "mammies." Their proper place was somewhere out of sight.

At the Lycée I studied history and science as background to my immersion in the growth of Gregorian chant. I was entranced by the elaborate, interlaced notes—like the Celtic knots in the Book of Kells. I wept with joy at the complex antiphons for Lauds and Vespers, the recitation of the psalms followed by a gentle refrain. At the end of my studies, I was admitted, with a scholarship, to the School of Medicine at the University of Poitiers in Tours. Already, five swift years had passed since I'd returned to visit my family in Texas. France had begun to shape me more than Fort Worth ever had.

9

Psychiatry was a fresh field of study at the university in those days; what fascinated me was the overlap between music and mental health care. Following pre-med, I became an assistant to the Director of the Asylum of Tours, Dr. Pierre Fromenty, a pioneer in experimenting with the physics of sound and the therapeutic effects of music—especially Gregorian chant—on previously incurable patients suffering from nervous disorders.

It seemed to me that the central problem shared by these men, exiled as "lunatics," was simply this: they appeared alike to an outsider but to each other the perceived differences among them were intolerable. They screamed at one another, attacked one another, murdered one another.

Dr. Fromenty was convinced that musical stimulation of the left pre-frontal cortex produced emotional, perhaps even spiritual benefits. We were just beginning to unlock these effects. Unfortunately, war-rumbles were causing mass mobilizations throughout the country, eerily reminiscent of the erratic behavior of the men inside the asylum walls. Many of our staff members were recruited into the army in response to German aggression on the eastern border. This ended our experiments. Americans were ordered to return to the United States but I refused to leave. France had molded my character and I couldn't abandon my friends in a time of crisis. Under Dr. Fromenty's direction, we arranged to disguise as mental patients the children of German, Austrian, and French Jewish families living in our region; we strapped them into straitjackets and used the asylum ambulance to transport them to underground allies in the countryside, who smuggled them to the port of Saint Nazaire and then on to England.

For several months we conducted this sober work until German soldiers occupied the town, requiring safe conduct papers for everyone. At barricades every few blocks, they stopped people and checked their documents. The remaining Jewish families had no choice but to hide in back-street boarding houses. One day I learned that an informer had passed my name to the soldiers. It appeared on a Gestapo death list. With help from my friends, I fled one night to Saint Nazaire. Finally, I was evacuated to England and then to the States. I arrived back in Fort Worth at the end of 1941.

Naturally, coarsened by experience, I saw the place differently now. Immediately, it was clear to me, as it had never been before, that the people I had always dismissed as laborers, as "mammies," were no less helpless than the people I had been working so hard to save in Tours. The hateful attitudes aimed in their direction, their contemptuous treatment by demagogues in the Texas power structure, were just as arbitrary, evil, and manipulative as those of the Germans toward the Jews. The word *other* began to lose its force for me.

My parents welcomed me warmly into their house, fed me, tried to fatten my "alarmingly skinny" frame. My mother insisted I see a doctor for a complete physical examination. That "immoral country" had undoubtedly infected me with *something*. My old doctor was dead now—lung cancer; smoking, a habit he had repeatedly warned me against as a child, a warning I'd ignored in Europe, learning from my friends a deep appreciation of the French Gitanes. The doctor had left his modest fortune to a friend of his, a man active in the Klan who would one day officially form the first local chapter, here, of the John Birch Society. He helped elect a succession of mayors running on the platform of "segregation forever."

My father offered me a job in his store—temporarily, until I regained my footing. He offered to speak of me to men who trafficked in oil field equipment, men who might find me employment. I couldn't see staying in Fort Worth. I missed the deep bass rumbles of the pipe organs in France's grand cathedrals. As long as war threatened to ravage these blesséd instruments, to sweep away all of my friends, the families starving in hiding, how could I concentrate on anything else?

I enlisted in the Army Air Force. As it turned out, I was not to be stationed in Europe, but rather in the Asian-Pacific Theater, first on a base at Guadalcanal, then in the Solomon Islands, finally on Morotai where, now, in the gusts of a gathering storm, listening to Beethoven's opus, I waited to be the single casualty of a Japanese invasion.

3.

Listen. Do you hear the thunder? It's faint, but this time of year, at this time of day, you can almost always catch the low clatter rolling through the hills if you're still enough and quiet. Perhaps I don't need to tell you this. Which newspaper do you write for? The *Courier-Journal*? Probably, in town, at your office, in your house, you listen every day for this. I imagine Tom here on the hermitage porch, in the rocker, straining to hear the sky speak to him just before Vespers each evening.

After absorbing the sparseness of this room, it's tempting to think of Tom sitting perpetually still, barely breathing, his eyes closed from dawn till dusk. Besides my typewriter, my radio, my wheelchair, my small bag of medicines, clothes, and the four framed photos you see on the shelf by the door—my wife, Elizabeth, my children, John Junior, Gregory, Susan—I've added nothing to the space. But as you can see, Tom was not a complete ascetic, and the image of him meditating round the clock is clearly off the mark. How would he have written all his books if that were true—though, as you must have experienced, writing is a form of meditation, or it can be. His cherished volumes: *The Divine Comedy* and Vernon's famous commentaries on the poem; Allen Ginsberg—the Beats accepted Tom as one of their own; photographs of the world's great cloisters. I'm happy to say I introduced him to photography and the camera seems to have given him enormous pleasure in his final years. On the wall above the hot plate—that's his print, not mine. El Greco. I found it tacked there four years ago, curling in the awful humidity, the day I arrived here in a cacophony of maddening crickets. An interesting choice, "St. Joseph and the Child," not one of the painter's best-known works. Take a close look. That's Joseph, the foster-father of the Savior, standing in his purple robe and golden over-garment, clutching the child to his waist. Below him, down the hill, the darkened city of Toledo, El Greco's adopted home—clearly, a stand-in, in this painting, for human community. Its eclipsed nature, the lack of light, doesn't speak well for humanity, and perhaps accounts for the tender melancholy in Joseph's face. Look at him gazing, almost aggrieved, at his son. He knows what this earthly life will do to the boy—God's grand plan notwithstanding. And that's precisely why I find this choice of images so remarkable. It's the sadness of the salvation story Tom wished to meditate on each day. Above Joseph's head, angels offer laurels of glory but he doesn't notice them. He casts his gaze earthward, at the boy, at the desolate town. At the coming anguish.

My eyesight is still not the best. I wear these polarized glasses to ease my sensitivity to bright lights so perhaps I am missing some nuances in the painting. But the image was the first thing to strike me when the Merton Trust asked me to become Tom's official biographer, and allowed me to move into this hut for certain periods of time each summer and fall, to *experience* his last years.

I know, from my conversations with him, that he was deeply troubled by the push-pull of the world. He hungered for greater communion with God, which required greater solitude; at the same time, he could not turn from the world's turmoil, the calls of his many followers to be more active in anti-war demonstrations, in civil rights marches and the like. To me, *that* is the significance of his choice to tack El Greco to his wall. The glories of Heaven await, its mysteries are open to revelation, but Tom's allegiance was also to unseeing humanity, to the poor child who would suffer as a result of the growing shadows. The child is the Savior, yes; his place is in Heaven. But he is also flesh and blood. I'm convinced Tom felt this schism in his body—as painfully as an actual muscle-tear.

The harshest thing the abbot here ever said to him—one year when he feared Tom was becoming too famous because of his books and ignoring his spiritual commitments—was, "What you really want is to be sitting high above Times Square beneath a neon sign flashing, 'I AM A HERMIT.'" The comment hurt Tom because he had to admit there was a sprinkle of truth to it.

Next to the hot plate, the portable record-player . . . you'd think it was mine, given my love of music, but no, I brought this transistor radio to listen to. The hi-fi belonged to Tom, and the album beside it—yes, take a look. Another instance, I think, of the world's increasing hold on him toward the end of his life. He told me he loved Bob Dylan. I can't hear the beauty—to me, it's all just electronic noise—but I've played this album again and again, in an attempt to draw closer to Tom. I was wary at first. After the lightning strike and the terrible shock from my typewriter—well, as you can imagine, I didn't want to touch *anything* here. Obviously, the hut was hopelessly wired. But I plucked up my courage for Tom.

Do you know his poem, "Fire Watch?" It begins, "Watchman, what of the night"—an echo of Isaiah 21, he told me, about the fall of earthly kingdoms: "Upon a watchtower I stand, O Lord, / Continually by day, / And at my post I am stationed whole nights, / And, behold, here come riders, horsemen in pairs."

As you must know, Dylan wrote a famous song paraphrasing this same passage, one of the reasons Tom appreciated the singer. I suspect he also sensed, beneath Dylan's public persona, a similarly reclusive personality trying to negotiate celebrity.

Dylan set Isaiah's doom-imagery to an upbeat tempo, foregrounding the tension between apocalypse and ecstasy.

Similarly, Tom's poem is a paean to the peaceful Kentucky wilderness: "The world of this night resounds from heaven to hell with animal eloquence." But Isaiah is its subtext—Isaiah, with its dire warnings that the "birds of prey will summer upon them (the people who flee the city) / and all the beasts of the earth will winter upon them."

Ecstasy and apocalypse: an unlikely twinning, perhaps, but Tom appreciated Dylan, I think—the way he appreciated El Greco—for seeing how inextricable they are.

Certainly, I felt the proximity of light and dark as dusk and squalls approached the island of Morotai, and I heard the first faint clattering of Japanese bombers.

4.

Fendler, Mills, and I had always called the Japanese war planes "Washing Machine Charlies" because of the rattling they made overhead. That night, at the first low approach of the sound—I was crouching in solitude on the island, the Beethoven drawing to a close—I caught a whiff of Fendler's lavender talc, a memory-trace tucked inside my sinuses, a manifestation of my longing to be with my friends, to be anywhere on the planet but here.

Earlier, I had checked to make sure the matches were dry. In the radar tent, I repositioned the gas drum nearer the files. Now I walked outside into puddles of stars—reflections of the sky in dirty ditch-runoff. Motors droned louder. Dozens. Hundreds? The eastern horizon brightened with moonglow . . . but the moon hadn't risen. Thunderclaps poured from the earth. Hundred-pounders, I estimated, smacking the ground every twenty-five yards or so. Headed in my direction swifter than I would have guessed. No time to do the job and also make the jeep. I turned back toward the radar tent just as a shell shrieked downward. Shrapnel whizzed past my legs. Hot coral peppered my face. I couldn't catch my breath—all the air on the island had been sucked to sea. I cringed beside the tent, looked up, and saw God streaking, silver, out of the night's stillness. My body split in two—the upper part, the brain-part, concentrated coldly on the bomb's angle of descent. The lower part drove like an overheated piston over the snowy coral toward a ravine we had used as an ammunition dump. "*Mater misericordiae*," I screamed at the sky at the instant an unseen force slammed my torso into the gulch.

Two days later, I woke in a hospital bed to discover that, miraculously, the rest of me had remained attached to my torso. "Concussion," I heard a doctor say. His face was a splotch of light. "Damage to the sub-arachnoid area of the brain . . . "

I was told I was "damn lucky": one bomb had landed twelve feet on one side of me, another had hit seventeen feet to the rear. The Japanese had confiscated the radar data and the jeep. Then they'd abandoned the island, figuring either it was not strategic enough to hold or planning to return with plenty of reinforcements to seize it. A team of our men had managed to slip in quickly to assess the damage to the camp and to find me twisted in the ditch.

I lost my musical scores and my books.

Over the next two weeks I began to realize something had happened to my vision. I received letters from home but the only way I knew they came from Fort Worth was by the familiar cheap feel of the paper. I couldn't read the addresses or the words. People in the hospital ward seemed to be moving through a moribund fog. Even low lighting in the room pained me, causing massive headaches. I had enough points by now to be billeted out of the army and to return to the States, but not if doctors kept testing me in hospitals. I pretended to be fine. I could see just well enough to fake my way through most situations.

On the day of my scheduled release, the chief doctor argued for my detainment. "He's still in a traumatic state," he told the other medics. "Look at his eyes."

"Please," I said. "I've been in the Pacific for over three years now. I promise I'll go to the best doctors once I get home."

"All right, soldier," he said at last, wearily. "Get yourself examined just as soon as you muster out."

As I was packing my duffel someone told me the news: the B-24 in which Fendler and Mills had been evacuated from Morotai on the day of the invasion had been shot down over the Sea of Japan. All crew and personnel were missing, presumed dead. Searches had been suspended long ago.

On the month-long boat trip back to the States, I kept testing myself for signs that my eyesight was improving. I'd blink unusually hard; close my eyes for long periods and then open them wide. Dark glasses helped reduce the daylight-pain but really, from the deck, all I could see was a surge of blue and an occasional white spume. When we pulled into the San Francisco Bay, I was dizzied by an assault of fluttering white blurs; the catcalls and hooting from my shipmates informed me I was watching rows of young girls wave their hankies at us.

Buddies guided me into the mess hall where we ate our first steaks and drank our first whole milk in years. We went back to the kitchen for seconds and thirds and even fourths. But for months, years, we'd eaten crap. The sudden introduction of wholesome nourishment acted like poison on our systems. I spent that night groaning in the shadows of the latrine.

Fort Worth felt no more like home to me now than it had when I'd first returned from Tours. "I'm sorry, honey, I promised myself not to cry, but I can't help it," my mother said to me, standing in the doorway of our house. Despite her sweet attentions and my father's patience, I couldn't relax. I found myself unable to remember the names of common household objects—telephone, spatula, couch. The bed was *too* comfortable to sleep in. I lay on the floor with a sheet each night for the first three weeks of my stay. I didn't try to hide my eye problems. The specialist I consulted sent me to a neurosurgeon who informed me I was going blind. He fitted me with thick-lensed spectacles and gave me a powerful magnifying glass for reading, but these would only aid me temporarily. He told me I'd be able to count on "usable vison" for a year or so, no more. I had no hope of continuing my medical studies.

This should have been devastating news to me, but I consoled myself with my love of music. I reasoned my hearing would grow progressively keener. My appreciation for Bach, Mozart, Chopin, and Stravinsky would deepen without the distraction of sight. With my magnifying glass I dove into Epictetus and Aurelius. "Tragedy lies not in any condition," Epictetus said, "but merely in humanity's concepts of that condition." Like Jews to the Reich, like "mammies" to my neighbors, I would become the *other*. As a blind man, I would become an object of revulsion and pity. I was determined to circumvent this inevitability as forcefully as I could.

The brother of one of my old colleagues at the Asylum of Tours was the guestmaster at the Benedictine Abbey of Solesmes in Paris. At my request, he received extraordinary permission from his superior to allow me to visit the monastery, to stay for three months in one of the cells, and, in my remaining time on earth as a sighted person, to conduct research in the *Paleographie Musicale*, in the archives of the Gregorian chant manuscripts.

Reluctantly, my mother let me go. She understood the fragility of my mental state at that point. Love is a matter of glances and gestures, I thought the day I kissed her goodbye. One needn't be eagle-eyed to witness such grace.

Shipboard, I listened to the deck's noisy planks, judged the angle of the sun and the salt-spray on my face, to sense our changes of direction; I felt the worm-pocked walls of my cabin to grasp the limits of my confinement—adjusting myself to a narrowing world.

The abbey monks proved the perfect companions for a man awaiting darkness: the great simplification they practiced in their lives had clarified their features and expressions. A single shadowy glance at each man, and I felt I could absorb his essence.

I arrived at the abbey one evening just before Compline, as the Great Silence was about to begin. "From then until Matins in the morning, no conversation will be allowed unless you have an emergency," the guestmaster told me. He showed me to my cell: a bare room with a simple night stand and a wooden cross nailed above a coffin-sized cot. Through a small window he pointed to a courtyard, at a squat stone structure surrounded by naked shrubs. "Those are the water closets. The nearest water for shaving and bathing is downstairs to the left of the door—a faucet in the courtyard. But you are requested not to leave this cell after Compline. Should you need it, you'll find a chamber pot in your night stand. Your pitcher here will be filled every morning. It is up to you to clean your cell each day." Again, he pointed through the window. "That tall building is where you'll find one of the world's great libraries, and either the originals or copies of every known Gregorian chant manuscript in existence." And with that he left me to reckon with my solitude. Always since, I've associated contemplative silence with the odor of straw—sharp stalks filled my mattress; the grassy smell was the first thing I became aware of as I stood alone in my cell.

The bells of Compline had not yet rung; I scurried down to the water closets and was gratified to find, on a nail driven into the wall, a sheaf of cheap mimeographed paper. Toilet tissue was hard to find in postwar France, and this was a luxury, one of the few the monks allowed themselves, along with an occasional glass of rich red wine. I returned to my cell and began my acquaintance with the solitary life to which I am now accustomed and which draws me so often to these thick Kentucky woods. It was different than the solitude I'd experienced in the radar tent. I don't mean the lack of anxiety; I'm speaking more of . . . *texture*. Something intangible, existing in the space created by stirring one's mental repose into the emotional atmosphere of a place. I dislike such abstract language, but I can come no closer than this in relating my first night in the abbey or most of my tenure here, over the last four years, inside Tom's hut.

My months in Solesmes passed more quickly than I would have thought, given the enforced physical discomfort, the bland meals of cabbage and potatoes, of yellow beans and onions. The rhythm of the bells, reverberating throughout the monastery, calling us to attend the offices, to eat, to retire, the joy of the chanting, the profundity of the silences entered my being, obliterating the cold days, the spare bed, the bad food, the distance to the toilet. Though the water in my pitcher was often frozen in the mornings, and I had to rub a towel across the ice to wash my face, I thanked God for this life-giving amenity. Though my eyesight was almost gone now, I whispered prayers of gratitude for the startling gray light reflected off the snow beneath my window.

Then there was the bounty of work. As Tom once wrote:

> How did it ever happen that, when the dregs of the world had collected in western Europe, when Goth and Frank and Norman and Lombard had mingled with the rot of old Rome to form a patchwork of hybrid races, all of them notable for ferocity, hatred, stupidity, craftiness, lust and brutality—how did it happen that, from all this, there

should come Gregorian chant, monasteries and cathedrals, the poetry of Dante?

Each morning, my suppurating tears left little snail-trails on the heavy pages of the chants.

The time came for my return to the States. On my final day at the abbey, I confessed to the guestmaster that the monastery environment held abiding appeal for me but I didn't trust myself to develop enough discipline for a life devoted wholly to God. I remembered Mills's imaginary choice between a lousy-looking "broad" and the Lord. I had not met a benevolent Being in the depths of my cell as I had hoped I would. "I know my appetites too well," I said.

"Do you really believe your belly is different than any other man's?" the guestmaster answered.

I admitted my biggest surprise of the last few months had been the abbey's smells. Prior to my arrival, I had assumed that men in communion with God would exist in some purified, almost immaterial, realm—that, somehow, their very physicality would be diminished. But no, the abbey's arched stone hallways reeked of dried, hot sweat, bad breath. Mop-water, lingering incense, piss and shit—these odors assumed a liturgical regularity in our daily lives.

"You seem to believe the Great Yes need only be spoken once," said the guestmaster. "God's grace will touch you and that will be that. No. The Yes has to be repeated again and again, and trust me, it never gets easier." He smiled at me. "Your doubt and your discontent are proper first steps."

Naturally, doubt and discontent only grew upon my return to Fort Worth. The oil fields were booming but total blindness engulfed me now; I'd be useless on a derrick. My father had sold off his wholesale business. It had not fared well during wartime. As a child he had raised cattle on his father's ranch. Now, presented with the opportunity, he partnered with a pair of friends to purchase a small share of a precarious farm twenty miles south of Fort Worth. He bought a few cows. My mother continued to earn a little money teaching piano.

Having, for the moment, no other alternatives, I moved into a small shed behind my parents' farmhouse. It was almost monastic in its sparseness, and that suited me now. A single bed, a walnut washstand, a lone lamp in case I entertained visitors. The simple acts of living required intense concentration but I learned to walk the farm's timberlands as though I were practicing scales and arpeggios, repeating movements and steps, recognizing by feel my regular trails, always placing the weight on my back foot rather than on the forward-pushing leg, so that if I bumped into something I would not stagger backwards. I learned the contours of my simple room and my furnishings by orienting everything around the sound of the radio.

In addition to cattle, my father bought chickens and pure-bred hogs. I discovered rather quickly that my deliberate, slow pace and my regular movements matched the animals' needs—they responded to consistency. By touch, I could recognize the flaws and uniqueness of an animal's bone structure that Father often missed just by looking. In this way, I became a livestock farmer. Every year, throughout the early 1950s, our Poland China hogs took the top ribbons at the Fat Stock Show.

5.

You're aware, of course: I almost denied your request of the abbot to visit me here. I am able to travel to Kentucky and to occupy this hermitage so few weeks out of the year, any interruption of my solitude, my communion with Tom's spirit, seems a terrible sacrifice. Naturally, I appreciate your interest in my story. But long ago I lost my pleasure at seeing my name in the newspaper, especially after journalists started referring so casually to my "stunt." I assume you wish to hear about *that* in addition to my work on the Merton project.

The Taoists say, "Desires unsettle the heart." I no longer desire worldly attention—not that I ever did, much.

Among the last pieces Tom ever wrote were his idiosyncratic translations of the Taoist poet Chuang Tzu—poems from the 3rd and 4th centuries B.C. Bob Dylan, Chuang Tzu . . . it's obvious Tom's mind was restless in his last years, though I dispute those who think he was planning to stray from the strict Christian path, to leave the monastery and the monastic way of life in order to engage in direct political activism against the war. He was a solitary at heart, and if he retained any earthly attachments, it was to this little spot of land, to the peace and isolation he had found here.

One of his translations of the Taoist reads:

When great Nature sighs, we hear the winds
Which, noiseless in themselves,
Awaken voices from other beings,
Blowing on them.

That is how Tom acted on me before I ever knew him. He was a gentle force whisking through the world, awakening my inner voice. I never intended to become a writer. In my shed, behind my parents' farmhouse, after feeding the hogs for the day, I would sit late into the night tape-recording my memories of the war, my experiences in Tours, at the asylum and at the monastery in Paris . . . my goal in making these tapes was simply to sort the chaos of my life, to see if I could discover any patterns worth studying for my own improvement. I was a lost and confused young man, existing quite literally in darkness.

A friend of my father's, an editor at the morning paper in Fort Worth, learned from my father that I was making these tapes and asked me one night if I had always wanted to be a storyteller. I'd never thought of myself that way. He asked me what sorts of anecdotes I recorded, and I repeated some of them for him. He said the details were marvelous, vivid —apparently, I had a "photographic memory," he said. He said I should consider writing. My blindness would be no impediment. Using the tape recorder, I could dictate my stories to a typist.

From then on, my efforts to shape what I committed to tape became more concerted. I'd always loved books, but I'd read Aquinas and Augustine for their philosophies—literary form was not something I'd been aware of. To me, structure in art meant *music*. The liturgy. And if I were to consciously write a story . . . well, it seemed to me that, out of the fragments of my life, I had been trying to piece together a spiritual autobiography of sorts.

Given my interests and experiences, then, Thomas Merton was an obvious author for me to seek. Of course, I had heard of Tom's memoir, *The Seven Storey Mountain*. The book had been an astonishing success in the late 1940s, a publishing phenomenon: the very public voice of a private man. A monk! Hidden away in Kentucky, at an obscure monastery called Gethsemani! He had broken the Great Silence and written a compelling and personal story of how it was still possible, in the modern world, to follow a spiritual path.

I asked my mother to find a copy of the book at our local library and to read it to me. After all these years, what I cherish most from the story— more than Tom's details of his spiritual practice, and the tale of how he came to Gethsemani—is his depiction of his little brother from childhood. Here . . . please hand me my copy . . . on the shelf over there, by my pills . . .

Tom says that when he was ten, he'd gather with his friends in the woods of Long Island where his family lived, and they'd fashion huts from boards and tarpaper they found at the building sites of cheap houses thrown up by speculators. His little brother John Paul, five years old, wanted to join the fun, but Tom and his older friends didn't want him around. They'd throw stones at him to keep him away. "And yet he does not go," Tom writes. "We shout at him to get out of there, to beat it, and go home, and wing a couple more rocks in that direction, and he does not go away":

> [H]e stands [perplexed], not sobbing, not crying, but angry and unhappy and offended and tremendously sad. And yet he is fascinated by what we are doing . . . and his tremendous desire to be with us and to do what we are doing will not permit him to go away. The law written in his nature says that he must be with his elder brother, and do what he is doing: and he cannot understand why this law of love is being so wildly and unjustly violated in his case.

From my very first acquaintance with this beautiful passage, I have felt the picture it painted is really of us, *all* of us—our relationship to the world, to the mysteries of God. Love, fascination, and perplexity.

After hearing my mother read Tom, and with my father's friend's encouragement, I decided to become a writer. No turning back. Tom's spirit had blown through me. "One call awakens another in dialogue," the Taoist says.

And yes, I suppose a desire for worldly attention played a part in my decision. In those days, I did seek it—telling myself I did so in order to spread inspiration, as Tom had. I admit I wanted to stage something, to catch the world's eye . . . but it was hardly a "stunt." I insist on this.

Do you know: I was nearly murdered one night on the streets of New Orleans. My son John was beaten at school because of his father's transgressions. However incendiary my actions may have been, to some—and I freely admit my naïvete now—they were not conceived in frivolity, or solely for the drama of the thing.

From Tom, years later, I learned that the Taoists speak of four basic virtues: *Jen*, human-heartedness, empathy; *Yi*, a sense of justice and obligation to others; *Li*, the ritual observance of veneration; and *Chih*, the living fulfillment of these virtues: an inner obedience to Heaven. In all my years, I have fallen far short of these exalted states of being, but their embodiment is what I sought when I offered up my soul to the American South.

6.

So. You want to hear about my "stunt." It was made possible by another encounter with God. On this occasion, it was not that I saw Him, but that He allowed me to see again.

By the time this miracle occurred, Elizabeth and I had been married for four years, Susan and John had been born. I had never observed their faces. I knew them by touch and sound and smell.

Elizabeth had been one of my mother's prized piano students, the sixteen-year-old daughter of one of my father's farm partners when I first met her. Naturally, her father denied her permission to marry me, an older, disabled man with no prospects in life other than feeding his father's livestock. In those early years on the farm, I suffered further health problems, blackouts, mood shifts, foot tumors, temporary bouts of paralysis, all stemming from what was discovered to be severe diabetes. These symptoms were complicated by latent spinal malaria which I had apparently contracted overseas during the war. Doctors told me the only known cure for my condition—in addition to the insulin I took for the diabetes—was to ingest small doses of strychnine: poison.

Hardly the ideal groom. I accepted Elizabeth's father's decision.

I went about my work, winning ribbons for my father's hogs, composing stories with the aid of my tape recorder, and even publishing a few pieces in local broadsheets. Meanwhile, cities across Texas, including Fort Worth, were railing against the U. S. Supreme Court's ruling to desegregate public schools. Crosses were burned in the Negro communities west of our farm. With the encouragement of my father's friend, I wrote newspaper editorials denouncing "white fanatics." The Fort Worth White Citizen's Council warned me to "mind my own business."

Throughout this period, I couldn't help but recall the asylum cells and the small, cheap rooms in Tours, made even drearier by the faded wallpaper, where Jewish families crammed together in fear—the tiny children no one would ever be able to save. I meditated on my own situation, isolated, exiled from the heart of society because of my difference from others.

You see, it was no great leap for me to embrace the Negro cause.

One afternoon I marched through downtown Fort Worth with a large group of white and black activists. We chanted in support of a lawsuit filed by the NAACP against the school district. Elizabeth came with me—she drove us to the march, in fact—and this, I believe, was the turning point for her father. He began to understand the strength of our bond and our mutual beliefs, our shared love of music. Further, he saw how committed I was to not letting misfortune exclude me from any activity.

With his help—his labor was his wedding gift to us—I remodeled an old chicken coop on the farm into a charming cottage for Elizabeth and me. We added a fireplace, a tile floor, and a wood beam ceiling. I continued to "write" in my shed, draping a quilt around my legs against the winter cold, forgetting to feed the animals until a dog or some geese came to my door, murmuring in hunger.

Occasionally, I would take a bus into Fort Worth to talk with a priest I'd met at the march. I confessed to him I feared I was drifting away from the adoration, joy, and peace that had filled my hours in the French monastery. Seeking reconnection with some measure of spirituality, I'd tread through the tired mechanics of worship.

With a local press, I published, one summer, a modest novel about a young man's education in the villages of southern France. I wrote a second novel about the war. Neither book sold well, but both received nice, if embarrassing, notices ("Blind War Hero Makes Book Debut"). It is a mark of my insecurity that I fictionalized my experiences rather than writing the spiritual autobiography I'd intended to tackle. Lack of self knowledge? Fear of exposing my shallowness? Yes, both, certainly, as well as painful awareness of my paltry literary skills. The most valuable aspect of those early efforts was the honest self-assessments I was forced to make. Was it fame I sought? Money? Neither were rushing my way. God had not granted me great talent. He *had* seen fit to inspirit me with a passion for work, and—for better or worse—no patience for injustice. With these qualities as my anchors, with soft cow patties oozing between my toes, keeping me grounded, I aspired to become, without knowing how to do so or even what I meant by the phrase, an artist of the spirit.

> *I do not wish to acknowledge my blindness for fear that this will limit me, yet to deny it is like listening for the footsteps of the dead.*
> *I tell my feet to uncross, yet they remain crossed.*
> *It seems I am rapidly losing the use of my legs.*
> *I am beginning to feel destroyed. I do not wish to become pathetic.*
> *I can do nothing but be silent.*

These lines from my tape-recorded journal, made in the first year of my marriage, reveal my greatest worry at the time: that I had given Elizabeth, for a husband, a wrecked husk.

Another taped remark: *Rarely has life ever seemed so good.*

One morning I fumbled for the telephone inside my shed and rapidly dialed the number of our cottage. Elizabeth's voice answered. "I think ... " I said. I fell into weeping.

"What is it? Honey, what's the matter?"

"I think I can see."

For some weeks, my regimen of insulin and strychnine seemed to have finally taken hold and produced positive effects, keeping the diabetes in check, reducing the incidents of paralysis, strengthening me. Then that morning, as I made my way by feel down the usual trail to my shed, a streak of red swirled before my eyes. I seemed to see a doorway—the back door of my parents' farmhouse—dancing, suspended in air. Suddenly, my eyes felt like two burning stones. My skull seemed to expand and contract.

"Call the doctor," I whispered into the phone. "Please hurry."

I sat in the chair in front of my desk. The room was a series of shattered triangles, yellow, pink, light blue alternately sharpening into vivid movement then fading. I shut my eyes, painfully. I kept them closed until Elizabeth arrived with the doctor.

When I heard her voice, I thought: If I saw her in the street, I wouldn't know her.

The doctor was a patch of blue, Elizabeth a blurry shadow behind him. "I can't stand this," I said.

"What color is my suit?" the doctor said.

"Blue, I think." It wearied me, profoundly, to keep my eyelids up. "Please, stop this. You've got to give me something. It's too much."

I felt the prick of a needle in my upper arm. "Demerol," the doctor explained. "A light dose I want you to be aware of everything. You're experiencing something few men ever have."

I heard him talking on the telephone to my parents. "Enough to distinguish colors . . . he's overwhelmed, very upset . . . "

I don't know how much time passed but I became aware of my parents' voices and my daughter's sweet giggling. I opened my eyes. Susan's round face flitted before me very clearly and then it blurred. It was like looking into the sun. I averted my eyes. "You beautiful little thing," I whispered, and then I passed out.

"Was it a brain injury that caused the blindness?" a specialist asked me. I did not remember coming to his building. It seemed to be evening.

"A concussion . . . ," I said.

"A concussion *is* a brain injury."

"Yes, of course."

"The eyes look fairly good." It was his opinion that the strychnine I'd taken may have had some impact on the optic nerves, but there was no clear reason for my return of vision and no guarantee it would remain. "We must work on restoring circulation to the eyes," he said. He gave me some prescriptions to that effect.

For the next several nights, despite my exhaustion, I was afraid to sleep, fearing that I'd wake blind in the morning. Yet part of my brain yearned for refuge in darkness. Light caused me unbearable fatigue. Elizabeth's pale face became a familiar pleasure, but when I held her now she felt like a stranger. The depth of touch I used to bring to our intimacies was missing. A curious depression accompanied the joy I felt as my vision came clearer. Would I no longer *hear* the rainbow in Bach's Goldberg Variations? *Smell* the yellows of Vermeer? I was trapped in the world of what I saw. It felt lonely.

One day in my shed I came upon my old cane and the dark glasses I used to wear. It was like bumping into a corpse.

I was thirty-seven years old.

I'm sure I would have fallen into lassitude were it not for a writing assignment. My father's friend, the editor, knowing of my monastery experience, learned that a small historical society in the oil-rich Permian Basin southwest of Fort Worth had received state funding to commission a book on West Texas' first church. Apparently, he said, a group of Carmelite monks had been drawn to the desert by railroad promotions in the early 1880s.

Initially, I was not particularly interested in this story; my realignment with my family remained uppermost in my mind. But I needed the money, and even more, I required activity. Perhaps I already suspected I would never fully adjust to sighted life or to family routines. My periodic need for solitude could no longer be ascribed to my "affliction" or my physical limitations. It was becoming clear to Elizabeth and me that I was, by nature, a partial ascetic: a confused and saddened child, standing just beyond the sting of the stones.

One morning in the fall of 1958, on a meager literary pursuit, I set out for West Texas in a rented Oldsmobile. In tumbleweed-infested Midland, I pored through library records to learn that, in the late nineteenth century, the Texas and Pacific Railway had laid iron across the thirty-second parallel through what had once been Comanche country. The railroad's profits depended on families ignoring the dangers of conflicts with the Indians and the rigors of desert existence. The T & P mounted a vigorous publicity campaign to encourage settlements. The first takers were a sect of German Catholics in desperate rebellion against their Kansas diocese. They were solitaries, too. Drawn by the railroad's promises of fresh opportunities, a limitless horizon, the future monks arrived at the extreme Western frontier, in one of the loneliest spots in the world. There, they established a Carmelite colony. Their patch of blasted earth they called Mariensfeld, "Field of Mary."

One chilly October night, I took a bedroll, a coffee pot, and some ham sandwiches into the desert, near where I calculated the monks first alighted from their train. The moon was high but it did not obscure the stars. I heard the yowling of coyotes in the distance, in the cold Carthusian silences. It is not overstating matters to say that, in that vast nothingness, I felt joined to Eternity. My new sight was of little use to me. Except for dirt and sky, nothing appealed to the eyes. The present was erased; everything here was just the same as it had always been. All distracting elements were absent: no beauty, no mountains, no trees. To stay here, I reasoned, trying to imagine the monks' first impressions, a man must face himself squarely, face the realities of life and death.

One of the last surviving journal entries rescued from the colony, before all traces of the sect vanished around 1890, read, "... burned and withered stubble ... sandstorms reign supreme ... "

In the morning, I drove into Midland for some breakfast. I asked the café regulars if anyone had ever heard of the old monastery. Most had not, but one of the waitresses said she thought the ruins of an ancient building, "something to do with the Catholics," still stood in Stanton, a small town just north of Midland. At the mention of "Catholics," the coffee-drinkers sitting on padded stools at the counter, roughened men wearing overalls and baseball caps, stiffened a little.

In Stanton, my nosy questions, in gas stations, in the courthouse, eventually led me to a large, two-story wooden building drooping behind the town's new hospital. Dusty, autumn-browned weeds littered a small yard in front of it. Boards had fallen away from the porch, which had warped badly and showed just faint traces of paint. An outside staircase leading to the second floor had long been boarded up. The second-story stood barely intact. Dust-fogged windows allowed no visible access to the place. From somewhere inside, I heard the monotonous pounding of rock and roll rising from a cheap-sounding radio. Squatters, I guessed: a cruel electric parody of the call to worship.

Later, over a cold hamburger in another dim café, I asked follow-up questions. The answers suited me well enough. I figured I *had* found the old church. Once again, the word "Catholics" prompted the locals to mutter, hostilely. This is a *Protestant* place, they said. *Good folks* live here.

On my last evening in Midland, as I strolled the outskirts looking for a place to eat supper, I noticed a man shuffling through wind-blown alleyways, pawing through metal trash bins for food scraps. His skin looked dark. "An old Negro," I thought. Then the man stood; a streetlamp lighted his face. His skin color had been a trick of the shadows. He was white ... to my shame these revelations rattled me more than if he *had* been black. Briefly, he battled a tumbleweed that had blown against his knees, and then he vanished behind a liquor store.

He never left my thoughts. Throughout that winter, as I worked in my shed on the West Texas book, it was the beggar in the alleyway, the mistaken other that plagued me. He had seeded my "stunt."

Quite simply, to confront my shame, my mistake, I needed to take his place.

Guilt, I have learned, is the difference between loneliness and solitude.

It was Elizabeth I worried about most. Patiently, she had permitted my withdrawals. She never complained about the amount of time I spent writing. She never begrudged the chores or the child-rearing that fell to her, always. She never objected to my trips into the city for church services, now that I had converted to Catholicism. The rituals of worship still felt mechanical to me, but I pursued them fervently. It was not a matter of belief. Throughout life's many stages, I've discovered, we embrace whatever we need, whenever we need it.

My dear wife assured me I was not a "bad" husband, "Oh no no no!" She freely accepted my "requirements." She felt fulfilled as a mother and as a piano teacher. Of course, in spite of her denials, I knew she wished I'd practice, more often, presence.

There are solitaries. And then there are saints like Elizabeth (I don't mean, by this, to simplify her nature).

But now, in any case, I was asking her to imagine me—to see me—as someone other than I was.

I suppose it was another experiment in blindness.

When I first made the appointment with the dermatologist, he didn't grasp my proposal. As a doctor, he could not see past his assumptions: specifically, the belief that I had come to him with a problem in need of healing.

Here was my strategy. It hatched in church. A man I'd met there suffered terribly from psoriasis. One Sunday he told me about a "miracle" drug he was taking. His condition had vastly improved. Oxsoralen, the drug was called. He said doctors used it to treat vitiligo, an infection among Negroes that caused white spots to appear on their skin.

In my shed, I dragged my medical textbooks out of storage. The books said Oxsoralen altered skin color when ingested over a period of six to twelve weeks, along with controlled exposure to a sun lamp.

The man in the alley. People's responses to me as a blind man. The Jewish families in Tours ... I can only surmise that, inspired by Tom's memoir, I'd come to value "right work." Almost without knowing it. Sometimes, Tom had written, one must become a "martyr to the love of one's neighbor."

Additionally, at this point in my life, experience had inclined me to suspect that society's major trouble was selective inattention: the strange ability to perceive what we're taught to mis-perceive, while bypassing what is actually in front of us.

This was the problem in need of healing that I had presented to my baffled dermatologist. My harassment wore him down: yes, it was possible, he supposed, that Oxsoralen combined with a week of fifteen-hour-a-day ultraviolet lamp treatments, might sufficiently blacken my skin.

He'd need to conduct regular blood tests to monitor possible liver damage. There was a risk of skin cancer. My pre-existing illnesses made me, if not cavalier, then oddly unconcerned with side effects. I suppose I had grown accustomed to the inevitability of suffering.

Armed with the doctor's assurances, I had no trouble selling a proposed article to a local magazine, securing some advance money: I would darken-up, take a bus to the heart of the Deep South, pass myself off as a Negro, and record my experiences. I would martyr myself to America's racial prejudice—to *all* discrimination against others—in an effort to promote greater tolerance.

And to grab a little worldly attention. I confess it.

"You're going to make yourself a target of the most ignorant rabble in history," the magazine editor told me. "But if you actually live to write it, it'll be one hell of a piece."

What will this do to my wife and children—not only in the unpleasantness that we might anticipate from racist neighbors, but in some deeper realm of our experience? We are, after all, white Southerners.

I will no longer be loved as myself. Even my wife will think of me as a Negro stranger.

I tell myself I am acting out of duty to my society. What about my duty to my family? Am I really an ethical man? Am I escaping something? Am I a scoundrel?

I am tampering with the mystery of existence.

These notes from my journal at the time reveal my harried state of mind. Whatever was going to happen, I had brought it on myself.

"Now you go into oblivion," the dermatologist said to me on the final day of my treatments in the fall of 1959. That afternoon, a chilly day in mid-November, I boarded a Greyhound bus for New Orleans.

It's hard to recall from this distance, but I think I remember believing that despite my painstaking efforts, I wouldn't *really* pass. Surely I couldn't pull this off. My skin was the color of creamed coffee now, I had shaved my head, but my eyes were blue, the hair on the backs of my hands remained brown, almost blond, and my face lacked anything resembling African bone structure. My speech patterns, my inflections, my vocabulary were bound to give me away.

A man in my church, a retired policeman to whom I revealed my plan one Sunday, assured me none of these details would matter. "Folks'll take one look at you and peg you as a nigger, no questions asked," he said. "Trust me on this. Nothing tighter than skin. If they start to wonder about you later, it still won't make no difference. Nothing'll shake that first impression."

On the bus, I took a seat near the back with the other black folks. No one said a word. Near the Texas-Louisiana border we made a stop in a small country town. A white woman boarded. She roamed the aisle, searching for a vacant seat. None were available. Out of habit, I rose and offered her my place. She gazed at me in horror. She scurried to the front of the bus. The driver glowered at me in his rear-view mirror. The black people, muttering quiet curses, wouldn't look my way. Everyone had accepted me as a Negro. And both the blacks and the whites hated me.

Within the week, I was rooming at a YMCA on Dryades Street, well-known as a Coloreds-Only hostel. I worked as a bootblack in Jackson Square near an unpainted wrought-iron bench where Faulkner was said to have scribbled some of his stories. Each night I scrounged turnips and rice or catfish stew in the alleys behind friendly cafés.

I assume the story's trajectory is familiar to you . . . if not, you can look it up in newspapers of the time. *Black Like Me*, I called it: only a few weeks passed between the appearance of the magazine article and the book contract. It took only a few months after that to extend the story with further texture, then the printers did their work, and I got what I thought I'd wanted. All the attention I could handle: my little "stunt," now the stuff of bestseller-dom.

When my neighbors in Fort Worth learned what I'd done, the Klan hung me in effigy from a lamppost downtown. A sign tied to the cloth dummy said, "Traitor to His Race."

My wife didn't know who I was anymore: the black man who appeared at her door one night, just off the bus from the Big Easy, or the white man who delivered the book to his editor several months later, once his pigment had faded.

And before that . . . in the Quarter, say, or along the shores of the Mississippi River, who was I? People looked at me. Lord knows what they saw. They saw who they wanted to see. Or they saw no one at all.

One incident I didn't dwell on in the book: the night four white sailors off the *U.S.S. Antietam* followed me up Canal Street, yelling, "Boy! Boy! Come here and shine my shoes!" Then they caught me, shoved me into the gutter, beginning to kick—urging each other, "Go for his liver!" They found their target. At that very instant, as my knees cracked against

31

the curb, as one of the sailors retched gin, I turned my head and saw the dark face of God grinning madly.

Of course, it was my face reflected in a window—a fried-chicken place, I recall.

7.

Black Like Me still sells thousands of copies a year. Every month I receive dozens of invitations—sometimes more—to address schools and civic organizations all across the country. People want me to describe the prejudice I experienced when I "became a Negro." Long ago, Elizabeth and the children got used to my hectic travel schedule . . . I considered it my obligation to speak . . . if you earn worldly attention, you should use it to promote harmony, I reasoned . . . still . . . is it any wonder my solitary nature began to chafe against constant exposure?

A break, of sorts, arrived in the form of a letter from Thomas Merton. I was astonished. My book had made its way even to him. He had read it and wished to talk to me about the state of America's cities, he said. Cloistered here at the monastery, he did not have up-to-date information; still, even as a recluse, he remained concerned about society's "fraying." He craved "ground reports on the nation's soul." A remarkable man.

I wrote to say he had been my literary inspiration. He was delighted. So I received my first invitation to Gethsemani. Immediately, I was suffused with peace here, an inner quiet I had not experienced since my days in the French abbey. I'm sure my reaction was heightened by my gaffe in the Louisville train station just hours before arriving at the chapel; I walked into the Jim Crow waiting room, old habit—this still occurs to me sometimes; I don't seem to know where I belong any more—and the Negro faces grew tense. After that, it was an immense relief to see the monastery entrance, to feel the freedom of enclosure, to marvel at the silver steeple in the moonlight, shining amid the dark folds of this endless rolling country.

Tom's first words to me were, "Are you cold? Does the silence trouble you?"

His gift to me was to return me to myself; to remind me that, in spite of my public observances, I need the solace of retreat now and then.

It seems my gift to him—aside from *Black Like Me*, which he said awakened him to the intransigence of American racism—was the camera. Following my blindness and the recovery of my sight, I'd become fascinated with *visual surfaces*. The surface—the skin—had such power to shape our responses to the world. Photography enabled me to explore the purely visual, to study a static image, to find what if anything might be discovered *beneath* it. Tom shared my intrigue; I suppose it's the business of any spiritual person to negotiate the hidden and the manifest.

I showed him how to operate the equipment. In time, he became a profound recorder of shifting light during the course of a single year here, of the living and dying woods all around us.

During our first week-long visit, in 1962, Tom and I discussed the paradox weighing on us both: as he put it, "The monk in hiding himself from the world becomes not less himself, not less of a person, but more truly and perfectly himself, perfected by union with God."

And yet, he said, "Those who are poor for the love of Christ are often poor in a purely abstract sense, separated from real poverty in a safe and hermetically-sealed economic stability, full of comfort and complacency."

He said to me one day, "You know, Griff, Saint Thomas taught that there were three vocations: to the active life, to the contemplative, and a third to the mixture of both. This last is superior to the other two." Tom smiled and shook his head. "But then, in the *Vita contemplativa*, he appeared to contradict himself. He claimed that, by its very nature, the contemplative life is superior to the active."

I knew my Saint Thomas. "Didn't he also say the active life is not to be continuous? It's an answer to a temporary emergency?" I said.

"Yes—motivated by an overwhelming love for God."

"Which can only be measured through contemplation."

We agreed there was no satisfactory resolution to this paradox. The only answer was to live with it and pray on it constantly.

In solely human terms—in the bone-dust of our daily existence—I was jealous of Tom's peace and quiet, and I believe he relished my activist role. We fit together.

Often, after our lengthy talks late into the evening, before retiring to my guest-cell in the dormitory, I would walk the narrow dirt road behind the powerhouse and the laundry, witnessing the dark hills against the stars, and meditate on matters we had discussed. It was in those moments I missed my family most, felt guilt for abandoning them, for that is surely what I had done: whether speaking in public, or retreating to the monastery, I had left Elizabeth alone with the children.

In time, I would find a better balance. (I admit my deteriorating health has had something to do with this.) I'm pleased to say that for the most part, in these last four years, I've forfeited the road. I remain in Fort Worth except for the weeks I spend here in autumn, in the hermitage, trying to write Tom's story.

And what did I learn, speaking to crowds about my life as a black man wandering the South?

I learned what any person smarter than I am already knows, and knows quite well: I was never *really* black. Despite the power of visual surfaces, and the undeniable hostility I absorbed, I can never fully

34

inhabit the soul or the experience of another.

Do you know . . . the worst suspicions . . . it's when I glanced in a mirror. That black face. The hatred I felt for myself.

I have learned how naïve I remain. I have learned the burden of optimism, in a world that tells us, *Death is the only effective educator*.

Forgive me. Besides the joys found in these peaceful surroundings, there is, here, an inevitable engagement with death. I don't think of it as grim. Not necessarily. Much of the work of solitude is preparation for an eternal communion with God.

You've noticed that my stories of Divine encounters—the lightning strike here, the bombing on Morotai, the beating in New Orleans—well, they're horrific. What can I say? I was ill-prepared. The prospect of meeting God in those moments was truly terrifying.

Even now, I can't sit here and proclaim my readiness. I still have work to do—writing Tom's story is central to my task. My final obligation.

Was he prepared to meet Eternity on that dreadful day in Bangkok? Who can say for sure? But if any man had trained for that moment, it was Tom. He was more disciplined than an athlete in his prime, aiming to hurtle a previously insurmountable barrier.

Like mine, his preparatory work involved, in part, wrestling his literary ambitions. The problem of the ego. The last time I saw him, shortly before his last journey, he told me, "By now, I should have been delivered of any problems about my true self. My vows should have divested me of the last shreds of any special identity. But this shadow, this double, this writer has followed me into the cloister. He's still on my track. He rides my shoulders, sometimes, like the old man of the sea. He, too, calls himself Thomas Merton. He's supposed to be dead. Instead, he keeps generating books in the silence that ought to be sweet with contemplation. Maybe in the end he'll kill me. Maybe he'll drink my blood. Nobody seems to understand that one of us has got to die."

8.

Well. Now they are both dead. The writer *and* the monk. And their story—his story—has fallen to a man who may well die before he can complete it.

That battery of pills on the shelf is exactly what it seems: a rickety support system for a man in imminent danger of collapse. Last month, before arriving here, I had two separate surgeries on my feet. Neuropathy. The nerves in my legs are starting to fail. My eyesight is dimming again, this time the result of diabetes. So I inject myself with insulin, gobble my dymelor, and stock up on extra portions of probanthine. I eat my creamed rice, listen to the talk of the rain as it drips into the barrels on the porch, and chant my "amens." The Amen of the Blue Firs. The Amen of the Countryside Awaiting Snow. The Amen of the Iced-Over Pools. The Amen of the Fragrance in the Fireplace.

Then I re-read Tom's journals.

The public life I'd come to loathe . . . I felt compelled to continue it for so long because of America's spiritual crisis, most apparent in its racial violence and the on-going war. But I managed to keep traveling only because I knew Tom didn't have to be in those alleys, those meeting halls, those rallies. He was back here doing what I wished I could be doing. The knowledge of this made me happy. A man who sorely needed it was experiencing the ravishment of solitude. "I am in a condition of ecstasy over the human race," he wrote to me once, after a period of intense meditation. I carried that sentence on a piece of paper in my suit pocket as I delivered speeches to the crowds, in the nerve-shredding smog of unrestful cities.

From time to time, between engagements, I'd ask permission of the abbot to stop by and visit Tom. We'd climb a cold hill near the hermitage to gather wood for the fireplace; at the end of the twenty-minute hike I'd be gasping, trembling. Whether or not I had the discipline for long-term solitude, I didn't know, but certainly I lacked the physical stamina necessary to the life of the true ascetic. Tom laughed at me gently and dubbed the hill "Heart Attack Ridge." Then, a day or so later, I'd be off again on a bus, on a plane, living the existence I was clearly meant to live, at least in those days, just as Tom belonged precisely where he was. "I will consider it a failure of my friendship for you if I ever hear from you again," I wrote him. "Please do not interrupt your contemplations to contact me."

He mailed me letters, anyway. "As for the spiritual life," he said, "I don't worry about it. It just takes care of itself." I didn't believe him, quite.

I knew how he struggled. Still, I was always pleased to get word from him. "One lovely dawn after another," he reported to me. "Meditation with fireflies, mist in the valley, last quarter of the moon, distant owls—gradual inner awakening and centering in peace and harmony."

He was working hard, he said, to insure that his solitude "met the standards set by his approaching death."

But the writer in him, his shadowy double, could not remain as silent as the monk. When, in November 1965, a member of the Catholic Peace Fellowship burned himself to death in front of the United Nations Building in New York, protesting the Vietnam war in solidarity with self-immolating Buddhists in Southeast Asia, Tom wrote newspaper editorials expressing his shock and anguish, his belief that such actions did not accord with the spirit of non-violence so necessary to the peace movement. Militant groups took issue with his "passivity"—as they did with Martin Luther King, Jr. It seemed the world could not be kept from the monastery gate. And it seemed to have devolved into madness. Tom received hate mail. One day, local police arrested an armed intruder lurking just across the stone wall from the chapel. The young man wore a T-shirt spray-painted with a green peace insignia. He said he'd come to kill "that traitorous monk."

Tom tried to take the incident in stride. "Sometimes I wish it were possible simply to be the kind of hermit who is so cut off he knows *nothing* that goes on," he wrote to me. "But that is not right, either." He admitted he was more shaken by the death threats than he'd let on to the abbot. He feared the abbot would force him to quit writing. He'd tried to do so once before, when he suspected Tom's "ego" had become "too invested in seeking readership." Tom had agreed with him—and with the Taoist, who wrote. "Achievement is the beginning of failure. Fame is the beginning of disgrace."

But still he couldn't stop writing. Solitude was both the problem and the solution.

One night, he was awakened by a brutal thunderstorm. A lightning bolt struck the compound's electrical system, down the hill, and was grounded. "I felt the click of it through the whole valley," he wrote me. "I even felt as if electricity were coming out of my feet in bed." He rushed to the porch to check for fires in the woods and witnessed a wounded deer, apparently frightened by thunder, limping through the pines. Tom knelt in the mud beside the hermitage and began to weep uncontrollably—a sign, he said, of his shattered nerves. He prayed not to fear a violent death, but to seek a "flowering" of death in his life "as a part and fulfillment of it."

9.

"Too much humbling," he wrote to me during Passion Week, the following year. "Too many hours in prayer, bent double on the floor." The nerves in his back had become severely strained. X-rays indicated surgery would be necessary. "If something goes wrong on the operating table and my heart stops," he wrote, "the thing I'll miss the most are future afternoons burning brush, watching flurries of snow fall into the flames."

What he could not have anticipated, when he entered the Louisville hospital, was a temptation to re-engage with the world that troubled him even more than the lure of literary success.

Of this part of his story, I know little: only what he wrote in his journals. He skimped on details, and he may be criticized for that. His detractors will say he did not want to leave traces of information that would sully his noble reputation. And yet he *did* address this period in his notes, however sketchily—aware that the pages would be studied after he was gone. Tom did nothing carelessly. And I will say: through-out his life, he would have done anything for the truth except lie about it.

Margie Smith was the young woman's name, a registered nurse who did much more than insert thermometers and check blood pressure while Tom recovered from the surgery in his hospital bed. Unlike the other nurses, she spoke to him. She told him she had been assigned to handle the compresses and to give him warm baths and to keep his room tidy. She had read *The Seven Storey Mountain* and she admired his discipline, his practice.

A familiar tale: the patient's gratitude—*need*—for kindness; the young woman flattered by a revered man's attentions. A clichéd situation, and Tom knew it—the *writer* in Tom knew it. Yet he was helpless to stop the process or change the dynamic.

The power of smiles, tender eyes, fingertips.

The minute to minute agony that he and Margie Smith endured over the next six months, as he made regular visits to Louisville for medical check-ups—such details are missing from Tom's journal. Also missing is any mention of sexual encounters and I do not believe they occurred, though Tom does confess many secret meetings full of urgent touching and affection. He speaks of the "obvious impossibility of human fulfill-ment of his love." He says Margie told him one day he did not know what he was getting into: "I might make you love me in a way that would harm you." He responded, "There is no such thing as an ideal self." He loved her, he said, for the "frailty and indestructibility in her."

Finally, all we know from the journals is that Tom recommitted himself to his spiritual vows and eventually Margie moved from Louisville. They both admired Joan Baez's recording of "Silver Dagger" ("Don't sing love songs / You'll wake my mother / . . . in her right hand / A silver dagger / She says that I can't / Be your bride"). From now on, they would each play it at a certain time of day (1:30 a.m.) and think of each other: an expression of their abiding passion.

Tom hunkered in the hermitage, playing on his hi fi Ravi Shankar and the Beatles, John Coltrane's "A Love Supreme," Dylan's "All Along the Watchtower." Margie had awakened a restlessness in him, a desire to confront the world more fully than ever.

His critics—the militants who considered him *too* withdrawn from the conflicts of his day, the religious traditionalists who decried his activism—have seized upon his relations with Margie as a reason to brand him hypocritical or worse. I see the couple's bond as evidence of his strength.

He once told me he didn't believe a person could be whole without the experience of solitude.

I believe the opposite as well (though I rush to say I have not been a suitable husband or father): wholeness is not possible without some experience of human intimacy.

"To untie a knot, learn how the knot was tied," says the Taoist.

After the last mention of Margie in the journal, Tom writes, "Snowflakes melt on the pages of my breviary. Empty belly. I need this continuity." Following that, a nearly year-long gap. Then this: "Rainy night. Radio. Nashville. Louisville. Indianapolis. Jazz. News. Ads. M. L. King gradually coming clear through all the rock and roll as definitively *dead*. This murder will weigh on America like the carcass of an animal on top of a traveling car, a beast of the Apocalypse."

A few pages later: "I am not really living as a hermit. The world is too much with me. Things are finally, inexorably spilling themselves out. Why? Are things happening because people in desperation *want* them to happen? Is the Christian message of love a pitiful delusion? Or must one just love in an impossible situation?"

From the road, at about that time, I wrote to him that earthly kingdoms were crumbling: America seemed to me to be revealing itself as a totalitarian society. I felt that those of us on the front lines of activism were doing little more than emergency work to hold off holocaust.

He wrote back, saying the world had always been saved by an Abrahamic minority—people like Schweitzer, Einstein, Gandhi, Boris Pasternak. This minority keeps justice alive, Tom said, and now it is it is charged with the heavy burden of averting the needless destruction of humanity.

10.

He died of everything.

That's what they'll say of me after I'm gone: total physical collapse, complete organ failure.

Tom's death was less expected. He should have outlived me by a hundred years. His journals tell us that, a week before he left for Asia, in mid-October 1968, he watched REA workmen string an electric line to his hermitage—at last, the abbot had granted his wish to "modernize" the hut, having received Tom's assurances that technological conveniences would not weaken his rigorous spiritual practices. "The light is coming!" Tom wrote. "Venit lumen tuum Jerusalem!"

Then, on October 18, with the abbot's permission, he boarded a plane for Bangkok. Ostensibly, the purpose of the trip was to attend a conference sponsored by leaders of ten major religions to discuss the relevance of worship in the modern world. Tom would be Gethsemani's representative. (The choice of Asia for the meeting made the Vietnam conflict the unspoken subtext: new methods of fighting, covert activities, undeclared wars, and massive world-wide protests were among religion's strongest challenges.) For Tom, I think the trip served several purposes: a chance to engage robustly with like-minded folks, to meet the Dalai Lama, to study, he said, the "silence of extraordinary faces" (it pleases me to know he took his camera with him), and, not least, to take a break from Gethsemani . . . not from exhaustion with the place, or any desire to suspend his rituals of solitude, not permanently. No, I think it was fear. The grounds no longer felt safe to him. It wasn't just the armed intruder. It was readers of his books showing up at the gate, day and night, demanding to meet him, curiosity seekers, members of the press . . .

The plane's lift into the clouds was a great relief to him.

Lyndon Johnson was about to call a halt to the bombings in North Vietnam.

Richard Nixon was about to be elected the 37th president of the United States of America.

On December 11th, at the Bangkok Red Cross Center, one of the conference sites, Tom delivered a paper on monasticism and Marxist perspectives, arguing that these two paths shared certain values, but this did not mean that materialist culture and transcendental searches overlapped. To his consternation, a Dutch television crew filmed his talk. Afterwards, in response to questions, he insisted he was not a "spiritual rock star."

The meeting broke for lunch. Tom, sweating copiously in the torrid humidity, returned to his hotel room for a shower. Four hours later, conference organizers found him lying on the terrazzo floor of his room. According to the official report made by a Korean nun who was also a medical doctor, "His eyes [were] half open, no breathing, no pulse, no heartsounds, no light reactions of the pupils. The face was deep bluish-red, and the lower hands and arms showed spots of the same colour. The arms were lying stretched beside the body. The feet were turned inside as in convulsion. F. Merton was only wearing shorts. An electric fan of about 150 cm height was lying across his body. The electric cord was pulled out of the plug lying on the floor. A smell of burned flesh was in the air."

220 volts of current, direct from the faulty fan. In the moment he tried to plug it in, barefoot, still slightly damp from his shower, did God appear to him?

I think about that, often.

A poor death for such a rare man; he, who loathed the military's daily cataloguing of casualties . . . he became just another mortality number from Asia ("No. 388/2511: Officially Recorded, December 11, 1968, by the Office of Civil Register [Nel Amphur] Muang District").

Six months later, the Merton Trust, noting my close friendship with Tom, our shared love of writing and photography, asked me to compose his official biography. The Trust arranged with the abbot for me to stay in Tom's hut, absorbing the atmosphere that nurtured him, reading his journals, working.

And so you find me here today, reciting my psalms. The Psalm of Coughing and Sneezing. The Psalm of Heat Rash. The Psalm of Numb Feet Wrapped in Gauze.

I am not the spiritual athlete Tom became but I keep my own rituals. At first light, when the valley is full of mists, I sit beneath bees swarming above the porch, next to spindly spiders on the posts. I contemplate the soaked green countryside, the leaves of the trees just beginning to shade scarlet. I tend to the body's things, shaving, brushing teeth, combing hair, treating minor wounds. I read and write until noon. Then I listen to the radio: Lili Kraus performing the Beethoven Concerto Number 4, say. In the evenings, I meditate on El Greco—the all-too-human Savior, that sad little boy. I eat my simple supper. Macaroni and red beans. Meat patties with onions. The night sky turns the color of a monochrome film strip. I listen again to sublime music. Then I close my eyes in even sublimer silence.

Like Tom, I seek not self-fulfillment but self-abandonment; not to become something, but to become nothing.

42

And the writing? Now that Tom can no longer make his own record, I want the world to remember him. And yes, I hear my own contradictions. How do you remember nothing?

Solitude is both the problem and the solution.

I keep a journal as he did—not to *capture* daily moments (they are lost the instant they occur), but to make note-taking a meditative practice, part of the nature of the hours, man and moment breathing together. I think this was Tom's truest aspiration with his writing: for the words to exist for no reason.

But then something happens. Like yesterday: the shooting of Alabama's Governor Wallace. Ah: you reported the story for your paper? I didn't see it. The news came to me over the radio.

The tragedy itself was lamentable, of course—another leader attacked in the streets, as though we've become a military junta. But even more disheartening was how the shooting unmasked people: those who shouted Wallace was the only man who could save us from the "niggers," and those, equally strident, claiming the "bastard" got what he deserved.

On my radio last night, both sides rushed to invoke Hitler to demonize their political opponents.

In these circumstances, the writer in me has a hard time staying quiet, even as I recognize how useless words have become. Poisoned by these hateful debates. What is a Contemplative or a Writer to do when the word "prayer" sounds as cynical as "peace" or "justice"?

Tom once told me that prayer is not something you "do," but something you "have done to you."

Well.

Tell me, then. The story you will write. What approach will you consider?

If I may, while you think about the shape of your narrative, I'd suggest meditating on a certain modest image: a sad and confused little boy, not weeping, not speaking, not moving, while the brother he longs to embrace hurls deadly stones at him.

Is God the little boy? The brother? Or both?

To prepare your story, I'd suggest plenty of solitude. I'd suggest praying as you write, praying, writing, until you perceive no difference between them—these lonely, lovely acts.

THE EDUCATION OF JACK ELLIOT MYERS

The Story of a Poet's Story

To you is left (unspeakably confused)
your life, gigantic, ripening, full of fears,
so that it, now hemmed in, now grasping all,
is changed in you by turns to stone and stars.

—Rilke

Obituary

From *The Dallas Morning News*, November 29, 2009: "Jack Elliott Myers, born on November 29, 1941, passed away peacefully at home in Mesquite, Texas Monday evening, November 23, 2009. Jack grew up outside Boston, where introspection, discourse, and youthful experience led to a profound love of language."

Beautiful man. Remember your unimportance.

The Vocation

Jack always remembered the afternoon he understood he was a poet. He was twelve years old. He was standing in his parents' back yard on a windy, salt-encrusted peninsula just east of Boston. The peninsula was crowded with third-rate shoe manufacturers, alcoholic lobstermen, and Jewish immigrants, mostly from Russia.

The year was 1953—an already-forgettable interval between devastating storms hawked up by the frozen Atlantic. Always, after a hurricane, the yard filled with sea-debris and litter snatched through holes in broken roofs: a padded wool jacket, shredded, missing its sleeves, deposited by the wind on the family's barbecue grill; an empty box, pristine, dropped into the tomato bed, still smelling of El Productos; a scuffed leather belt, caught like a snake in the fir tree, made for a fellow as big as a carousel pony. Jack's mother, Ruth, called these wayward piles "trash"—"like God emptied his stinking garbage on us again"—but Jack liked to take and rearrange the objects. Not physically—as patterns in his mind, *belt-box-jacket, box-jacket-belt*. He savored the differing lists in his head, the alternate rhythms: *jacket-belt-box*. This mental exercise should have been Jack's first inkling of his poetic inclinations.

Instead, his insight occurred on a late-summer day—the sky going green, pre-hurricane—when Alvin, his father, ordered him to mow the lawn and he refused. He was busy reading the paper, he said. "Reading ain't busy," Alvin snapped. "Get out there and get the job done before the sky falls on us." They argued. Nothing new. What was new was that, later, one of his sisters did something—who could remember what?—that made her father proud: solved a crossword clue, recalled the name of an old actor in a classic movie, something silly like that, and Alvin said, "I've got such smart kids. My kids are my garden!"

Jack walked into the yard. He stood above the dahlias, the roses, the stalks of blue iris long past blooming. From school, he knew the words *metaphor* and *simile*, but not until now, with his father's pronouncement, had he witnessed such a powerful demonstration of what language could do. His father's ridiculous statement changed the way Jack experienced the world. Bright-cheeked Ellen was a rose, pale Sandi a dahlia; Marshall, the athlete, the older brother, his temper quick to flare and subside, was a fading iris.

Now Alvin, still mad about the mowing, worrying about the storm, glared at Jack through the open kitchen window. *Me?*, Jack thought. *I'm a wild onion sprouting in the yard.*

The Vocation, Seen from the Other End of Life

When Jack could no longer write poetry because of his diminished physical and mental capacities, he saw every poem he'd composed in a forty-year career as if from a great distance: they were gray pup-tents pitched on sloping snowbanks in the Himalayas. Red flags whipped above them, dyed by the heart's-blood he'd smudged into every word: the little shelters remained visible even in the worst whiteout.

He imagined crawling inside the poems, one by one, working his way back down the mountain he'd climbed all his life. He'd shut the tent flaps behind him, warm his hands over a pot of brewing leaves. The structures were carefully designed but they were no match for the wind and the snow. Soon, he knew, an avalanche or a landslide would wipe them all out in a single stroke. But, he figured, if just for a while he'd left behind a nurturing space, a port of refuge for some other exhausted traveler, he'd made something sacred.

The Long View

Occasionally, when Jack was a child—late 40s, early 50s—Alvin took him fishing on the crappy creeks tumbling to the Atlantic from the peninsula's granite outcrops. "A glacier smoothed this out," Alvin told him one day, waving his arm at a gully through which muddy water spurted, trying to be a river. "Nothing but ice here, once. Now look at the abundance!"

"Where did the glacier come from?" Jack asked.

"I don't know."

"Where did it go?"

"I don't know."

"Will it ever come back?"

"I don't know. But that's not the point. The point is, always take the long view."

Why? Jack wanted to ask, but decided it wasn't worth it.

In a down vest the color of dung, Jack's father always carried two items: an old cottage cheese container packed with moist earthworms dug from his garden and a small glass flask. Grinding his wide buttocks into the cleft of a rock, he'd turn to his son. "Two things Jews never do," he'd say. He'd raise Jack's pole, stabbing a worm onto the hook. "Jews don't fish." Then he'd pop the cork on the flask. A stinging smell. "And it's for damn sure that Jews don't drink." He'd laugh like hell.

In those days, he didn't add that "chasing skirts" was something else Jews didn't do, but Jack would learn that lesson later. When he did, it took him a long time after that to grasp how his father could lie with strangers and near-strangers when, most days, he could barely tolerate sitting in a room with his family.

If someone asked his father, "How are you?" Alvin snapped, "How should I be?"

When someone knocked on the door of the house, Alvin shouted from down the hall, "Goddammit! Who the hell is it?"

Eventually, from his own life, Jack would understand that sliding into bed with a stranger was not the sort of intimacy his father chafed against at home.

Jack began to take the long view around 1972 when Boston Edison built the Pilgrim Nuclear Power Station on Cape Cod Bay. The strings of unintended consequences knotting the plant's operation started immediately with cost overruns tripling the initial estimate until over 23 million dollars had been committed. Jack read in the paper that 480 million gallons of seawater were cycled as coolant from the bay into the plant, and re-deposited into the tides. Inadvertently, small aquatic creatures got sucked into the system and trapped against sharp intake screens. The screens ground the sea-life into sediment. Released back into the ocean, the granular waste clogged the water's oxygen content and blocked sunlight from above, killing hundreds of other species and gradually warming the currents. Plant shutdowns due to excessive sea temperatures, rendering the water ineffective as a coolant, grew more frequent. Later, when the U. S. government deregulated the nuclear industry, Boston Edison was forced to sell the Pilgrim station to a Louisiana-based company. The plant's new managers lacked any knowledge of local conditions. It was like putting a flounder in charge of an owl habitat.

Jack imagined nuclear reactors popping up beside the creeks he fished with his father. The recycled water would heat the streams until— in the way of unintended consequences—underwater weeds bloomed, snuffing all life in the marshy beds. So the plant's out-of-state managers introduced weed-eating carp into the creeks; in turn, these fish got so big, they outgrew the gullies and the shapes of the gullies, and even the need for water. Crawling warily from the waves, they challenged foxes, voles, and wolves, muscled Dodge Rams out of the way for control of the roads.

Meanwhile, cities sparkled at night, powered by the plant, and people snuggled warmly into beds, hugging strangers or near-strangers. No one was aware that the gullies glowed and echoed with menacing growls. No one knew that, secretly, toxins hummed under dazzling streams of light.

Of course, Jack figured, I must've been an unintended consequence of my father's not-doing what Jews didn't do—getting drunk one night and forcing his wife, whom he could barely stand to talk to, to do things with him she never imagined doing. And now his recycled blood lubricates my veins, blocking my light, choking off my air, pumping through me the toxins I depend on to survive. Dad, I've got it now, I have the long view, Jack thought whenever he wrestled—every day of his life—with what it meant to be a man.

Mystic Whispers

At the end of each week, Ruth switched off the electric bulb in the living room and lighted the candles for the Sabbath.

The year he turned thirteen, while preparing for his bar mitzvah, wondering what it meant to be a Jew, Jack stared at the candle flames on Friday nights and asked himself which was truer, that the candles illuminated spaces inside him, interior caves and tunnels where the voice he called his *self* went searching for the voice of God, or that the candles made every object in the world, and all the voices in them, a single space of whispering light?

Early Memories

The kosher butcher on the north end of Providence Avenue . . .

Jack's mother trusted Jack, as soon as he turned seven and learned to ride a bike, to pedal downtown to buy a pound of hamburg each week. Lou, the butcher, stood like a god in a kingdom of those he'd afflicted: headless chickens, amputated turkeys and calves. Animal tongues clicked in the breeze on little hooks in the windows, like the old ladies in synagogue *tsk-tsking* noisy children. Yellow bird-claws swung on strings from the rafters, as stiff and shriveled as Jack's grandma's arthritic hands —the hands he'd shrink from whenever Ruth took him to visit Nanna at the Hebrew Home for the Aged.

"What'll it be, young man? Livers, hearts?" Lou boomed from behind his shiny glass case.

"He's a goddam crook!" Ruth yelled at Jack once he'd sped back home and parked his bike in the yard. "A dollar a pound for *that* piece of rat-gnawed gristle?"

For the rest of the day she'd exhaust her anger on the laundry, pounding wet shirts then hanging them on the line behind the house as if lynching every horse thief and marauder that had cheated her family for generations, from Boston to the steppes of Odessa.

Alvin arrived home from the steel factory at dusk (after a short detour to Ray's Bar, at the end of the block), stared at the supper table and lectured his wife, "Ruth, damn it, all day I work surrounded by the whole smorgasbord of stupid humanity, and then I come back here and have to look at *this* on my plate? Like some stupid son of a bitch tore off a piece of my flesh and threw it in the oven?"

Jack lay awake at night, dreading the next time his mother would ask him to visit the butcher. He liked riding his bike in the streets, enjoyed the independence and the responsibility, but he didn't relish being in the middle of someone else's battle. It was like hurling his body into his father's box of tacks, out in the garage.

But then, this was *his* battle, too. After all, the butcher was cheating the whole family, not just his mom.

One day after school, Jack propped his Schwinn against the pale brick wall, where the word "Kosher," painted in white, was starting to fade. He startled when he opened the door and the bell above it chimed. The bell always surprised him, no matter how many times he heard it. The sawdust on the shop's floor seemed more slippery than usual, or maybe he needed a new pair of shoes, the soles worn thin. The little wood-shavings smelled like his sisters' doll houses, the high pine scent of perfect lives that never moved, never changed, never yelled, and never grew old. Lou stood behind gleaming glass wearing a bloody apron. He smiled like the Angel of Death.

The shop, stuffed with its lopped-apart birds, smelled like shit and molted feathers.

"My mom says take your thumb off the goddam scale!" Jack blurted while he still had tongue to speak (he glimpsed a silver hook in the window, waiting to snag him like a fish).

Lou didn't say a word. He leaned over his glass case and stared Jack, hard, in the face.

Usually he wrapped the ground beef tight, neat and clean, in thick waxed paper. Today, he handed Jack a gory mess in a leaky plastic bag. It rolled in agony in his bike basket all the way home: his mother's heart, torn from her chest.

Rejects. Tossed in a pile in the asphalt lot behind the shoe factory...

Sometimes after school Jack dropped his bike at the curb and stared through the chain link fence at the useless shoes—each hole in the fence like some lost part of himself, matching the footwear's gaping mouths, emitting silent screams: loafers, Oxfords, slippers, boots, each one missing a partner, right or left, but never a complete pair, and each one tragically gashed or stripped of its polished skin.

After the photographs appeared in *Life* magazine, the pictures of Buchenwald, of skeletal survivors, of the piled possessions of the dead, the shoes acquired a different reality for Jack. Each was a ghost, a silent reproach. Not a mistake whose flaw lay in its making; rather, *that which should never have been.*

Days of Atonement...

"To each one of these coins whisper a sin you've committed in the past twelve months," said the adults, "then toss the coins into the sea. The waves will carry off your transgressions... or at least you'll feel unburdened and promise to do much better next year, won't you?"

None of this made any sense to Jack, and wouldn't have made sense even if he hadn't fasted all day, becoming delirious with hunger. The rabbi didn't require fasting on this particular occasion, but Jack's mother insisted: "Atonement means sacrifice!" she said.

Shivering on the sandy shoreline, Jack did as he was told: slowly, he brought Abe Lincoln's coppery face to his lips and blew into the president's beard, "Impure thoughts," borrowing the phrase from a Roman Catholic friend of his down the block. Then he hurled the penny into the air. Seagulls scattered and settled like scarves on the breakers. The bad part of Jack—but also, he feared, the vital part—tumbled and vanished in the dirty surf.

When he'd dispersed all the coins, when he'd thrown himself away, he slumped on the beach. Starfish oozed at his feet. He gripped his belly. He imagined a sea star trapped behind his ribs, curling its arms into a ball, scraping and dislodging his inner organs, heart, liver, lungs: full atonement for all he was and ever would be.

His mother handed him a cheese sandwich: "Stand up. You're hungry, that's all."

One year, his father, blind on whatever he poured into his flask, ran onto the beach, weaving violently among gently davening figures. He screamed, "Quick, get me a wagon! I'll load up everything I own! Chairs, silver, tools! Everything I've earned with the sweat of my brow... take it ... take it all ..."

His buddies sat him down to sober him up. Jack tried to imagine the wagon it would take to cart away his father's splinters: wooden slats wobbling, metal brackets bursting at the seams. Its wheels turned in one direction only, forcing the contraption to travel backwards. Anyone sitting in the wagon would witness the beginning of Alvin's life crushed by the future rushing toward it. The poor horse hauling all this shit to the shore, its eyes milky and thick, lifted its head in a swarm of gnats and flies...

The old man's performance on the beach that day was no different than a typical Sabbath night, Jack thought. His mother lighted the candles while his father crashed through the house, shouting and shattered from work. Jack watched smoke trickle from the wicks, each puff a silent prayer.

One mild December, workers in the shoe factories went out on strike. Riding his bike, Jack saw men and women picketing for higher wages in the shadows of rejected boots. Most of the workers were Jews. The factory owners mocked them, "Here's your Christmas bonus," and brought in replacements, Italians mostly, a few young Poles, on midnight trains. The owners collected the coats, shoes, and metal lunch pails the striking workers had left inside their lockers when they all walked out, bundled the stuff into trucks, and drove the piles to the shore. The scabs threw the whole pitiful lot into the waves retreating in brown foam to the world's edge.

It seemed to Jack that God, not sin, was the burden Jews carried. The God that made Jews made them poor and ashamed so they'd get hammered each night to forget their emptiness. Maybe it was God they should lug to the shore. Maybe it was God they should hurl into the salt and the wind.

How, and how much, would He change the taste of the sea?

The ragman—Jesus, yes—another early memory, another mysterious figure. Roaming the streets at dawn...

"Bring me your knives! Your cutlery! Your scissors!" he'd yell at sleepy housewives, their heads in curlers poking out of upper-story windows. He'd sharpen whatever had gone dull in their lives.

He walked beside a lopsided wooden wagon, round oak wheels, pulled by a limping mule. The mule's clopping appeared to clear away the ground mist. The ragman took away skirts and blouses, shirts and pants, bibs and overalls that families didn't want anymore. Ruth gave him the purple chiffon nightgown Ellen had outgrown, Sandi's baby jammies, Jack's favorite old sweatshirt—its collar had torn and she'd told him she didn't have time to sew it.

"What does he do with all those clothes?" Jack asked his mother one day.

"Turns them into paper."

"How?"

"Oh, I don't know . . . Mrs. Tuttle told me, once, you boil the clothes in scalding water, thicken it with baking powder, maybe . . . then you beat the cloth and strain it. . . "

Up and down the block, everyone's histories, phone numbers left in pockets, lipstick smeared on a fraying glove's fingers, a collar ripped in anger, a lonely night, a joyous reunion, an unexpected encounter— pulped to snowy blanks.

War

Maybe, just maybe, the problem had always been this: the ocean had swallowed his father once and he'd never been the same. In the belly of the *U.S.S. New Orleans*, far below the water line, Alvin had stirred vast pots of Shit on a Shingle for his fellow sailors. Above, on deck, the big guns bucked and recoiled.

Into the pots he shoveled dozens of pounds of dampened salt.

Back home, at the tip of the salty peninsula, Jack swam in a sea of his own inside his mother's belly. One day she spied a starfish on the beach, stooped to pick it up, and felt her body buck. Jack was ready for the world, ready to fight his wars.

By the time his father came home, billeted out, Jack was already running through the garden aiming a wooden rifle at his brother. His father—this stranger—looked like a cloud of smoke roiling in the doorway: the after-effect of some distant, massive discharge.

Beautiful man.

The Worst Night

Hard to pick just one. The evening of his thirty-seventh birthday, perhaps. 1978. He'd just gotten a raise at the university, but that year Jack didn't celebrate his birthday because, three weeks earlier, his wife had left the house with his two young sons. Boxes of junk she no longer wanted blocked the curb, wilting in the merciless Dallas sun: purses, shoes, board games (*board games, purses, shoes?*).

"I know," she said, just before slamming the car door in his face, the kids screaming in the back seat. "You don't drink. And you don't chase skirts."

Waltzing

One night, the year, the very month he turned eight, he came home late from playing with a friend. His parents' bedroom light was ablaze.

He shimmied up the spindly apple tree outside the window to get a better view inside.

Who *were* these crazy people?

They faced one another across the bed, his mother and his father, Ruth wearing a peach chemise, Alvin in khaki shorts, no shirt. Gray hair grizzled his puffy chest.

The discussion was intense—not unfriendly, but fraught, somehow. The mystery of adult concerns. Jack's mother gestured to her right; his father responded by waving his left arm. It looked like they were rowing a boat together across a river, not quite in synch. The water was rough but they were managing—just barely. Then the sun went down: his mother turned out the light.

Jack sat in the tree watching the stars come out, feeling taller, bigger than he'd felt before, and larger than he knew he'd ever become.

Another night, a few years later, his parents were going to a club dance, invited by some friends of theirs who were members. Ruth came spinning into the living room wearing a blue, sparkling gown. Alvin, in a suit and tie, twisted her awkwardly around the coffee table where she'd laid out late-night snacks for the kids: potato chips and tuna fish sandwiches.

Who the hell were they Who did they *think* they were? Marilyn? Fred Astaire?

Jack's mother blew his father kisses from across the room, gyring her arm—great, broad gestures—smacking the backs of her fingers. It was the saddest, ugliest display he'd ever seen, Jack thought: two old people trying to be sexy, pretending they were happy.

Decades later, sitting alone in the house his wife and kids had left, he decided he'd made up his mind much too soon about permutations of beauty, and he longed to tell his mom, who was dead, "You're a knockout, babe."

Teacher

Sometimes his mother made him pick up his sisters' dolls, dresses, and shoes, scattered on the floor. "But *they're* the ones who made the mess!"

"But I asked you to clean it!"

He'd throw the shoes in a closet, stuff the dresses into drawers. Then he'd arrange the dolls against the wainscoting in his oldest sister's bedroom. Barbie and Ken and Tammy. He'd shake his finger and lecture the stiff figures as if they were his pupils: "Listen, guys, next time, I better not find you all over the damn house! You got it?"

He discovered he liked being Teacher. His teeth flashed, extra bright.

Sombreros

If someone had told him, "One day you'll be an educator, and you'll raise your boys in Texas" (retrieving them every other week, in tense consultation with their mother), he'd never have believed them. But it was Texas that hired him to teach, out of school.

The up side: Six Flags, the Cotton Bowl, mom-and-pop market stalls along the lazy river in San Antonio. Lots of boy-friendly souvenirs. From visitation outings, Ben and Seth came back to their mom gripping plastic six-shooters, football pennants, and velvet-lined sombreros, hideously pink and purple.

One day, when Jack arrived at Nancy's house (a circus of scattered buttons, Lincoln Logs, dirty BVDs), Seth, who'd been on a comic book binge, leaped from his bed into Jack's open arms. He wore a blue terry-cloth towel safety-pinned round his neck. "Don't worry, Dad! I'll save you!" he shouted. By that evening, exhausted, overheated, sick from too many hot dogs, he buried his head and wept into his Mexican hat. The hat's dark bowl was so wide, it swallowed half his body.

After that, whenever Jack thought—from an impossible distance—of these beautiful little men, he imagined great sombreros soaked with tears wobbling in their beds.

Desert Trees

What can you say about a Hebrew School teacher so frightened of his students he feared the consequences of arming them with lessons, much less wisdom?

That was every teacher Jack ever had.

They didn't trust these kids to grow up and have kids of their own.

Early in his education, he dreamed of becoming a teacher so he could teach his students not to trust teachers.

The teachers saw themselves as gardeners, cultivating recalcitrant young sprouts, except their idea of gardening was to pound the plants with shovels and hoes until they flourished or withered. In the class-room, this approach translated directly into frequent beatings with rulers.

As a result, Jack linked being whacked on the butt with Moses's wide grin, displayed on a wall poster behind the teacher's desk. Jack always faced the poster during his punishments. The old patriarch was gesturing at sunny blue clouds, pleased by some cosmic joke Jack never got.

"Bend over! It's for your own good, boy!"

The school smelled like the butcher shop, clammy and dank, the scent of battered flesh. Beatings became especially severe when Jack and his pals began to wonder what bubbled the girls' blouses—particularly Rita Kurlansky's, so tight the buttons were about to fly loose beneath her long, dark braids.

On some days, school seemed like a gangster movie, a giant extortion racket: "Take that, you little twerp—and give me all your dimes. Why? So we can purchase trees to plant in Israel. Don't you want the desert to bloom for your brethren? Are you holding out on me? You little *macher* . . . How's *this*, then? You want another? What? We've told you: each dime is a leaf in the Sinai. You keep hoarding coins, boy, the tree in your name will be shrunken and black, barren and full of thorns!"

Wrong, Jack thought. *I'll close my eyes and make a better tree than God's.*

Recalling the Days of Atonement, he whispered to each dime, "Sin, sin, now you're infected with sin," before dropping it in a teacher's open palm.

Clearly, sadists were drawn to the teaching profession. "Please, sir, may I go to the bathroom?" "You may not!"

So the boys shat in paper bags behind the buildings and set the bags on fire. When the teachers ran to stamp out the flames, crapping-up their shoes, the kids laughed until their stomachs hurt. They could do sadism, too. What the hell else were they learning?

In class, in the last seat of the back row, Jack daydreamed of lying with Rita Kurlansky, holding hands, in the cool shade of his desert tree.

Remember your unimportance.

Immigrants

He learned far more at the Hebrew Home for the Aged than he ever did in school—though he hated going there just as much.

His grandma, dumpy and soft as a mound of mashed potatoes in her bed, always knew who he was, though she didn't seem to know quite *where* he was in the room. She'd pucker her lips, strain her head in what she thought was his direction, and end up kissing air. He'd reach for her hand, gristly as a fried chicken wing, and ask her how she was. She'd launch into regrets: how much she missed so-and-so, how fervently she wished for this or that. She longed to go wintering in Miami, the way she used to do (Jack's folks had taken him to Miami on vacation once—rows and rows of roasting Ashkenazis stretched on towels, white grease slathering their noses; he swore he would never be one of them, just as he would never wind up in an old-age home). Watching his mother, now, tend *her* mother, he learned that, when a person deteriorated past a certain point, the only thing you could do for them was to say, "It's okay. Go back to sleep."

Sometimes Ruth told him, "I'd like to sit with Nanna a little while longer." She'd pull a hankie from her purse and dab at small tears. "Here's some quarters for the soda machine in the lobby. Wait for me there. I won't be long."

In the bathroom in the hall, shaky black graffiti: "Inside every old person is a young person asking, 'How the hell did this happen?'"

Old men wearing threadbare coats, waving canes, wandered through the lobby. Occasionally, they'd stop and talk to Jack, almost always in a soupy, eastern-European accent. It didn't seem to matter how long they'd lived in America: when they heard how well-spoken Jack was, they'd ask him about language. One day, "*Fall* I've never quite understood," said a meaty fellow with a beard like moistened flour. "I mean, the season . . . "

"It's just another name for 'autumn,'" Jack answered.

"Does it refer to what the leaves do when the trees let go?"

"Hm. I've never thought of it that way. But I like that."

"Words are strange."

"They are," Jack said.

On another occasion, a man who said he'd fled Poland in the 1940s (Jack had met him here once before) wobbled by and asked Jack what he was doing. Jack was seated in a leather chair, drinking a bottle of Coke and scribbling on loose sheets of notepaper torn from his school binder. "Writing a poem," he admitted shyly.

"It must be lovely to be your age and to be studying poetry in school."

"We don't read poems in school. Except from the Bible."

"Ah! A secret vice! Who are your favorites?"

"I don't really know," Jack said.

"Shelley? Yeats? The Americans? Whitman?"

Jack shrugged. "I don't know them. I just like to make up rhymes."

"Yes, an amazing power, no? Unlocking secret correspondences . . . the way *night* sounds like *nigh*, as in, 'The end is nigh,' just like night brings an end to the day."

Jack nodded, not quite following.

"When I first came to this country . . . " The man's eyes misted. ". . . nothing gave me more pleasure than learning a new word in English. Tasting it on my tongue . . . *evening, whole* . . . it was like kissing a woman while being pulled inside her . . . oh, forgive me, forgive me, young man, I'm . . . "

"It's okay," Jack said. *Go back to sleep.*

"A word a day. That was my regimen. Still is—and tomorrow I turn ninety-seven!"

The old man shuffled down the hall, back to his room. The rooms smelled of unguents. Jack glanced out the lobby window. "*Unguents,*" he whispered, savoring the vowels. Leaves were falling. Jack felt he was rising instead.

Liver Fluke

In biology lab, the teacher made the students observe amoebas and liver flukes under microscopes. The flukes looked like splotches of pissy Jello or gray, flattened footballs. "Yuck," Jack said, and Rita Kurlansky laughed.

"Parasites," said the teacher. Jack heard *pair of sights*, and staring at Rita Kurlansky's chest, thought, *They certainly are*.

"Profusion," the teacher said. "The way life wants nothing more than to live. To spread and spread. Essentially, the fluke survives by turning everything it touches into itself."

Rita Kurlansky batted her eyes, knowing Jack was watching her, but the teacher's last words ... what had he said? ... *profusion* ...

Like a riot? A riot of life? Unstoppable, everything becoming everything else ...

He looked again into the microscope. This time he saw a river of flowers.

Knock Turn

On hundreds of shelves in the school library, he found only one book on poetic form, and no one had checked it out since 1932. When he opened its cover, its spine broke, and dust spores peppered his face.

A *nocturne* was a "night scene," he read, a genre first tried by John Donne in 1633 ("'Tis the year's midnight, and it is the day's"). Spiritual contemplation was frequently the subject of nocturnes, said the book, as night was a "threshold" time where human and not-human blurred in dreams, and altered states of being seemed "imminently possible."

The dust made him sneeze. He couldn't keep reading. He replaced the book on the shelf and it fell apart even more, pages flaking. Was he the only one in the school, student or faculty, who cared about genres, thresholds, altered states of being?

That night at home, he sat in front of the Magnavox with his brother Marshall, watching the fights. Marshall did a little competitive boxing down at McInally's Gym. He'd tried to teach Jack to "defend himself, 'specially since you're a Jew. Don't kid yourself. Somewhere, sometime, boy, somebody's gonna come after you." Marshall crouched barrel-like in the living room, his burr haircut a square of black sandpaper, his pug nose shiny in lamplight. He ordered Jack to "put up his dukes." Then he popped his little brother on the chin and Jack went down. "Get up!"

Marshall yelled. *I will*, Jack thought. Then he thought, *I will not*. His mind seemed to wobble like a broken clock. It wasn't so bad, his scrawny body heaped on the floor, his mind floating somewhere near the ceiling. "You're hopeless!" Marshall said. *Is that what this is?* Jack thought. *Hopelessness? Well then, here's to it.*

Tonight, a pair of flyweights fluttered across the television screen. Marshall stood inches from the screaming box, joining the noise of the crowd, shadow punching along with the pale fighters. "Yah! Yah!" he huffed. He seemed thoroughly alien to Jack—like his fellow students, like his teachers.

Jack's world was a meditative nocturne.

Everyone else's world moved to the choreography of aggression and self-defense. Knock. Turn.

"Oh, come on! My sister could've taken that punch!" Marshall yelled at a black and white figure, no bigger than a bug, sprawled in the middle of the ring on the jumpy screen. A skinny Puerto Rican, down for the second time in only the first round. "Fuck. He's vulnerable to the short right cross," Marshall said.

No, he's vulnerable to not wanting to fight, Jack thought. Look at him. Down again, grimacing on the canvas (imprinted with a Corona beer logo—the fight's sponsor).

"Where's your spine?" Marshall fumed.

Broken, Jack thought. Jack could read the boxer's face, even though it was infinitesimally small on the TV, and the screen wouldn't sit still: it was the face of a young husband scrabbling to make ends meet, enduring another hellish screaming bout from his wife; the face of a disappointing son being told by his father to get the hell out of the house and get a fucking job. All he wanted, this kid, was for someone to help him up and say, quietly, "All right, all right, go on home now." But no one made a move while he writhed across the ring, except for the ref, counting down his end.

The camera zoomed in on him, highlighting his helplessness: worse than absorbing another haymaker. He was trying to remove his mouthpiece, a glistening bar of plastic, but he couldn't manage with his clumsy leather gloves. He was a man trying to pull himself out of himself, and throw himself away.

Jack couldn't watch anymore.

A few days later, after school, he took his bike to the shore and went for a long, slow walk on the beach. Earlier that afternoon, he'd discovered that the book on poetic form was gone. Probably some librarian had noticed its tatters and tossed them out. The book wouldn't be replaced. The other volumes on the shelves continued to claim space . . . *in this corner . . . and in that corner, weighing in at an impressive 450 pages . . .*

Jack was starting to find his tribe: the losers, the hopeless, the ones with busted spines.

He watched a dingy gray seagull poke holes in the sand. Stupid bird. Every day, taking whatever the sea hit him with. Well. What choice did he have? Jack picked up his bike and pedaled into the wind.

"I'm Coming to Kill You . . . "

. . . said the fluke in his dream, quivering like a spoonful of Jello. Then everything turned into everything else.

First Job

Delivery boy, on his bike. For Louie the Fruit Man. Round as a Halloween pumpkin in his blue Hawaiian shirts. "Don't break my heart for a nickel!" he'd yell whenever a customer caught Louie trying to short-change him. "A lousy five cents? What's it to you?"

If someone insisted Louie was a thief, Louie smashed an orange or whatever fruit he could find from the buyer's sack and squeezed out the pulp, maliciously. Behind the counter, Louie's fat wife huddled by boxes of poppyseed bagels, trembling. For her, every encounter with the public was an attack of angina. Every few minutes during the day, Louie screwed up his little red mouth, an expression of pure agony, as if God was stabbing him in the chest.

Jack didn't know how the man stayed in business but he was grateful for the after-school work. If Louie was cheating him, Jack didn't much care. He was happy to have any amount of pocket change. Louie would load the basket of his bike with an avalanche of apples and hand him an address on a juice-smeared slip of paper. "Ten minutes, you're back here, right? Don't let Mrs. Weisberg throw you off track. Woman gabbles like a goose. You got seven more deliveries to make today!"

It was a peachy arrangement—until Bill Smithson, the undertaker's son, stole his bike. Pure meanness. Smithson already owned several sparkling Schwinns. Spoiled by his dad, who feasted on the dead. *Parasite*, Jack thought. Smithson just didn't like him—never had. Jack figured it was because he was a Jew, and Jews didn't support his daddy's business. In any case, the bike went missing from Smithson's neighborhood one afternoon when Jack had a delivery in that part of town. He was in Mrs. Orlovsky's kitchen no more than five minutes, but that was enough. The next day, on the street, Smithson smirked at Jack—*you-can't-prove-a-damn-thing, kike*—signaling he was the culprit.

"You're no good to me without a pair of wheels," Louie said. He fired Jack. Jack said that wasn't fair. "It's not my fault. You know what I mean?"

That day, Jack learned most people don't have the courtesy to say, "I know what you mean."

After school one cold October day, near the rejects behind the shoe factory, Jack spied Smithson walking home alone. He waited in the shadow of the shoe-mountain. Then he stepped around the corner and basted Smithson's nose. The boy fell to the street, glassy-eyed, spurting blood. Jack didn't say a word. His fist hurt but the rest of his body felt like a beacon shining clear across the ocean, lighting all the dark huts in Odessa where his ancestors had dwelled.

Smithson came to his senses and grinned, a twisted jack-o-lantern, teeth rivered with blood. "It's okay, Myers," he said. "It's okay. You're going to be poor all your life. You'll never own anything more than a crappy old bike. Me, I'm going to work for my dad. Believe me, I'll have another chance, someday, to lay you out."

That night, Jack sat in the little apple tree outside his parents' bedroom window, remembering when he'd watched them, wondering who they were. Now, he thought about himself. Who was he? A poet. A poet who'd relished knocking someone to the pavement today. He should tell Marshall. His brother would be proud of him. But then the thought of bragging about what he'd done—the memory of Smithson's ugly, ruined grin—sickened him a little. What was important? For the Fruit Man, it was a few extra pennies shaved off a customer's change. For Marshall, it was getting up once you'd been flattened. Jack listened hard to the night-sounds of his town. Voices, cars, TV music, the buzz of electric wires. It all blended into one vague hiss and flew away on a chilly wind packed with salt. Jack sat for a long time in the bare tree, pretty sure nothing mattered.

Another Bad Night

His sixty-fourth birthday, when the woman he was with suggested they eat raw fish at a restaurant called Thai One On.

Seven months later, he took medical leave from the university. In the chemo ward, when his doctor pronounced the word, "Cholangiocarcinoma," Jack asked him what it meant. The man said, "Bile duct cancer—a rare form. Caused by Asian flukes."

"Rare, eh? Lucky me," Jack quipped. On a silver pole above him a plastic bag quietly dripped. His head was melting.

"Yeah."

"How do people get this thing?"

"Oh, you know, bad sushi? Something like that."

Heaven

How did I get to be an old man? Long after he'd gotten over his astonishment at where his life had taken him, Jack thought often of Alvin and Ruth, many years dead, and he saw them as he'd seen them as a child: giants on the earth. He remembered sneaking into their bedroom and combing through the garments in their wardrobe: pants, shorts, suit coats and ties, gowns and girdles, panties and skirts. They contained multitudes! (A gent at the Hebrew Home for the Aged once told him a poet said that.)

Now that his parents were gone, Jack still imagined them as a child might picture Heaven: sitting on an afterlife cloud, staring down at him. Were they still disappointed?

His poor mother. She wore herself out on him until she was just an old rag on the rocks. If he did something wrong (and never a day went by ...), she'd come at him, waving a mop or a scrubbing brush as if he were one of the household impurities it was her duty to eradicate. "Jack!" she'd scream, like she was having a heart attack.

As she got older, weaker, her voice cracked; a miner inside her was chipping away at her once-formidable walls.

She looked at Jack so sadly when he told her his wife had left.

And later, when *he* left his second wife.

Jews don't do that, her eyes seemed to say. "Oh well, whatever you do ..." she croaked, waving her papery arm. "As long as you're happy."

And Alvin. Did it please him just a little—could he *admit* he was pleased—when Jack defied his teachers' predictions (that he and all his classmates were going nowhere in life, or at best to jail) and became the first kid from their God-smacked town to work his way through college, driven by his desire to learn poetry?

Alvin couldn't grasp it—not a bit of it.

If he appreciated the irony that Jack made something of himself while the Hebrew School eventually closed in a scandal of mismanaged funds, became a weed-lot for nearly a decade before reopening as a private, minimum-security prison, he never let on. After Ruth died, he threw himself into a Vegas-style party life, traveling cross-country on his retirement funds with one ditzy girlfriend after another until lung cancer caught him somewhere between Reno and the Florida panhandle.

Nights, as he lay dying, Jack sat by his hospital bed, whispering, "Go to sleep now."

One early morning, machines beeping, he startled Jack, waking and whimpering, "Was I a good father?"

Instead of being honest and saying no, Jack was honest and said, "In part, I am what I am because of you."

Alvin grimaced as if his son had slugged him. Then he nodded in agreement and drifted off again.

Last call, Jack thought. *Drink up, old man.*

Now, older than his father was when he died, Jack asked himself how was it possible that Alvin and Ruth got so miffed whenever someone broke a glass in the kitchen, or one of the kids dulled the scissors trying to cut through wood, or mud got tracked across the carpet. None of it was important. How could it be that they didn't reserve their anger for the bigger things to come? Abandonment, sickness, death? From the vantage point of age, their domestic explosions struck him as freakish—and as incredibly magisterial as Moses parting the seas.

Death and Fish

The terrible ghosts of his adolescence were every bit as frightening as his folks.

The fish tin men! Lined up like judges in Heaven, droning louder than locusts inside the synagogue.

The building might have been a hive or a larval cocoon . . . and the smell! Drifting through the temple's open door as the chanting soared: briny fish forked from little tins; the sour lunch-breaths of a dozen fathers, the humid stench of their debts . . .

On his bike, passing by the synagogue late in the day, Jack was always fascinated by the spectacle of the minyan, but if he lingered too long by the heavy oak door, they'd snatch him inside and make him kiss the Book of the Dead.

Death smelled like salted herring.

In the chemo ward, death *still* smelled like salted herring.

And always, all over town, muddy shoes. Loafers. One cold winter night, he found, abandoned by a bench on the beach, a left and a right, not a mismatched pair. Someone had left them there, someone the size of his father, maybe drunk and forgetful or maybe suffering from a pinched toe or a burst blister on a heel. Or maybe the shoes had had enough and would no longer go where their owner wanted them to go. Twelve at the time, assigned that day to write an essay on his ambitions, to recite how his surroundings had prepared him for the future, Jack sat on the bench for a very long time, staring at the empty shoes. They seemed to say everything there was to know about his town.

And then there were the peppermint cabanas on the beach, mini Big Tops, red flags waving . . .

This was a few years later. Jack was maybe fifteen. He marveled at the town's attempt to draw tourists: *See how festive we are! We have an ocean! Come swim!* Already, Jack foresaw the future: the town's purpose (its drive to be a town) had collapsed years ago, before he was born, shattered in the surf, tangled in coils of kelp, heading for the bottom. No amount of striped cloth or colorful flags could resurrect its soul. As a child, idle, bored, poking broken crab shells with a stick, he'd been right to grasp that a boy's only choice, if he remained here as a man, was a lobster boat. Someday, he figured, he'd work the nets.

In the meantime ("my greatest ambition . . . "), he was free to dream, a poet.

After school and on weekends, he sat on the sand, staring at the ocean. Sometimes he imagined the Old World, his ancient family. Poet-farmers, poet-merchants. He'd picture lifting rocks, thirty-pounders or more, dragging them one by one into the water, pieces of a bridge to the past. He'd walk to Europe, shedding all his flaws along the way, like the surfaces of the rocks eroded by the water, and he'd arrive like the best idea the world had ever seen.

The bridge would be his temple to himself.

But of course he didn't have the strength to carry rocks. *I believe the rocks are there*, he thought. *I believe, if I look long enough, I'll find the perfect stones, in just the right number, fitting back to back, taking me wherever I want to go in the world.*

Eventually, he concluded that his faith in the rocks—like his faith in poetry—was enough. It was his way of building the temple.

Finally, of course, it was the lobster boats that helped him escape. Summers, all through high school . . . the first paid work he'd done since Louie let him go. Ruth urged him to order applications from junior colleges, and to practice drafting Statements of Intent for the schools (Alvin stayed silent, as though he'd given up on his boy). But Jack apprenticed himself to small-boat captains, aiming to save enough money to get to Harvard Square. He'd seen pictures of the "new breed of college student" in *Life* magazine. Though at first he had no intention of going to college, he figured, from the photos, the prettiest girls in the country lived in Harvard Square. That's where he'd go. He'd write poems and make love to a different muse each day.

The lobster boats made slow circles in the sun, lazy little dances. The experience was almost pleasurable. The captains carried sloshing flasks, like his dad. Occasionally, they offered Jack a swig, and he learned to keep the fiery ripples down.

Naked from the waist up, he hauled dripping cages to and fro—contraptions as wide as his chest. Beyond the twelve-mile limit, Russian trawlers dropped traps the size of small hotels, and scooped up half the sea.

Inside their cages, the writhing black lobsters snapped at Jack's hands: deadly, slow machines. The first time he caught one, he propped the cage on the gunnel. Prehistoric bastard. He looked it in the face. It existed at one end of the evolutionary scale, Jack at the other. Its bright eyes bulged, bigger than his: two creatures, staring down the centuries.

"Boy, you look like a Sephardic wanderer. You look lost," the fishy men yelled at him from inside the synagogue. He'd spent the summer in the sun, getting darker. They meant, "Boy, you don't look like one of us."

No, Jack thought. *Not anymore. Soon enough, you creepy old schmucks, I'm out of here.*

He didn't write a Statement of Intent—at least not then, late May, 1959—but the week before he moved to Harvard Square, he reflected on his childhood. He asked himself what his teachers had taught him. He'd learned that he'd come from a stubborn tribe, that his DNA inclined him toward milking, skinning, roasting animal flesh—useless maneuvers in a failed industrial town on the east coast of the United States. He'd learned that his teachers hated teaching. What had school prepared him for? Bewilderment. Oh yes. He was fully primed for that.

Hell, Louie. Call the cops. We both got robbed.

Mystic Whispers

Late in the day, as the flukes swimming inside his liver tried to turn him into whatever they were striving to become, his mind drifted. He dreamed of his childhood beach . . . he saw himself as a father sees his son . . . *Remember,* he asked his younger face, *remember that day you wanted to die, not believing in the future? Do you remember what stopped you from harming yourself? Finding that wreck, that shell of a boat on the shore . . . the thought of repairing it, caulking its seams, painting it as blue as the sea so that, when you finally set out, no one would be able to tell you from the water. Well, guess what? I'm the future you couldn't imagine. The ocean you'd sail. The possibility you thought God teased you with, holding it just out of reach. How about that? Nice job, kid. Not bad. You got pretty damn far on a wreck you never tried to fix.*

A Beautiful Man

For a while, in the fall of '78, after his wife and kids left him, he supplemented his teaching pay from Southern Methodist University with a moonlighting stint as a bartender in a little pool hall near campus, next to a Dr. Pepper bottling plant. He didn't need the money, especially.

66

Who knew that, in America, a poet could earn a comfortable living as a teacher? Own a mortgage? (Hell, that was news to his dad! News to Jack, too.)

Back in Russia, the poets were in jail. Here, they assigned homework every day.

No, he didn't need the money. He just didn't want to sit alone in the house at night. The silence was worse than his boys' screams when they were toddlers.

Sometimes, some of his poetry students from the college came to the bar to chat with him. One he especially liked: a depressed young man from West Texas, son of an oil driller who expected him to inherit the business. Child of the desert, completely besotted with words—how could he not be depressed? Tracy was his name. Nineteen, twenty. Jack felt certain he was a virgin: half the trouble, right there. The kid had an ear. In class, it was almost uncanny the way he picked up the rhythms of the poems Jack read aloud as examples of villanelles or *a-b-a* or end-stopped lines. He keyed to Jack's voice, to his body's metabolism. He was serious and malleable: a real student.

But a mess. So much to learn. *Was I* that naïve, *growing up?* Jack thought. *Probably worse.* Ben and Seth, snatched from his hugs on these unholy nights . . . they were ten and eight now, engaged with plastic soldiers, armed only with Crayons as their primary means of expression. Jack's students were practice, for when the boys matured.

Who ever thought I'd be a dad? Jack thought. *Who ever thought I'd have something to teach? In goddam Texas, so far from the ocean!* Randomly, it seemed, he'd been swept across the land, the scarred valleys, the serrated plains—all his life, at the mercy of his childhood storms.

Maybe, at last, Jack was learning to treat *himself* as a son.

Around ten on Friday nights, the girls from Dr. Pepper's early-evening shift clocked off work and marched in a big sexy group to the lounge. They carried plastic bags holding changes of clothes. They'd head for the bathroom in back, step out of their overalls, jeans, and tennis shoes—their baggy work garb—and slip into short cocktail dresses. Red, black. High heels or boots. Then they'd crowd the bar, asking men to light their Virginia Slims, ordering sweet, green drinks. The first thing Jack taught Tracy: you see a gal grab a beer or a straight Scotch—not one of those goopy concoctions—*she's* the one you talk to, right away.

On break, every two hours, Jack taught him to handle a pool cue. Between shots, they'd stand at the table, watching the girls. "Which one do you like?" Jack asked. Invariably, the boy pointed to a quiet one or one who hadn't slipped into a slinky little skirt. Obviously, the beautiful, bold girls, the ones who laughed loudest and acted like they owned the place—hell, they did, didn't they?—scared the shit out of him.

"She's got stubby legs," Jack would say. "Watch her when she stands." Often, during these evenings, he was reminded of Rita Kurlansky. The memories made him laugh. Dazzled by her other attributes, he'd taken a long, long time to notice her legs.

"Oh."

"Don't idealize women. I mean, nothing wrong with stubby legs, if that's what you like. But look."

Hopeless. The kid couldn't see it. He couldn't see the table, either. Passed up obvious shots, misread the angles, left his opponent spectacular opportunities.

Knock. Turn. Well, he'd learn.

One night, chalking his stick, Jack said to Tracy, "See that fellow over there? Big guy by the jukebox?"

"Yeah."

"He and I are about to get in a fight."

"Why? Do you know him?"

"No."

"Jack, you haven't been near him. How can you get in a fight?"

"He's been looking at me."

Earlier, behind the bar, Jack had finished four Lone Stars. Swing an arm and smash something solid, he thought. Knock yourself silly. Tonight, he was missing his brother. Missing his boys. "I don't like the way he's staring."

Missing his folks.

Someone had taken them all away. Loaded them in the back of a crappy wagon. Who?

Where would they all wash up?

The Pepper girls danced with one another. Slow. Close. The men at the bar sidled up to them. Jack looked for the one *he* liked. Soon, the place would empty out. Shame and addiction, anger and need, arm in arm, stumbling through the beer-stained door.

"I don't understand, Jack."

No. No, of course you don't, beautiful man. Because you can't read the room. The angles of incidence, the territorial claims, the distance from here to there. How we become who we are. Tonight, fates will be cinched. Believe it. Futures decided.

Ah well, Jack thought. Probably a poem here, somewhere. Not exactly an epic. Jack laughed to reassure him—this young, bewildered soul lingering by his side tonight instead of his boys. "I gotta get back to the bar," he said. "No fighting. Promise." Soon, it would be Last Call. He gave the kid a hard, affectionate pat on the neck. *Remember your unimportance.*

First Kiss

April. Tenth grade year. When Rita Kurlansky's parents announced they were taking a pleasure trip to Europe, leaving Rita and her older brother alone for two weeks—"You're responsible young adults now"—Jack seized his chance.

No. It was Rita. *She* made the move.

Her father was a dentist. The Kurlansky's house overlooked a private golf club, a nine-hole course. In front of the giant living room window with its view of the manicured fairways, a bright green pool table sat at a ninety-degree angle to a wet bar and an expensive B & O stereo system. One Friday night, Jack brought his Bill Haley and the Comets and Buddy Holly records to Rita's, and they played them while Rita taught Jack to play eight-ball—an attempt to wait out her brother, who said he was leaving the house soon with his buddies to watch a high school baseball game. Rita's father had taught her to play pool. She was pretty good. She leaned on Jack and draped her arms around his waist to show him how to position the stick for a particularly difficult shot. He was quick to calculate the table's angles, the concept of English, and the speed at which to hit the ball, but the glancing touch of Rita's skin against his wrist, her perfume (sugar and apples?) rattled him so, he didn't sink a thing. He caught his reflection in the living room window: pale, skinny arms, nose like a twisted parsnip smashed into his face. What was a schlub like him doing with Rita Kurlansky—Rita the lustrous, the bounteous, black-haired and gliding?

No one had ever just *liked* him!

The game bored her. Jack was no competition. Her brother still hadn't left for the baseball. Jack heard guttural laughter—three or four boys—from her brother's room. To kill more time, Rita showed him her violin. She was a member of the school orchestra. More than the instrument, which was exquisitely beautiful, honey-brown, delicately curved, the plush, velvet-lined case intrigued him. The velvet was cool and blue, an endless night sky. Close the lid, snap the silver locks, and you tucked whole galaxies beneath your arm, the Music of the Spheres.

Rita bowed a couple of notes. Then she sighed. "Fuck it," she whispered. She locked away the music and nodded for Jack to follow her out the sliding glass door to the patio. On her way across the room, she ducked behind the wet bar and snatched a bottle of Scotch.

They ran, giggling, down the sloping lawn toward the golf course, Jack realized, then, that Rita had exceptionally short legs. She couldn't keep up with him. They collapsed together on the seventh green. A little red flag, stuck in the hole, fluttered above their laughter.

The ground smelled like chickpeas—some pungent chemical meant to keep the grass green.

The velvet sky spread above them.

The Scotch stung his mouth.

Before he'd left his house, Jack had slipped into his pocket a small piece of jade from his mother's vanity cabinet. She'd kept it there so many years, Jack was sure Ruth had forgotten it. She'd told him it had been a gift from his father. He'd brought it to her from the war, from an island in Asia where the ship had stopped on R & R.

"Green is the color of eternity," Jack told Rita—the explanation his mother had given *him*.

"For me?" Rita said. Jack set the jeweled lozenge in her palm.

"For you," he said. His mother's little piece of timelessness.

Rita bent to kiss him.

"Rita! Rita, where are you?" her brother yelled from the deck. Behind him, Buddy Holly cooed.

"Shhh," Rita said to Jack. He imagined the boys sprinting down the slope, swarming him, kicking him senseless in a sand trap.

After five minutes, her brother gave up. He screamed, "We're leaving!" The sliding glass door slammed shut.

Then Rita's breasts were bare. Her tongue was down his throat. With his hands he weighed her warm flesh, like creepy Lou behind his scales. He brushed his palms across her nipples, a blind sculptor memorizing what was real.

In the grappling of their eager, young bodies, his mother's immortal chip fell to the ground. They never got it back. Jack assumed someone must have found it the following day: a grumbling duffer slamming his club into the grass after three-putting the seventh.

Harvard Square

"How can you live like this?" Alvin growled, promptly leaving the room.

A different muse each day, Jack thought. Goddesses exposing Rita Kurlansky as plain and mortal.

Well, that was the plan. It didn't work out that way.

He had a single room in a residential hotel one block east of the Harvard Bookstore. No kitchen—just a hot plate and a coffee pot, a Murphy bed fitting poorly into the wall. Often, it crashed into the middle of the room, threatening brain injury.

"You're on your own," Alvin had told him. "Expect no help from me unless you decide to go to college and make something of yourself."

Jack had saved enough money from the lobster boats to survive for six months. Six months was an eternity—especially in a paradise of bookstores. Grolier's Poetry Shop: Kenneth Rexroth, Lawrence Ferlinghetti, Allen Ginsberg, Gregory Corso, Arthur Waley's translations from the ancient Chinese . . . Where to begin?

At night, knowing no one, he'd head up cobblestone streets to the Brattle Theatre and watch a double feature, alone. The Brattle's patrons didn't say "movies." This was *cinema*. Buñuel, Hitchcock, Kurosawa, Bergman. Quiet stories of post-war Japan, of Eastern Europe. Mountain villages and desert outposts. In rich black and white, lives unfolded: Jack couldn't believe people survived them. A dozen kids stuck in a single bed, sleeping in an attic stuffed with straw. A woman massaging fat, naked men in rooms made of paper.

In daylight, in the square, he was dazzled by a carnival of street-corner buskers, pamphleteers ("Ban the Bomb!"), pimpled boys from Harvard, and svelte, worldly Radcliffe girls. People retreated into shadows, sharing acrid, hand-rolled cigarettes. On Read Block, Jack spent hours at Tasty's, sitting on a wooden stool, scribbling rhymes and spooning down chocolate ice cream. Or he'd grab an all-you-can-eat-sausage-and-kraut at the Wursthaus and spend the rest of the afternoon regretting it.

In the evenings, after a "cinematic experience," he'd slip down an alley to Club 47, a former coffee house featuring jazz and blues. Black men—*black men!*—with stage names like Mississippi John Hurt and the Reverend Gary Davis made their "git-boxes" cry. The place smelled of grenadine and clover.

One night, before the last set, Jack heard a black pianist tell one of the waitresses, a gaunt, pale girl, he'd been arrested two nights ago in the subway station. "What'd they bust you for?" He shrugged. "Told me I'd made the mistake of 'being abroad in the night.'" Together they laughed, and the pain inside their laughter made it sweet.

How can I live like this? How can I live without it?

Tai Chi

The first woman he slept with after his wife and kids left reminded him of the first girl he slept with, years ago, in Harvard Square. Both women performed Tai Chi, naked, before making love with him. They balanced on one foot and held up their palms as if predicting a distant wind. Then they brought their hands together in prayer. They might have been cupping butterflies inside their long, curved fingers. Their breasts dipped upwards, excited by the cool night air.

He found it remarkable—a woman from his youth, a woman from his jaded middle age, perfect mirrors. But then, women had been practicing, on the planet, precise and delicate movements for centuries.

The long view.

For centuries, moonlight had slanted, blue, through windows onto the quivering bodies of expectant lovers. At thirty-seven, Jack thought, *I am no more myself now than when I turned twenty*. Draped across the bed, his empty clothes were the shape of every man who'd ever lived. And also the shape of no one.

Kabbalah

His lover in Harvard Square was a Radcliffe dropout, the only daughter of a prominent internist in southern Connecticut. Her name was Sheila Schwartz. Jack met her one night in Club 47. She was short and slender, with a bob of black hair and a nose as finely chiseled as an arrowhead. She'd "sloughed off" college when she'd discovered Jewish mysticism. Jack joked with her—the only thing mystifying about Judaism, he said, was why people still practiced it. She introduced him to Kabbalah. "It's about losing the ego," she informed him, "becoming other-centered."

This didn't mean anything to him, but then she shared with him her meditation practices—for instance, she said, composing a mantra, or taking a pen and scrawling the same word repeatedly on a piece of paper, each time changing the style of the lettering, increasing or decreasing the spacing between the letters, and doing this until your mind loses its conscious awareness of the hand, the pen, the paper, the word. He became intrigued. She told him about an ancient rabbi who authored over forty books, each volume consisting of a single short word. On his deathbed, he asked that the books be burned: the fulfillment of his life's wisdom.

"That's poetry," Jack said.

"It is," Sheila said.

He'd found his muse.

Within six weeks of his arrival in the square, he'd moved in with her: a solid white apartment just off Eliot Street, north of the trolley yards. Together, seated on a leather couch beneath a burgeoning ficus plant, lighting bundles of incense, they read the teachings of the Tzadik of Zitshav, of the Baal Shem Tov. They pondered parables: *One day, a journeyman arrived in a village and spoke about a magical bird he'd witnessed in a faraway land. Its face was human and it possessed the spindly legs of a young giraffe. No one believed him. One of the villagers became determined to prove him wrong. He retuned years later, telling a similar tale, except the face of the bird he'd glimpsed only resembled that of a human being and its long legs only reminded one of a young giraffe. No one believed him. A third villager sailed to the faraway land.*

Years later, he returned to the village hauling a bag on his back. He reached inside the bag and produced the fantastical bird. No one said a word.

"What does this teach us about skepticism?" Sheila asked.

Jack didn't know, but he said he'd think about it.

She encouraged him to grow his hair, to wear a beard. To his surprise, his beach-brown hair turned red and delicate, long. He liked the way he looked, serious, mature. Sheila bought him lengthy black caftans, increasing his rabbinic allure.

"What are you, a fuckin' holy man? Lost your mountaintop? You look ridiculous," Alvin said one Sunday, when Jack returned for a visit to his family. He thought the family would be pleased that he'd immersed himself in Judaism, but his spirituality was as foreign to them as a steaming, fat pork chop. Marshall was working at the post office. Jack's sisters were dating fiercely, searching for Mr. Right, fulfilling their destinies. Jack caught the first train out that night.

Sheila got him a job tending bar at The Blue Parrot, where she waitressed. He added the tips to his lobster boat funds. He could stay here forever, pursuing enlightenment, teasing himself with his girl's astounding body.

Mystic Whispers

Sheila taught him:

Understanding the mechanics of motion means learning the essence of movement. *Without the motion.* It's like opening and closing your eyes until you can see either way.

To lay a foundation for shelter, dig a hole in the ground. Each bucket of dirt you cart away: name it after one of your faults. Anger. Impatience. Mistrust. When the buckets have disappeared, and you're standing chest-high in an empty pit, begin to build your house.

A man searching for himself, counting on his intellect, is akin to a man shining a flashlight into a mirror, blinded by the reflection of the beam.

One night in the jazz club, Jack met a physics student in his last year at MIT. The boy tried to explain what he did. He told Jack that "hot solids like the human body are perfect light absorbers. They emit an invisible light called black radiation."

"So—you're saying I cast *light* instead of shadows?" Jack said.

"Huh?"

"And I live in the shadows of things I can't even see?"

"No no, I'm—"

"The Bible says God separated darkness from light." Jack sipped his beer. "But you're saying light is *not* the absence of darkness."

The boy stared at him, gripping his glass.

"So what is the opposite of light?" Jack asked.

The boy walked away.

I guess it depends on who's talking to whom, Jack thought.

Abraxas

Sheila joined a group on the square demanding a halt to America's pursuit of energies based on splitting atoms. At noon each day, the group gathered on the cobblestones, a dozen women or so, to march in front of bead shops and vegetarian cafés. The women carried cardboard placards: "No Nukes!," "Practice Love—The *Natural* Energy!"

Jack spent his days, before going to work at the bar, reading paperbacks in the stuffy aisles at Grolier's. His reading had taught him that poetry didn't need to rhyme. But he wasn't sure he'd learned anything more than this. Without rhymes, what held a poem together?

Increasingly, in his mind, abstract imagery from Eliot's *The Waste Land* mixed with parables from the Baal Shem Tov, with Sheila's politics. Whatever else his poetry contained, he thought, it would be spiritual and socially engaged. Like the Torah scribes, like the rabbis composing midrash, a poet was a prophet, yes? And his people were *all the people*—everywhere. Therefore, he had to be "oracular"—a lovely word he'd read in a book in Grolier's, a primer on poetic form.

What held a poem together? The poet, beneath his willowy caftan.

At The Blue Parrot one night, a swarthy young fellow in a red blazer, wearing a pencil mustache, approached Jack at the bar. "Your girlfriend tells me you're a poet," he said. He said he owned and managed a small press here in Boston. "Broadsides, chapbooks, limited-edition posters. I'm looking to do a full-length volume of poetry in the next year or so. You pull a manuscript together, let me know. Name's Hal. Hal Coyne."

He said his sole aim as a publisher was to raise the planet's consciousness.

That night, after Last Call, Jack returned to the apartment, mulling a poem in his head. In his notebook he wrote: "... my daddy's blood ... / lay siege to the vertical city / rising in its tide of business and transgressions."

In his readings of Kabbalah, Jack discovered "Abraxas," a concept from Greek Gnosticism, with roots perhaps in Hebrew. It meant something like a blessing or a curse, depending on how the term was used and who was using it. In the classical world, the word was often carved as a charm on amulets. The seven letters corresponded to the seven planets of the ancient cosmos, invoking symmetry and universal order.

Another word for "Poetry."

"I have entered the sun's palace / not the walls of memory or womb," Jack wrote.

Up a flight of rickety stairs in an alley around the corner from Club 47, a note in ballpoint scrawled on an index card tacked to a scuffed pine door proclaimed the office of Hal Coyne. Jack knocked three times. The staircase swayed with his weight. When he got no answer, he stepped inside. A single room with a thin, beige carpet. An open file cabinet stuffed with manila folders. An old Rita Hayworth poster from Jack's father's time taped to the wall above a plywood desk. Behind the desk, Hal Coyne, still wearing the red blazer Jack met him in, four months earlier.

Jack set a stack of pages, bound by a blue rubber band, on the desk.

"What's this?' asked Coyne.

"My manuscript."

"Of?"

"I'm the poet. Remember? From The Blue Parrot."

"Oh, right, right." Coyne tapped his temple. "Girlfriend . . . that cute little thing frightened of the bomb."

Jack didn't answer.

"So. Your masterpiece, eh?"

My cry from the heart, Jack nearly said. *My will and testament*. "It's . . . the best I could do."

"I'll look it over. Write your phone number on this top page here."

He phoned the next day. How could he have read the whole thing, much less absorbed the poems' layers? "Brilliant stuff, Myers. Deep. Wise. You're an important new voice in American poetry."

"*Really?*"

"I'm proud to publish this book."

"Really?"

"Listen, you know, we're a small, independent press, and this'll be our first full-length volume . . . we could use a subsidy, to help defray, you know, expenses . . . "

We? Who else, Jack thought. Rita Hayworth? "I'm just a part-time bartender."

"I know, I know, but sometimes sacrifices are necessary . . . something this important . . . adding your voice to . . . you know, *enriching* the culture . . . "

Damn. A fucking player. He didn't even have faith in his own bullshit, the way Louie the Fruit Man did. Still, Jack couldn't help himself: he was flattered, even if the flattery was false. No one else besides Sheila had taken him seriously as a poet. If Coyne's reasons for courting him were self-serving, well, it still meant Jack *came off* as a poet. Something solid.

Okay, so I still have an ego, Jack thought. Like Narcissus: fascinated, watching parts of myself drop to the bottom of the pond while remaining attached to the face on the surface.

If he got a book into the world, he could begin to be other-centered, as Sheila wanted him to be. His reach would stretch . . .

"Okay," he said. For the next eight months, he delivered a third of his monthly paycheck up the rickety stairs.

Breathing wind into my sails, Jack thought. *Filling the sails until they're full.*

150 copies of *Black Sun Abraxas* sat in rough stacks behind the leather couch. Whenever Jack watered the ficus plant, droplets rained from the watering can onto the covers of the books, curling their edges.

"What'd you think?" Coyne told him on the phone. "We don't have an ad budget. It's up to you to distribute the damn things."

So Jack took a spot among the buskers in the square each day. Black men pounding bongos, Joan Baez look-alikes. Arrayed like Moses, he offered copies of his book, imploring passersby to "take a little sip of eternity." Who was he kidding?

The cover was a beauty. Coyne had found the image, copyright-free, in a photo warehouse: a Japanese ink drawing of a solar eclipse behind a forested mountain. The big, black disc caught strollers' attention, but as soon as they understood this was *poetry*, and that Jack was asking money for it, they hurried on by. Directly across from him, in the plaza, Sheila and her cohorts had phenomenal success passing out anti-nuke pamphlets.

Finally, he began carrying handfuls of the books to the Parrot each night. He set them on the bar, by the door, next to the Smirnoff's. *Gratis*, he told folks. The important thing was to spread his vision.

The books didn't move.

Sheila complained that the stacks made it difficult to vacuum the apartment.

So. Now he was a poet.

He wasn't really sure what he'd wanted. But he'd thought there'd be something more.

Student

One day, Tracy, Jack's shy student, came to his office at the university to discuss a poem he'd written for the creative writing workshop. The poem wasn't very good. So far, none of the kid's work had clicked. He took himself too seriously. Nothing to say yet. But Jack had his eye on him: he was a member of the Bewildered Tribe, the ones who wound up making art because making art was a useless thing to do. Uselessness was the only thing that made any sense in a world determined to use its effects to hurt us all. Synesthesia of the soul: just as, for some people, music evoked color, and vice versa, Jack's beautiful, damaged young poets experienced absence as vivid, the past as present, joy as sadness.

Jack himself had arranged sadness on his office shelves, among his many books, because its talismans brought him pleasure: souvenirs from his outings with his boys, reminding him of their enormous vitality but also of their absence from his daily life—a piece of driftwood from Galveston Beach, picked up last year when he'd taken Ben and Seth for Labor Day, a geode Ben had found for him in the foothills of the Davis Mountains on their last camping trip together.

Tucked between Jack's framed diplomas and a plaque announcing his membership in the Texas Institute of Letters was a snapshot of Seth running through his mother's kitchen wearing a yellow bucket on his head, laughing like a loon. Jack kept it there to remind himself that no matter how decorated we become, how weighty with achievement, deep down we're all just a bunch of bucket-heads.

For a week or so, Jack had been re-arranging his books alphabetically. Volumes sat in stacks around the room. On a pile, Tracy noticed a copy of *Black Sun Abraxas*. "Is that yours?" he asked. "I've never seen that before."

"My first book," Jack said.

"How come you've never mentioned it?"

"I've disavowed it. I should never have published it. It embarrasses me."

"Why? Beautiful cover."

"Yes. The cover's the best thing about it. I wrote it before I'd read enough, knew enough. I was full of my own importance. Steeped in a lot of religious gobbledygook. No. No, that's too harsh." He sat on the edge of his desk. *Be gentle with yourself.* "I thought I had the answers. I didn't. But I still respect the questions." He laughed. "Now then, about this magnum opus of *yours*—"

"Oh God. I'm sorry. I know it's awful. I'll do better."

"The opening conceit has promise, but in the second stanza you start to—"

"Jack?"

"Yes?"

"How do you know when you're ready? I mean, when you'll stop embarrassing yourself?"

Jack picked up and examined his book. The sun's blackened disc. "Like I said. We don't have the answers." He smiled. "But the questions are essential."

Ambition

Early in the evening, when the first hospice nurse had left the house and the second one hadn't yet arrived, he lay, goofy on morphine, recalling how driven he'd been to become a poet.

Was he ashamed of his ambition now—now that he knew how little it mattered, how little it had amounted to? Ashamed of his desire to hurl his achievements at his teachers, his parents, like tossing raw beef into a cage of aging lions? Ashamed of wanting to rhyme everything he wrote with an expletive, along with the defiant shout, "I told you so"?

No, not ashamed. Well, maybe just a little. Mostly sad for that lonely young man. Whatever he thought he'd come here for—*here* meaning now, this moment, this life—he knew, in the shadow of death, that he had only been the sum of processes set in motion by light from a distant sun. Success and failure, the distilled byproducts of youthful ambition—they had always been irrelevant. The process churned, and it just kept churning.

Funny: in his morphine dreams he often pictured Rita Kurlansky's violin lying still in its blue velvet case. Once, he had wanted to *be* that expensive, gleaming instrument, vibrating with exquisite music. Now, he felt his body yearning to dissolve: the silence before and after sound. Not an exclamation. An innuendo.

Obituary

From *The Dallas Morning News*, November 29, 2009: "Over the years Jack Myers produced 9 full volumes of poetry, became a beloved professor, and was honored as the Texas Poet Laureate."

The Essence of Movement

"It's crap."

The old man, his beard like early morning fog along a cluttered shore, leaned across the bar. He sneered at Jack. He'd been pawing through a copy of *Black Sun Abraxas*, after spilling beer on it.

"What do *you* know about poetry?" Jack snapped at the man. Sea shanties, maybe—he seemed the type.

"Listen to me, sonny boy, I've hitchhiked all over this country, ridden the rails, done every kind of shit work there is to do, from digging raw coal to burying soldiers. I know the poetry of humanity."

Jack laughed at him.

"Plus, I taught Jack Kerouac everything he knows." Offered matter-of-factly, not as a boast. *Could be true*, Jack thought.

The room got busy. Jack lost track of him. Every guy in the place looked like Bogey. Slouching, adjusting smashed gray hats on their heads. For a week now, the Brattle had been staging a Bogart revival: *Casablanca, The Maltese Falcon, To Have and Have Not.*

The unruly beard twitched at him through a noisy huddle at the bar. "'I have entered the sun's palace / not the walls of memory or womb,'" the shanty man shouted: quoting Jack to Jack. "Trust me, sonny, *memory* and *womb* are exactly what you should enter. *That's* what you should write about. 'The sun's palace'? What the fuck is that? It's crap."

"Yeah, yeah," Jack said, wiping a glass.

"Memory, womb, your daddy's blood." He tossed the book on the bar. "You're circling the real stuff in *those* lines, but you never get there. Why waste your time on the sun's palace when you've got your daddy's blood?"

Shit. That's a beautiful line, Jack thought. Poetic. Because it was true, wasn't it? He looked around. All these wasted kids, stumbling, weeping, laughing, nudged by needs they couldn't name, needs sliding through the sludge in their veins.

He served up a couple of bourbons then turned to look for the beard. Gone. Just the sun on the book's slick cover, eclipsed in a puddle of beer.

"Can we store these books in the closet?" Sheila had been saying this for months. Or: "Maybe it's time to move on."

He could tell she was disappointed he hadn't stepped into Walt Whitman's boots, but more than that, she was impatient with him for nursing *his* disappointment.

Her impatience materialized as indifference. A fading libido. Most nights, Jack threw himself on the couch after his shift at the bar. When he woke in the mornings, the bed was rumpled and empty. Sheila was marching, out in the square, saving the planet.

One night, someone left a catalog of classes on a chair—the University of Massachusetts at Amherst—discarded in a wad of napkins stained with catsup. Jack threw the mess away, but later in the evening, when things got slow and he was straightening up behind the bar, he spied the pages in the trash barrel. He plucked them from a pile of soggy fries, wiped them with a rag, and tore through their sticky columns. Introduction to Literature. American Poetry since World War II.

His self-education—long afternoons sitting in Grolier's, in aisles surrounded by paperbacks, chapbooks—hadn't advanced him very far. He was swimming in the shallows. The books were fine, but his reading was scattershot and random. He had no coherent sense of tradition. What rules was he was supposed to be breaking?

All he had was crap.

Even sea shanties served some purpose in the world.

Over the next few weeks, he figured he'd saved enough money to enroll in two classes for one semester, and to pay the bus fare to Amherst three times a week and back. What he'd do after that, he wasn't sure, but he convinced himself: he had to make a start.

The bus trip was ninety miles either way. He and Sheila saw even less of each other than before—worse, they didn't make the effort. Obsessed with politics, Sheila seemed fine with that, other than complaining that their spiritual training was slipping. Usually, when Jack stepped off the bus at the end of the week, he returned to bras and panties scattered on the floor, cardboard signs in the corner: "No More War!"

Two lives, no longer fitting. The day he noticed the ficus was dead, he told Sheila he wanted a clean break.

She wept while he packed his shoes. He left the caftans hanging in the closet. She dismissed his need for change as childish restlessness, a lust for novelty ("just like a man")—responding to the mechanics of motion. Instead, he insisted he was pursuing the essence of movement. He did not see his abandonment of Sheila—she would always be dear to him—as the result of boredom or disappointment. Or shame when they looked at each other and realized they'd fallen short of the other's expectations (Sheila's explanation to her friends). He saw it as preparing for the long haul—accepting the unforgiving nature of art.

Amherst

Emily Dickinson. Robert Frost. The houses they had lived in, small and unimpressive—they were *houses*—were as close to poetry as Jack came in Amherst. He took a course on poetic technique. He learned spondees and trochees. He learned that spondees and trochees, lovely as they were, did not help him write poems.

The campus—ugly as hell. The architecture students, a truly conceited lot, sat in the student union discussing "modernism" and "brutalism," neglecting to add that what they were talking about was concrete. Slabs. Subterranean bunkers. The campus was an accurate reflection of Dante's inferno, the only advantage to studying here.

Jack landed in a garage apartment three blocks from the Frost place. Soon, it became apparent he couldn't keep paying tuition along with the rent. He'd be damned if he'd ask his father for money. So he dropped out of school. He shaved, cut his hair, went to work as a housepainter.

Gorgeous Georgian Revivals and Victorian-era bungalows prettified Amherst. Their complex eaves and angles leveled Jack. He ended each day with a searing headache. His hands became grizzled bear paws, the colors of washed-out prisms. Every morning he'd slap a house in the face, yelling, "What do you need more yellow for? You think you're the goddam sun?"

Middle school girls wearing T-shirts and shorts slid past him on the streets, riding sleek bikes. They muttered (but Jack could hear), "He's watching us. Pretend you don't see. It's only the painter."

He had to pee behind bushes, hiding from the neighbors. For lunch he ate cheesesteak sandwiches. The bread was hard as rocks.

At night, he dreamed of stepping off his ladder into space, tumbling into nothing.

He'd fled to Amherst to become a poet. To learn the essence of art, to understand professionalism, the difference between a *real* publisher and a hack like Hal Coyne. Instead, he'd become an amateur bird-watcher. Each day, he'd squint into the sun and wonder which sort of wing—sparrow, robin, hawk—would make the best twenty dollar paint brush?

Nanna

She died at a hundred and three, while he was living in Amherst.

He didn't return for the funeral.

His mother squawked at him on the phone.

For weeks, he wept uncontrollably for that horrible old woman. He didn't understand himself. It was as if an elderly man nestled inside him, snug behind his rib cage, tucked behind his heart, shaking a bony finger and saying, "You're missing it, boy. What's important. It's passing you by. Just you wait." Patiently, without further comment, the old man coiled a long—but not endless—piece of rope. With each new coil, Jack's shoulders hunched a little more.

Nancy

He'd made her drop her Chagall. She was leaving a frame shop next to the deli he went to on Saturday afternoons. Stuffing his change into his wallet, paying no attention to the sidewalk, he bumped into her. The large framed poster she was gripping fell to the ground. The glass rattled but didn't break. Before he gathered his wits to apologize, he glanced at the poster: a fantasia of colors, pink and orange discs, a green-faced man staring a cow in the eye. Floating freely in front of the cow, a tiny milk maid (the cow's dream?). Above the man, a miniature ploughman danced with a jolly woman wrapped in a flowing scarf. The woman tumbled upside down, wielding a scythe. A playful defiance of gravity, a magic spell in the middle of the street. "What is that?" Jack said.

The rest of your life, the stranger might have answered, so beguiled was he by her smile (she wore no make-up), her long black bangs, her violet eyes, squinting at Jack to pull him into focus. All week, he'd been painting a three-story English Tudor house—his hands were as garish as the poster.

"Sorry, sorry," Jack said. He invited her for a cup of coffee. "Can we sit and examine it carefully, make sure the frame's okay, the glass . . . if anything's amiss I want to pay for it, of course."

Her name was Nancy, a Boston girl who'd moved to Amherst three years ago to study art history. She'd run out of money and gone to work for the phone company. She was obsessed with Chagall, she said. She loved the way he combined images of Old World labor with dreams-capes invoking Jewish mysticism. Yes, yes, she'd read the Kabbalah. Jack liked how she talked about it, not as overt and doctrinaire as Sheila. She had a gentler, more aesthetic appreciation of the texts.

Together, they ran their fingertips across the glass, feeling for hairline cracks. They found none. Their hands touched. Jack asked for her number.

Over the next several weeks, a stroke of orange, a dollop of yellow would instantly remind him of her. They met at the deli on Saturdays—coffee dates only, at first. She knew nothing about contemporary poetry and he didn't know art. They enriched each other. One day she said, "I think you have the heart of a Chagall. Rough, earthy, but shining with light." She laughed, self-conscious. "Do I sound like an art historian?"

"You do. You should go back to school."

"What about you?"

"I'd like to."

He'd had enough of his gruff Italian boss. "Don't die on me!" the bastard yelled at Jack from the foot of the ladder, face redder than a slice of salami. "What the hell are you doing up there, Myers? The house won't paint itself!"

And the taverns he prowled at night . . . now that he'd met Nancy, and dreamed of spending nights with her, the bars seemed like funhouse Halls of Mirrors. In the burnished light, people saw their bodies distorted: a weak man's shadow loomed high in a darkened corner, an ugly pug stood firm as Cary Grant. Deluded by laughter and booze.

By the end of the evening, fellows sprawled on the floor among broken peanut shells. They stared at hardened gum stuck to the bottoms of the barstools—as if studying snapshots of themselves: faces never changing, stiff and dry, all the freshness gone.

The night Nancy invited him to her apartment, a second-story efficiency around the corner from the deli, they both felt shy. It was clear she'd not wanted to ask him, she'd tried to put him off, but he'd been quietly persistent.

Finally, she admitted, "It's my time of the month. Will that bother you?"

"Not at all," Jack said, eagerly shucking his jacket, tossing it on a folding chair against her kitchen wall underneath the Chagall. Rinsed, empty cans of baked beans filled the tiny sink. Dying ivy dangled like rope from a pot hanging on a hook in front of a balcony window.

"My hands are calloused. Tough. Like sandpaper," Jack said, sitting heavily on the bed. "I'm sorry."

"I'll be fine," she said, but she did flinch a little when he stroked the small of her back.

They rolled together. Soon the sheets grew moist with blood. Sticky. Warm. Jack stood. "I'm not . . . I don't think I can—"

"You said you were okay with it."

"I know, but . . . "

Naked, he walked outside, onto the balcony. Nancy picked his jacket off the chair, wrapped it around her shoulders, and joined him in the moonlight. Their legs were smeared—black, beneath the moon, like bruises beginning to thicken.

"I'm sorry," he said.

"This is it, Jack."

"This is what?"

"This is life."

She hugged him from behind. He placed his hands on hers.

Artist

Years later, when he was thinking of leaving his marriage (in the end, Nancy beat him to it), he spent four weeks one summer at a writer's and artist's retreat in northern New Hampshire. He'd applied for a residency there and been awarded room and board, time to work on his poems. Twelve hours a day or more, no communion with the other guests, meals left by members of the staff on the wooden porch of his cabin.

The first week, he was so lonely he took long walks in the moonlight. A life-sized statue of a pioneer woman—the indomitable spirit of New Hampshire!—rose in a quad among the cabins. Each night he'd crawl onto the pedestal and cup her copper breasts. "I'm not made for solitude," he told her. "What about you?"

In the second week, on one of his nightly strolls, he met one of the artists in residence, a delicate Asian-American woman named Mila. Ten years younger than Jack. She called herself a sculptor but he thought of her as an alchemist, transforming the ordinary materials of the world into magic. Collages of pebbles, wood, and glass; origami; mobiles made of nylon, feathers, twigs. She was gorgeous, pale and angular. She spoke

83

softly with a remarkably low voice, forcing listeners to lean in to her: an enormously seductive power.

Jack ate suppers with her on her cabin porch—picnic baskets left by the staff, turkey sandwiches, carrots, chips, brownies. She showed him books on Asian art, the pen-and-ink traditions she'd learned from. He spoke of his love of Chagall. One night, they ignored the baskets. They sat on her porch, side by side on a wicker settee, kissing for hours. Her lips were as gentle as one of her sculptures. She was white in the rising moonlight. Glare through leaves of the trees cast blue hexagrams onto the porch's worn slats. Mila became a beautiful moth fluttering on the periphery of Jack's awareness.

He had been unfaithful to Nancy three times in the last three years, with students from his poetry classes, but this was a more perilous situation. He could easily fall in love with Mila. A mature woman. An artist. A poet of the senses.

She stood, gripping his hand. He rose beside her. She intertwined her fingers with his in such a way that their touch became a lovely work of art.

"Before we make love, you should know something," she said.

"Yes?"

"Jack. Jack, listen. I've had a double mastectomy."

He didn't grasp her meaning. Everything about her was perfect. She must be referring to an art prize. The coveted Mastectomy. She was so gifted, the judges doubled the honor!

"Do you understand what I'm saying?"

Slowly—like a toilet bowl resetting after a flush, he reflected later—his mind brimmed with the truth.

"Jack. Is it okay?"

He squeezed her hand. Squeezed it again. Then he pulled his fingers from hers. "No. Mila, I'm . . . I'm sorry, I'm afraid I couldn't . . . I mean, I wouldn't be able to . . . "

She closed her eyes. She nodded. Then she slid without a word into her cabin.

The following morning, he stepped onto his porch to retrieve his breakfast basket. Sitting next to it was a small white bowl. It was topped with a round glass lid. He smiled. An offering. No hard feelings, Jack thought, relieved. When he picked it up, he felt the bowl's breast-like contours.

He removed the lid. A swirl of orchid petals, yellow, purple, pink, and red. Dazzlingly bright. Underneath them, a different texture, brown and thick. Jack brushed away the flowers: a pile of dead bees.

Remember your unimportance.

Advice

What was it about the birth of his son—Ben, his beloved first boy—that prompted him to compose a long poem in the form of a posthumous letter of advice? The sudden awareness that beginnings require an end?

Maybe it was the waiting room outside the maternity ward in the small Amherst hospital. The attending nurses asked nervous, expectant fathers to remove their shoes while they paced. The floor was creaky and old and sounds carried through the walls, disturbing the mothers and babies resting in the ward. Jack stared at the empty loafers, lined up against the baseboard. Prisoners at an execution.

Maybe it was that annual bad joke, his job. His back cried each night. His muscles ached in the mornings. When Ben was born and he picked him up in the hospital, Jack nearly collapsed, an enfeebled old man in the body of a twenty-eight-year-old. After an impromptu wedding in the downtown courthouse, Jack and Nancy had merged their belongings and moved into her place. She said she had a plan: he should quit painting houses and re-enroll in school. A man needed a real career. She'd support him with her phone company job; later, he could return the favor. She'd finish *her* degree.

But then she discovered she was pregnant. They'd need more space. For another year and a half, Jack balanced classes, painting, and babysitting until Ben turned ten months old. Finally, Nancy urged him to leave work and make a final push toward graduation.

(After the wedding, he'd dropped his mother a card: "I'm married, Ma!" She wrote back, "As long as you're happy.")

Maybe he worked so hard on the poem because he desperately needed *meaning*. He'd become obsessed with the bubbles in the water glass on his bedside table at night. Endlessly, the bubbles rose to the top of the glass while Nancy breast-fed Ben. Sleep-deprived, Jack stared at the popping motion, becoming dizzier, feeling increasingly weightless.

Maybe the poem resulted from a blurring of time. It was the late 1960s. Street protests thronged the parks near campus, just as they had in Harvard Square. But instead of clear-cut demands ("No More War!") the demonstrators shouted, "Mao!", "I grok Spock," "Turn On, Tune In!"

Instead of marching on City Hall, groups of young women dressed in black and wore white theatrical masks. Crying, laughing, they stood immobile under willows. Their signs said, simply, "Truth." What they wanted, and to whom they were appealing, was not at all evident. Everything was tilting toward unreality, as if the future had arrived and Jack could not decode its signals. (He'd been lucky not to be drafted because of his date of birth, purely an accident of time.)

Maybe the poem was a meditation on Ben's perfect fit with the curve of Jack's chest. The planes of the baby's cheeks locked evenly into his father's collar bone. But Jack saw himself softening as he aged, just as Ben grew harder, stronger. Someday, there'd be nothing left of Jack but the goo of a former clown, a pair of wax lips floating in a puddle.

Of course the poem was an elegy—his long goodbye to Amherst. In the fall of '70, he and Nancy relinquished the apartment lease, bought a used 1956 Ford station wagon and packed it for the move to Iowa City.

By then, the epic Jack had begun the night Ben was born had swelled to several pages, still unfinished. He'd been working on it for well over a year, more concertedly since getting his BA and receiving his acceptance into the Writers Workshop at the University of Iowa.

Earning a college degree had gotten him no closer to poetry than he'd come his first week in town, when he toured the Dickinson homestead. But then someone told him about the Workshop: "If you want to be a poet, that's where you go." So Nancy quit the phone company. They pulled Ben out of day care—abandoning his pals there like a batch of broken toys—and hit the road.

The American prairie was brown and expansive. Behind the wheel, to keep from falling asleep as he drove, Jack imagined catchy slogans for Midwest license plates: *Iowa, Land of Land*.

"Advice to Ben": "Someday when you look up . . . / you'll want to find out who you are / and then you might read this. / Go on. / Like any mongrel, / you'll have to make things solid / with your body, as I did you. / Mark what's yours and keep it . . . / Follow your nose. All laws are an abstraction of this / crassness: Pick out a tree and take a piss. / Go on . . ."

Prairie

Nancy slept with Ben in her lap as the sun slipped behind cornfields. The highway never wavered: a strict, straight line cutting through valleys and hills. It mesmerized Jack, especially at night, the headlights dancing off scrub brush on either side of the road. Now and then the Ford's engine *pinged*, a small metallic whine in Jack's ears. Breakdown was imminent. They'd be the Donner family, lost in America, prey to jackals and grinning car salesmen.

Nancy stirred. "Go back to sleep," Jack murmured, patting her arm.

Twenty years would pass before he'd make a drive like this again, on vacation with his second wife and his second family, heading for the Mississippi River. He'd think, then, of this exhausting journey with Nancy and Ben, mid-1970, when the future was just a gentle bend in the road . . . he'd think of his marriage to Nancy, how its wheels fell off. He'd stick his head out the window, following the lilt of the high wires strung above the prairie. He'd wonder how Nancy was faring these days. He'd think of calling her. But the wires hissed at him with the sound of his own thin voice: Hello, who is it, are you there, hello, hello?

Iowa City

Married student housing had long been filled—the wait list for a one-bedroom bungalow was as long as the history of Western Europe. For the first three weeks, Jack, Nancy, and Ben stayed in a roadside motel, the kind of dump Hitchcock might have filmed a murder mystery in. A woman in the registrar's office told Jack he might check rentals in Cedar Rapids, twenty-five miles east of here. She'd heard there were affordable openings in the Czech neighborhoods, but Nancy said they were too close to the railroad tracks and rusty grain mills.

They settled finally into a couple of rooms in the back of a converted barn, just north of town. Jack shaved a third off the monthly rent by helping the landlady with small tasks around the farm. She had long rented to students and faculty at the Writers Workshop. "Though I gotta tell you," she said. "I think all poets are crazy. Harmless, maybe, but crazy. They drink too much, for one thing."

"True," Jack said.

"One poet I rented to, back in the 50s—*he* wasn't harmless. Not by a long shot. Lowell was his name."

"*Robert* Lowell?" Jack said. "My god, Robert Lowell lived here?"

"Nearly burned the place to the ground. Three times. Used to have spells or something. Cuckoo. Really off his noggin."

"Don't worry. I don't have spells."

"Hmph." She shoved a bucket into his hands and told him to go get some slop for the pigs.

He was impressed with the dirt. It worked hard.

For two decades, creative writing classes had convened in a series of World War II-era barracks on campus. The barracks still stood, but most of Jack's workshops met in new brick buildings or under trees when the weather was warm. His classmates came from all across the country, naïve about the power of poetry to change the world, but smart enough to know they'd never get rich scribbling verse. As graduate students, they taught introductory composition courses, earning a small stipend. The goal, after leaving school, was to land a part-time job at a junior college teaching comp, pursuing poetry on the weekends and during summer breaks. Jack didn't write Alvin and Ruth about his studies or his vague visions of the future. He knew his father's reply: "How can you live like this?"

The students sat in dim classrooms or under fir trees, watching leaves fall, smoking, considering one another's mimeographed poems. Purple ink smeared their hands. They said, "Why do so many animals die in your work?", "You overuse enjambment," or, "You're evading the real subject here!"

They went to weekend parties in crammed apartments. They danced, jammed together like football players scrambling for a fumbled ball. Old-timers, self-published poets who came to Iowa City years ago and never graduated, working now as cab drivers or dishwashers in Chinese restaurants, reminisced, "John Berryman would've said of your bathroom, 'It's too damn small to get drunk in. Where am I supposed to fall down?'"

Jack enrolled in a class taught by Dick Hugo, a squat, granite block of a man. He reminded Jack of one of those figures on Mount Rushmore. A Westerner, he wrote tough-guy poems about the comfort of bars, the sadness of shut paper mills. Towering blondes you never got to kiss.

To Jack, the West was all wilderness.

In class, Hugo said, "People say, 'Write what you know.' I say, 'Write what you *want* to know.' Better yet, 'Write what you don't *know* you know.' Go to a town you've never been to. Hang around. See what it does to you. It'll pry loose your secrets." Jack didn't know what he was talking about, but he sure as hell *sounded* like a poet.

After Hugo's first class, Jack returned to the barn, his hands spotted with purple ink. He slopped the pigs then he sat beneath Chagall, hanging in the bedroom. He scrawled into his notebook, "Here begins the education of Jack Elliot Myers, 1941- ."

Hugo told the class he had served as a bombardier in the war. In a B-24 Liberator, he flew thirty-five missions over Italy, pressing his rock-like face against the tiny range finder. One day he missed the enemy target and bombed Switzerland by accident. That was the day he knew he was a poet, not a fighter, he said.

In his small office on campus, he'd tacked a photo to the wall: his younger self standing dazed next to his burned and twisted jet. Not a reminder of the past—a perpetual warning, he said. For Jack, it was always *the* image of the poet.

Sometimes, in workshop, while his fellow students ripped his poems apart, Jack felt he was tumbling through the sky without a chute. He wondered if the day would ever come when he'd feel he was rising, instead.

88

The Worst Night

The still house felt even emptier, on his thirty-seventh birthday, three weeks after Nancy drove off with the kids, because Dick had just left town. Jack had invited his old mentor to Dallas, on a visiting writer gig. Hugo had given a guest lecture at the university and a poetry reading at a local bookstore. Jack spent a marvelous time with him, reminiscing about his student-days at Iowa, toasting Dick's continuing successes as a teacher and a poet.

He'd put Dick on a plane that afternoon. Standing in the airport, watching the airliner lift into the clouds, he felt his past *and* his future were departing.

A week before Hugo's visit, Jack had been tending bar one night in the pool hall. Tracy was there, watching the Pepper girls. On a break, Jack mentioned to him,"Dick'll be coming in just a few days. I've got to buy him a chair."

"Jack, you've got lots of chairs. Why do you need another chair?"

"Have you ever seen a picture of Dick?"

"No," Tracy said.

Jack spread his arms, wide as a fridge.

Now, in the empty house, his thirty-seventh birthday, Jack sat in the expansive recliner he'd bought for Dick, watching Tracy. The boy was seated on the couch across the room from him, curled fetus-like against a black leather pillow. A single lamp burned in the corner, enfolding the two of them in a soft yellow circle. The chair was so big, Jack felt he was swimming in it, breast stroke, backstroke. As if Tracy was drowning and Jack couldn't reach him.

The kid needed help. But Jack was in no shape to save him. He remembered Dick's photo, the one tacked to his office wall: the dazed young man, wrecked fuselage steaming all around him.

Tracy stirred. Jack tensed. A suicidal night. How was he going to get them through it?

Sea-Chaser

Jack's second son, Seth, was born to chase waves. But he came into the world on a dry Iowa prairie. Jack saw the swirl of the sea in the baby's gray eyes, caught the scent of womb-salt sprinkling his delicate skin. In Seth's flailing little fists: an impossible desire to hug the swiftest currents.

Ben was three now, delighted to "own" a baby brother. He had the gift of charming strangers. On the sidewalk he'd reach for them; they'd swerve, put their lives on hold, stop and talk to this beautiful little man. Jack envied his pull.

"Too many!" Ben screamed one day, tired of bumping into knee caps, doorknobs, lumbering house pets. "There are too many feet!" *Exactly right*, Jack thought.

Jack and Nancy were anomalies among the students in the Writers Workshop—slightly older, married with kids. They rarely attended parties together. One stayed home, babysitting, while the other enjoyed a night out. They both relished chances to be on their own, dancing and flirting. Sometimes they fought about it. Nancy leavened her jealousy with resentment that she'd never got to go back to school. It was impossible now with two young boys in the house and Jack on a path to teaching.

When Seth came along, Jack, drunk with words, marveled at his son's ability to express himself silently. The miracle of it gentled him— Nancy, too—and for a while they were happier with each other than they'd ever been. "He's like those poets—like Rimbaud—who gave up writing to *become* a work of art," Jack said.

"Well. We'll see to it he never gives up anything he doesn't *want* to give up," Nancy said.

"Holding on and letting go. Learning the difference. Isn't that the secret?"

"You terrify me," Nancy said. She laughed. But he knew she meant it.

Wings, Roots

In Iowa, the birds hung like doubts in the trees: black, brooding shrouds rustling on wind-stirred limbs.

For two years, he'd been a farmer and a teacher. He didn't know if he'd become a poet.

He'd learned the rituals of fathering. A husband's limitless capacity to disappoint.

He'd learned to estimate morning temperature by listening to sparrows' songs. He could tell rotten fruit by feeling it even though its skin looked perfectly fine.

He could tell the difference between a bare tree branch and its reflection in a barrel of rainwater. But poetry had taught him not to value that difference.

The difference was false.

So Long

Overturned trucks rusting in patchy yellow fields. A collapsed farmhouse swarming with wasps, a ripped mattress lodged at a ninety-degree angle in its doorway. Red oaks burning on the blue horizon. Rabbits bounding in a ditch.

"Wave goodbye," Jack said to Ben.

Nancy sat beside Jack in the rattling old Ford, cradling sleeping Seth in her lap. Ben stood in the back seat, staring out the window. "So long," he said. "So long."

Metroplex

Seen from above at night, through the window of an airplane, it looked like a chandelier floating in space. At ground level, stuck inside freeway smog and the misty aftermath of a late-fall thunderstorm, you felt you'd entered a jewel, trapped in an abstract, glassy maze. Once you penetrated deep into the city, away from the traffic hubs and onto side streets, the place resolved into specific, more comprehensible zones, shopping centers, neighborhoods. It began to seem possible for people to live here.

Dallas: Jack's new home. In the early 1970s, the chair of the English Department at Southern Methodist University noticed that creative writing programs were sprouting on college campuses across the country, modeled on the Writers Workshop at Iowa. They attracted more students, more tuition money, than traditional literature courses. "Get me a poet," he told the head of his hiring committee.

"Jackpot," Jack's classmates called him, his last year in the workshop. He managed to publish a dozen poems in so-so literary journals—short verses full of farm imagery and vague emotional content. Whatever energy the poems had sprang from his irritation at changing diapers and facing his wife's scowls in the mornings. The length of his poems, rather than quality, was the key to success, he figured: he pursued magazines with severe space restrictions, and wrote to their lack-of-room. How he came by this strategy, he didn't know, but he took great pride in his pragmatism.

The poems were enough to land him an interview with SMU at the annual Modern Languages Association conference, held that year in downtown New Orleans. (It was his only interview, though he'd mailed dozens of applications across the country.)

What got him the job was the fact that the head of the hiring committee, an Emerson scholar, was an old Boston lad. As a high school kid, he'd worked the lobster boats. He and Jack spent the interview reminiscing about the sun and the sea.

Three classes per semester, annual salary $21,000, tenure-track, subject to review and promotion in six years. Jack Myers, Poet-Professor!

Nancy found a two-bedroom, Spanish-style house near campus, and they filled what they could of it with their small possessions. Chagall claimed the whitewashed wall above the living room fireplace. Prior to this, Jack's views of Texas had been shaped by the movies. Cowboys and horses, oil derricks, big-haired girls. Instead, Dallas was a sophisticated, international city. The big hair was everywhere, but Jack saw none of the other stereotypes. Generally, his neighbors were friendly, worldly, surprisingly diverse in their politics, tolerances, personal pursuits.

Parochialism wasn't entirely missing. One Saturday morning, Jack stood in his tiny front yard, underneath maniacal bird song in the trees, wondering how, or even if, he could get a garden going. From across the street, one of his neighbors called, "That's black clay you're tilling. Awfully tough to work with." He walked over and introduced himself. Bill was his name. He chatted with Jack, eyeing him closely, offering advice about fertilizers and various potting soils. Finally, he asked, "What denomination are you? My wife and I are Lutheran." Jack said he was Jewish. "I see, I see," Bill said, made a quick excuse, and wandered back to his house.

A few mornings later, Bill called to Jack from his driveway, "You know, you and your wife are welcome to join us as guests at our church." Jack nodded politely: "No, thanks." "Okay, okay, that's fine," Bill said. "Perfectly fine." As the birds groused loudly about who was going to get the best food today, and from which lousy yard—surely not that black-clay disaster?—Jack knew he'd never see Bill again, except from a distance.

Wildcats

Most mornings he woke early to write in the kitchen, before Nancy and the boys stirred. That first year he was remarkably productive. A book was taking shape, and individual poems appeared in quality journals, *The American Poetry Review*, *Kayak*, *Poetry*, *Antaeus*. After a bagel for breakfast, he'd walk to campus, a quiet ten-minute stroll, giving him a chance to compose more lines in his head. The sight of the clock tower atop the social sciences building broke his reverie; it was time, then, to turn his mind to syllabi, assignments, appointments.

SMU was an expensive private school. Many of the students, Jack learned, came not for education but rather for the fraternity and sorority experience. Social bonding. Sowing oats. They didn't worry about the future. They'd go to work for their daddies. The boys would marry sorority queens, and invest with their former frat buddies.

Not so, the student poets. The black sheep. The outcasts, the misfits. God knew how they wound up here. Family pressure, scholarships— whatever initial path they'd followed, a handful of them discovered they felt safe only in creative writing classes, among other lonely introverts.

Beautiful women, beautiful men, Jack thought.

He wished classes like this had been available when he was young.

He taught them Lorca's *duende*, the dark uncertainty inside their guts giving them enormous power. He became their guru. They flocked to his workshops. They wrote down his words: "Allegory is most effective, used sparingly." "Too many animals are dying in these poems!" Inseparable, they drank with him after class in bars near campus. Jack referred to them as the Poetry Wildcats. Like an intramural sports team.

The biggest challenge? Not lighting up in the classroom, a lazy habit he'd developed at Iowa. And it was agony not to respond to the adoring stares of star-struck coeds. They saw him—schlubby Jack!—as the embodiment of lyricism.

During Finals Week, first semester, he decided on the spur of the moment to throw an end-of-term party at his house. It would provide a further bonding experience for the Wildcats, good for morale going forward, improving workshop chemistry. In class, the last day, he told the students to bring snacks and drinks to his place that night. Dance records, too. His wife had an old hi-fi set. He'd not informed Nancy of his plans.

She squinted unhappily at him when the first students arrived at their door that evening carrying six-packs of beer and Donna Summer albums. He gave her what he hoped was a charming grin. She retreated down the hall. She'd put the boys to bed, she said.

By midnight, disco kicked Motown off the turntable. Dancers stamped the floor. Dishes rattled on thin kitchen shelves. It occurred to Jack: some of these kids were under eighteen. If the cops came, summoned by a noise complaint from the neighbors, well . . . too late now. The party was a great success.

He saw Tracy in a corner, talking to no one, staring at a girl across the room. A drunk young beauty flung her arms above her head. She twirled across the floor and stumbled against the fireplace, knocking her hand against Chagall. The print wobbled. It tumbled from the wall.

The glass cracked in three places. The dancing stopped. The music continued to blare. Jack swept the shards with his hands. Suddenly, Nancy's bare feet appeared in front of him. He looked up. "Be careful," he said. "Glass."

She folded her arms across her lacy nightgown. The students backed against the walls. "You think you're going to live forever, don't you?" Nancy said.

"I don't know what you mean."

Smoldering cigarettes. Half-empty glasses. "Kick the children out, Jack. It's time to come to bed."

The Schmooze

It was common sense, and a solid aesthetic principle: success is harder to write about than struggle.

Jack pondered that thought one morning. He was standing in front of the antique armoire Nancy had bought last week at a flea market. While preparing for the day, for his classes, he liked to check his look in the door's full-length mirror.

Today the door stood open. He'd shuffled across the room, half-asleep, expecting to see his face. Instead, he was confronted with a tangle of wool, corduroy, and cotton: his clothes, folded badly on the shelves. "Wow, Jack, you look like shit," he said. Like the inside of his brain, a ragged mess.

The armoire, the clothes, the shiny leather couch in the living room. The freshly-framed Chagall. They were all measures of success.

The leisure to rise in the mornings and plan the day over hot coffee and a bagel.

His neighbors, with the exception of Bill across the street, fanning his quiet anti-Semitism, were pleased to have Jack in the neighborhood. They always smiled at him and waved. A dignified man of letters, a professor: his presence here conferred respectability upon them as productive members of the middle class. All was well!

They didn't know he had rags-for-brains. He shut the armoire door and grinned at himself in the mirror.

He used to sit in the kitchen with his coffee and an onion bagel, drafting new poems. These days, he graded papers—a successful working teacher. Even if he had time to write poems, he'd have nothing to say. When he was younger, struggling to find his way in the world, words came easily. Struggle was laden with conflict and drama. No shortage of material. Now that he'd become Professor Myers, cushy in his tenure-track job, what was he going to meditate on? His lovely armoire?

One Saturday morning, weary from grading, unable to concentrate on writing, he spent hours shoveling clay in his garden. Seth, claiming he wanted to help, picked up a plastic hand shovel and poked a few holes in the yard. He stuck his face into a divot he'd made.

"Honey, what are you doing?" Jack asked.

"I want to see where the darkness comes from."

From me, Jack thought. *The darkness comes from me.*

Seth dug another hole.

Jack wiped sweat from his neck. *Jesus*. What prompted *that*? Whose voice was it?

Mine, Jack thought. *My voice.*

He leaned on his shovel. *You're a roaring success. Jackpot. Don't fuck it up, boy.*

But the past . . . he removed his garden gloves . . . the past was like a vagabond, wasn't it, lurking somewhere, just out of sight, in the neighborhood. Sunburned. Mottled with house paint. Smelling of the butcher's blood-soaked blades.

Seth gashed the dirt.

One night, the past was bound to come pounding on the door: *Pay me what I'm owed! You can't ignore me like this, asshole, just because you're a fucking big shot now!*

Once a semester, the chair of the English Department asked Jack to join a handful of other "distinguished profs" at what he called "The Schmooze," an informal fund-raiser held at the house of a hefty university donor—usually a mansion on Turtle Creek, in Dallas's Highland Park neighborhood. Since Jack's arrival, enrollment in creative writing classes had skyrocketed. Poetry had become a steady revenue stream. The chair wanted to establish an undergraduate creative writing major.

One night, Jack, itchy in a gabardine suit, the one suit he owned, stood talking to an investment banker, an SMU alum, beside the banker's back yard pool. The yard was big enough to accommodate three tennis courts. Jack was explaining to the man, "Poetry-writing is not as impractical as it sounds. Naturally, it helps students develop communication skills, critical thinking: good preparation for the legal profession or most business fields."

"Yeah, I hear good things about your program, really good things," said the banker.

Bullshit, Jack thought. *You and me both, buddy—we're so full of it, your pool's about to crest.*

"We certainly do like winners here at Southern Methodist."

But the losers have more to write about.

Look at me. A domesticated house pet. De-clawed, de-fanged.

He had to get spectacularly drunk just to make it through an evening like this.

Why can't *I flirt with the women who flirt with me? Let's do the dance we do!*

The banker walked to the other side of the pool to talk to someone important. A California film crew had been invited to the party tonight —the smell of United Artists money permeated the chlorinated air. The crew had come to Dallas to film a movie about the 1960s' counterculture. A location scout had decided SMU would make a fitting backdrop for staging an anti-war demonstration.

In fact, in the 60s, SMU had been asleep. It was a quiet, conservative place—a primary institution *funding* the war, Jack thought.

With Hollywood here, who needs the History Department?

He went to the wet bar and ordered another Scotch.

Sometime later, in the light of a rising half-moon, a young woman dressed in black—a sequined gown with a slit up its side—approached him poolside. In one hand she waved a slender cigarette, in the other a slushy gin and tonic. *So, we've all gone Hollywood*, Jack thought.

"And what do you do?" she said.

"I'm a poet."

"Oh, how cute."

He tugged the hem of his coat. The jacket pinched him under the arms. "And you?"

"I own all this. The lady of the house."

Jack glanced at the glaring, Italianate windows overlooking the yard. "Must be nice inside."

Smoky and low—Lauren Bacall: "Would you like me to show you around?"

"I would," Jack said. But when she turned toward the sliding glass doors: "Actually, no, I'm sorry. I'd better not." *I am, after all, Professor Myers! An accomplished man of letters!*

"Okay, poet." She raised a bare, dismissive shoulder. A display of what he'd nearly had. Then she walked away, trailing ashes.

He stared at his reflection in the pool: floating rags.

Where does the darkness come from? Oh, my little Sea-Chaser, if you only knew!

Desert Trees

After his second fling with a student—which failed to ease his restlessness—Jack began eating sack lunches in the Meadows Museum, a small, neglected space in the campus art building. It featured a fine collection of Spanish paintings.

He thought he remembered reading, once, that Picasso, whenever he moved into a new phase of work—the Blue Period, Cubism—found a new woman to inspire him.

Jack particularly liked the Goya Room. No one went there. It was narrow and dim. He sat on a bench eating his corned beef sandwich. One tiny oil captivated him: four or five madmen beating each other in the pit of an insane asylum.

He didn't want to walk home at lunchtime to face Nancy's ire. Nor did he want to remain in his office where students could find him. He needed silence and solitude. He'd caught fire again. He'd finally finished a book-length poetry manuscript and sent it off to publishers.

In the evenings at home, the boys cried in their rooms. Nancy yelled at him for not getting the groceries or for leaving dirty dishes stacked in the sink—everything but what she *really* wanted to scream.

"The students love me. The department loves me," he said. "Everything's fine."

"Yeah, aren't *you* the cat's pajamas?"

So on Friday nights he'd spin out of the house in the rattletrap old station wagon, a couple of six-packs warming on the seat next to him. He'd leave the city behind, heading west into the darkness of Texas until the desert began. He'd drive for hours until even the few trees, the rock-hard mesquites, disappeared. Sometimes he'd pull over and sleep in the car on the edge of the road, sometimes he'd stop at a bodega in the middle of nowhere, a concrete block festooned with Christmas lights, the bulbs' red tips piercing the night like distant satellites. He'd be the only gringo in the place He had to watch his step. On at least two occasions he was so full of beer, so full of himself he *wanted* trouble just as much as he wanted a woman. He ached for the kiss of a fist on his mouth, just to feel alive.

One night, he came close to standing on the bar and shouting at the room, "Hey, I'm a goddam poet! What're you fuckers gonna do about it?"

What stopped him?

The memory of Dick Hugo's pockmarked bomber, lying charred on the ground. Out of nowhere. There the damn thing came, flaming in his head.

You could go too far. Push so hard, so fast you reached the lip of the atmosphere, the thin, blue epidermis keeping life intact.

You could outrun your air.

You think you're going to live forever, don't you?

Go home, damn it. Apologize.

Sometimes, in the remotest areas of the desert, where even the refinery fires fizzled, his headlight beam swept pairs of empty shoes lying in the dirt, traces of dying migrants walking thousands of miles to start their lives again.

The night Nancy took the car, Seth bawled uncontrollably in the back seat. Boxes blocked the curb. Ben hugged his mother's knees. Then he threw himself at Jack. "No no no!" he screamed. "No no no!" "Go on," Jack told him quietly, patting his head. "Go with your mom. I'll see you soon. Promise."

From across the street, standing in his open garage, Bill crossed his arms and smiled.

Therapy Session

"A form of suicide? Burn everything to the ground so you can start fresh, with renewed vigor?"

Jack didn't answer. Finally he said, "Can I smoke in here?"

"No."

The Worst Night

Jack didn't know, and didn't really want to know, what had happened to the boy. Young heartbreak Nothing serious. And yet it was.

A sensitive, self-involved young man, shy with women, jilted or rejected . . . probably, in a year, given how fast young lives moved, the incident would be forgotten. But the problem was tonight. Left alone, Tracy might hurt himself. Jack read the signs.

The boy was a little drunk. He wasn't used to so many beers. When he staggered, trying to leave the pool hall that night, Jack insisted he stick around. When Jack was done with his shift behind the bar, he said, "Come on. Come on home with me." He wasn't about to let this kid wander away on his own. Not until the sun came up.

At the house—the sad and empty house—Jack made coffee. *Just be present*, he thought. *Let him talk. Or not.*

Tracy patted the big, wide Hugo chair. "I loved his reading," he said.

"Dick's a treasure," Jack said.

"I couldn't believe he just stood at the podium, and . . . *spoke* his poems aloud, without glancing at the page."

"'You might come here Sunday on a whim,'" Jack quoted. Dick's most famous poem. "'Say your life broke down. The last good kiss / you had was years ago . . .'"

The boy slumped on the couch.

"Do you want to talk about it?" Jack said.

"No. It's good just to sit. Thanks."

"So. Do I know the girl? One of the Wildcats?"

"Really, Jack . . . it's not . . . truly . . . I don't want to trouble you . . ."

"No trouble."

Tracy shook his head.

"Stubby legs? Short nose? Nasty temper? What is it you're overlooking in your ridiculous idealization of her?"

A smile.

"You know, we're in the same boat," Jack said.

"What do you mean?"

"My wife left me. Took the kids. Just a few days ago."

"God. I didn't know."

98

"No."

"Why? I mean . . . Jack, are you—" Obviously, it hadn't occurred to him that anyone else might be suffering on this good green Earth, on this fair, tender night.

"I was a shit."

Tracy's hands trembled, dribbling coffee. Clearly, he'd never heard a teacher talk like this. Morality was black and white for him. Part of the trouble.

They sat in a circle of light, the rest of the room in purple shadow.

"You're a good man, Jack."

"Yes, I think I am. But I'm also a shit. So are you. So is this girl who's worrying you."

The paradox—*any* paradox—was too much for him. But it was precisely what Jack had to teach right now. At least until the sun rose.

Mystic Whispers

Only the troubled could help the troubled. He'd believed that, once, until sour experience taught him otherwise. It was a case of false humility—like floating a helium balloon modeled on your image over a parade you'd arranged to celebrate yourself.

Better to be the wind that blows the balloon, over empty streets once the parade is finished.

Wandering among Women

One night, he brought home a Pepper girl. He unlocked the door, flipped on a light. The girl nearly tripped on a toy fire truck Seth had left on the floor last week. She laughed, surprised. Jack recoiled. He didn't know why, but he no longer liked this person.

He made an excuse about not feeling well, drove her back to her apartment and dropped her off.

He had to get out of this house. It belonged to Nancy as much as to him. He needed a neutral space. A place to forge *new* memories with Ben and Seth.

He broke his lease and moved into a one-room flat in northeast Dallas, next to a power station. Here, he knew no one. That suited him. At night, naked, he'd stand on his tiny balcony in thickening fog, listening to the hum of the voltage towers. City lights pulsed wildly below him: the forests of his coming middle age.

He scribbled in a notebook: "Here begins (again) the education of Jack Elliott Myers, 1941- ."

He smoked. He drank alone. Each step he made, in or out, day or night, was a labored stroke across a choppy strait.

In the mornings, he sat at the kitchen counter writing poems. A mockingbird sang in an apple tree outside his window. The bird's meter wobbled. *I know*, Jack thought. *It's not easy, is it? Especially when you're alone. But it's the job, right? The whole point is to sing, and to just keep singing. I'm amazed, little brother—astonished at your courage.*

Some evenings, he'd invite a woman into his bed. He'd cling to her as though something catastrophic had happened in the middle of the day.

Psst—I've finished another coil, the old man twisting rope inside him whispered.

Creative writing classes continued to exceed their enrollment caps. Jack remained popular at "The Schmoozes."

Yes, indeed! We like winners here!

A publisher based in Fort Collins, Colorado—independent, non-profit—agreed to publish *The Family War*, Jack's first book of poems . . . his second, really, but he'd erased *Black Sun Abraxas* from his thoughts. The press couldn't promise wide distribution: "It's a labor of love for us," said the owner. "It costs us about $3,000 to print 500 paperback copies, and we work out of my mother's house to keep cost-of-business down. We depend on the poets to market themselves, otherwise we couldn't stay alive. Our goal is just to break even."

Sales weren't as important as recognition in the literary press ("About a third of the poetry books published annually in America fall out of print within two years. After five, almost *all* of them are gone," said his editor).

At least *The Family War* earned Jack tenure.

The day he signed the book contract, he drove to town to celebrate. He listened to a local band at a club called Randy Tar's at a trendy strip on Greenville Avenue. The singer, a young blonde named Karen Bella, an improbable cross between Joni Mitchell and Janis Joplin, was marvelously gifted. She belted out Motown, R & B, a handful of originals. She wore a silk blouse and purple hot pants. "She of the creamy, dreamy legs!" the emcee had introduced her. The audience seemed wrong for her music—too young or too old, fixated on fried shrimp more than steady groovin'. Jack considered approaching her at the break, offering to buy her a drink. He saw how hard she was working. It must be as difficult to advance in the recording industry as in the poetry world, he thought. Talent was the least of it. Two impossibly hungry souls. Karen and Jack. In a nation that didn't give a shit.

He didn't think so. He drove home alone.

In the chilly moonlight he stripped and stepped onto his balcony. He sipped his Scotch. He spread his arms and imagined leaping into the power grid. An electrical outage, cascading among thousands and thousands of sleeping citizens. So much strength he possessed! It gave him a mild, cold thrill.

A Vow against Good Health

Several years later, days from his 60th birthday, urged by his third wife, Thea, he agreed to moderate his bad habits. Just four months earlier, he'd undergone emergency heart surgery.

One night, he'd awakened nauseous, dizzy, tingling like he'd licked a live wire.

"You're lucky to be alive," Thea reminded him every day, after the double-bypass.

He didn't feel lucky. He didn't feel anything, really. At night, whenever Thea said a prayer of thanks, he thought she sounded like his dog barking at nothing through the open window.

He quit smoking. The effort made him keenly aware of tobacco. Like when he tried to kill a fly. The goal was to restore peace to the room. But all he thought about was the fly. The room shivered and disappeared.

He cut his drinking in half. The world became a bleaker place. Thea felt so proud of him. He'd added years to his life, she said.

He heard a persistent buzzing. He sat with his dog by the window.

The Kids in the Garden

What was so spectacular about living alone? he asked himself. It was 1981: the year of his second marriage. *You have many desperate gifts to give someone. And doesn't life begin (again, again) at forty?*

Willa had been a student in one of his classes. Not poet material, but a sharp thinker. Good critical acumen, quick with words. He was mightily drawn to her dark beauty and she knew it. She flirted with him. She called him a different name each day. Herbert. Sam. He'd laugh and say, "And how are *you* today, my bird-like bird?"

Her bright olive skin lent her a vaguely Spanish air. He called her the "exotic Juanita."

They'd meet on campus, over chocolate ice cream at a snack bar in the memorial union. They talked about her grades or her latest assignment. The melting dark chocolate in her hands, held against her shiny purple blouse (she wore a lot of purple), charmed him into mad carelessness.

Already, he pictured how sad his underwear would look tossed next to her skirts in the armoire Nancy left behind.

Perhaps because Nancy had returned to Amherst, taking Ben and Seth; perhaps because, as a tenured professor, he was mired now in university committee work, Jack tried harder, these days, to re-set the game board—to move, once more, from the "Quicksand of Despond" to the "Kingdom of Success."

Whenever he calculated the distance between him and his boys, he lost his breath.

Twice a year, he made a trip back East. Ben was twelve now, too young to grow a beard, but his hard stare suggested he imagined wearing one, a protective mask against his father's expectant smile. Seth showed Jack his bicycle tricks, popping wheelies in the garden, flying like Evel Knievel over his mother's tomato plants. "Watch this one, Dad!" Then he'd rise, flashing, in the sun. Perfecting his moves. He was doing remarkably well without his daddy's help.

Jack recalled *his* boyhood bike, stolen by the undertaker's son, that rotten son of a bitch. Well. These days, it was an iron sled of guilt he rode. No one could take *that* from him.

At the end of each visit, he muttered goodbye and the boys nodded glumly. Once again, their lives pulled apart.

By the time Jack had kids with Willa, Nancy wanted to erase the past entirely. Willa wanted to believe it had never happened. Jack prayed to a god he didn't believe in, "Help me gather them all, please, my lovely wives and my beautiful children, under one sturdy roof."

As long as Willa remained in his class they did nothing more than eat ice cream. Once she graduated, they "dated officially," she told her father, a retired army general living in Plano, a north Dallas suburb. "He's going to be famous, Dad! He's a *wonderful* poet!"

In the way of old army generals, the man grunted more than he spoke. Jack never knew what he was thinking. Probably, *Never marry a poet.* Right.

One day, the "exotic Juanita" said she needed a purple blouse. She asked Jack to take her to a mall. Dallas was lousy with malls. Jack hated malls and the people who shopped in them but he noticed, in this particular mall, a modeling studio. It advertised "discounted opportunities to unlock the secret women inside you!" For $150, a professional photographer would snap a dozen portraits of a woman wearing a dozen different outfits. (As it turned out, the owner was teetering on bankruptcy, and this was his last, desperate sales venture.)

Jack steered Willa into the studio. She didn't want to go, but once she picked a red, floor-length gown from a box of costumes, she got into the spirit of play. The photographer posed her against a tall blue sheet, a fake sky. "A little more," he said. "Wistful. That's it. Turn your head, just a little . . . there!"

Before she switched outfits for the second shoot, Jack held her hand. "Miss Scarlet, will you marry me?"

Next, a polythene jumpsuit, the rock star look. "More pout! Cock that hip! That's it! Show it to me, babe!"

"Miss Whipcrack, I'm singin' the blues for you," Jack said, falling to his knees.

A Western ensemble: checked shirt, red bandanna.

"Miss Kitty, will you have my humble hand in holy matrimony? I know, I know, my skin is rough from all that nasty cotton I've picked . . . "

Of course, marriage doesn't come with a fake blue sky, Jack thought. *The storms are frighteningly real.*

But the "exotic Juanita" was a dozen secret women. His dark beauty! Life with her would never be boring.

Later, in the parking lot, sliding into the car, Willa in her ratty jeans looked stunning.

Jack was *not* a dozen men. He was still the same small boy, sore about losing his bike, vulnerable to love's sucker-punch.

He stopped moonlighting as a bartender. He bought a house in Plano. He promised Willa: no student parties. Once more, a good trick pony, running straight down the track, wearing blinders.

At night her scent was like cinnamon. In the most casual situations —tilting above a sink, scrubbing dishes—she was gorgeous. Before falling asleep at night, she'd circle her nipples with her fingers, smile dreamily at the ceiling then drift off. Her hug was a crush. It floored her that she could not squeeze hard enough, far enough, to reach Jack's darkest parts.

She didn't wear jewelry. "That's because your laughter is a necklace of silver," he said.

"You're such a fucking poet," she said.

Jacob, Jack's third son, was born in the spring, in 1986, while thousands of miles away Ben and Seth went the rounds with puberty.

As soon as Jake could walk, he tottered into the garden with Jack. Jack planted seeds. Mud-faced Jacob dug them up, his blunt little fingers squirming like worms. "No no," Jack said, laughing. "Honey, we've got to leave them, cozy, in the dirt so they can grow." With each fresh burial, Jake became more and more upset.

He'd toddle to the edge of the yard. He talked to rocks. "Mm-duh," he said. When the rocks didn't answer, he cried. He appealed to the holly bush: *Why don't they say something?* When the bush didn't move, he

103

turned a wet, accusing face to his father. *What kind of broken world have you dropped me in?*

"Mm-duh," Jack said. "And I mean it."

Jessie. His daughter.

What did it mean to be the father of a daughter? When she hit puberty, it meant visiting malls so she could sample make-up and pierce her ears.

Once, to entertain her after a long day shopping, he sat beside her in a pedicure chair and let a woman paint his toenails. "Carrot Red." Jessie laughed at his thin, hairy legs, his khaki pants rolled to his knees: "You have feet like a crippled old woman's!" A teenaged boy passed the shop and gave Jack a big thumb's up.

Jessie said she wanted a nose job so she wouldn't "look so Jewish." Jack swore to her she'd get more boyfriends if she left her nose alone, and he was right.

Much earlier, when his second family was still in its infancy, when redemption for his previous failures remained a possibility, Jack spent a lot of time building swing sets and slides in the yard. Skateboard ramps. Kiddie pools.

One Saturday morning, the children insisted on a neighborhood swim party in spite of a rainy forecast, so Jack set up the pool. He tried to erect a protective shelter. He propped two inverted laundry baskets on a stack of folding chairs. Twice, the rig collapsed. He anchored the chairs to three wooden poles and some concrete blocks he found in the tool shed. Then he pulled an old, discarded waterbed from the back of a closet. He and Willa had once bought the bed on a whim. On it, they'd had their first romantic encounter. Then they tucked it away. Now, he slit it open to form a makeshift tarp, and spread it over the baskets and chairs, covering the pool. "Pretty good, Dad," he told himself. "You've earned a nice, cold beer."

Maybe it wasn't so bad, after all—petty bourgeoisie materialism. He popped the can and looked warily at the sky. "Goddammit, it better rain," he muttered.

Success

As Long as You're Happy he titled his next book. Seamus Heaney, a famous Irish poet, a future Nobel Laureate, chose it as one of the winners in the National Poetry Series, a prestigious prize ensuring publication by a well-established press. The Academy of American Poets invited Jack to join. He was promoted to full professor, and given a hefty raise.

One semester, he decided to teach Dick Hugo's first poetry collection to his students. He placed an order at the university coop for thirty copies of the book. The store manager informed him the book was out of print: "Unavailable at this time." Jack was heartbroken. Quietly, he spent the afternoon with Goya's madmen, wondering, *What is success? Where is it kept?*

Liver Flukes

He imagined the creatures in his guts, a little face attached to each: the faces of his forebears, his children, children never born, the progeny of possible futures.

Everything I am is coming to kill me.

Inevitable

That old vagabond, the past. Of course, it showed up one day, demanding everything in the house.

You are *me, you son of a bitch. Don't pretend you're not.*

He'd been living like someone else. A manufactured identity, like a man in Witness Protection.

Waterbeds? Kiddie pools? Accolades?

A North Texas suburb?

"Jack!" His mother's voice in his head, like a curse.

Black, snapping creatures dredged from the depths of the ocean. They pursued him in his dreams.

His father's ghost, wearing a yellow slicker and a soaked Nor'easter, appeared in the bedroom at dawn one morning: "How can you live like this?"

One night—the kids screaming at their mother in the yard—he jumped into his car, a brand new Honda Accord. He drove into the desert. As in the good-old-bad-old days, somewhere east of Lubbock, he almost started a bar fight, but he sobered up just in time.

Reflections from blue-white refinery fires rippled across his windshield.

Back home, the horse kicking the sides of his mind wouldn't settle. Too damned familiar—all of it. He hadn't written poetry in months. He stamped around on the white shag carpet looking for open prairie. *Follow me*, said the past, reaching to snag the reins.

Obliteration

Oh, and the shock he got, years later! Leaning on a cart in a discount supermarket, clutching his list: the things he needed to survive—*cereal, triple-A batteries, foot powder, bread.*

Then he realized where he was.

Where he *had been.*

His bedroom. It used to sit right here. In *this* spot, this very aisle, between the meat case and the fish counter. Razed. Years ago. The physical joy he'd known here with Willa, on a quiet suburban street, was long missing; in its place, hundreds of pounds of processed food.

Over there, at the pharmacy, by the racks of athletic supporters, Jessie used to hold sleepovers with her girlfriends. Jake watched football on TV, sprawled across the living room floor wearing his Dallas Mavericks shorts. Now, where the boy had sat eating late-night popcorn, a man in dirty overalls was reaching for a box of salt-free chicken broth.

An entire housing division, plowed under as the suburbs expanded and real estate prices soared. Hundreds of settled lives, liquidated— "Everything Must Go!"—shoved aside to make room for boxes, cans, delivery trucks.

He felt like a veteran of an obscure war, suburban hand-to-hand combat, suffering the pain of a phantom limb—except his whole body was gone.

He should grab that old lady's cart, stop her in her tracks next to the half-price Handi-Wipes. Ask her: Was she aware of the big sell-off, how someday it would sweep every last crumb of their lives from the shelves?

"No," he said aloud, softly. "No, Jack. Get your things. Just get what you came for and get the hell out."

Ruins

Once, in the desert, he visited the remains of a thousand-year-old Pueblo village. It astonished him, how sacred and mysterious silence felt, swirling around hollow cliff dwellings.

He wondered: Was it better to leave a ruin rather than a finished monument?

Horse Trainer

Another suicide? Or had he simply grown tired of Willa's dark beauty? Poor Juanita. Never marry a poet.

Poolside, at a "Schmooze," he met a wealthy young widower, a major donor to the Art Department. Marci was her name. She lived on a boutique ranch just outside the city. He introduced himself as Picasso. Marci smiled, said nothing.

She was drunk enough to need a ride home. He wasn't as drunk as he wanted to be, so he offered her a lift, to take advantage of her Scotch.

She owned a single black stallion. At the ranch, once she'd changed into tight jeans and poured Jack a drink, she walked him outside to the stable. Loamy and moist. The horse reared. Jack backed away from the animal, into a splintered fence post. The horse chewed the wood, addictively—so much so, Marci said, he didn't get enough nutrition from his meals.

"Make friends with your fear," she told Jack. "And then you'll make friends with the horse. I'll show you." She reached for the animal's neck, stepped in front of him, and breathed into his nostrils. The horse shivered, calmed. Gently, Jack brushed his fluffy mane, his chest. That massive heart.

Stars jittered above the open stall like old television test patterns when Jack was a kid. Marci tottered on her feet. Jack walked her inside the house, tucked her into bed, told her hoped he'd see her again. He never did.

Before driving home, he braved the stable to confront his fear once more. He stroked the horse's jaw. "What are you going to do?" he said. "Marry and marry and marry again? How useless is that? How hurtful?" The stallion jerked his head up and down. Snapped at a spiky slat of wood.

"You are alone with Alone, / and it's his move"—Robert Penn Warren

Jack was on his own again, living in an efficiency apartment in a sterile, modern complex a block off Greenville Avenue.

Willa didn't yell that night. She didn't throw books. She didn't even give him a chance to insist he'd not slept with the woman, when he returned outrageously late smelling of whiskey and horse.

All she said was, "You need to move out. At least for a while."

The biggest shock to him was that he didn't try to argue.

He didn't want a bachelor pad. He wanted to be with himself.

The dwelling was too perfect, the pool painted so blindingly blue no one wanted to dip in it. It was like the gorgeous girl in high school everyone was afraid to approach. Jack sat in his room, blinds half-open, smoking.

Occasionally, the girl from 1B below, who moonlighted as a stripper, slipped outside wearing a red bikini. While she tanned, splaying her legs in a nylon recliner, most of the first floor residents suddenly needed ice from the machine at the pool's far end. They popped out of their dark apartments, gripping plastic buckets, and fast-walked past the woman dozing in her chair. *My god, it's like Hebrew School*, Jack thought, watching from above. *Boys nudging each other, "How far did you get with her?" as if they'd traveled thousands of miles. Really, all they'd done was burrow deeper into loneliness.*

All his life, he'd defined himself against the physical realities of women. What they were, what he wanted from them (and could never have, given matter's essential flaws).

It was enough to make you gnaw wood.

He remembered, early in his marriage—he and Willa had taken Jacob on his first big vacation to a lake resort in southern Oklahoma. As soon as they checked into their room, Jake screamed, "No! Why do we have to move to *this* tiny place?"

Now Jake, with his father gone from the house, hugged his mother's knees. He demanded to know, "Why are you apart?"

Unlike the older boys—Ben, who *had* grown a beard now, an angry nest to warn away the world, and Seth on his bike, leaping like Icarus into the sun—Jake seemed unprotected, exposed, a creature missing its shell.

One night, refusing to hear again Willa's explanations of why Jack had moved out, Jake ran into the woods behind her house. He ran so fast he imagined his legs circling backwards, like the wagon wheels in TV Westerns he'd watched with his dad, spinning in reverse. That way, leaving felt like a grand arrival.

On days off from school he'd sit, late into the day, wearing a blue bathrobe and eating plums from the fridge. He talked to no one.

A few years later, when the worst had occurred, worse than the very worst night, Jack wrote:

> *I never told you this, but I remember the exact moment*
> *I conceived you, how I thrust all that was good in me,*
> *like a pink storm of storks taking off and blurring into the eternal,*
> *into who you'd become. But I forgot that all of the dark*
> *matter that also made me would eventually undo you, bring us*
> *to this dead-fall wall of absence each day is.*

Sort of Sad for No Reason

In the last two years of his life, trying to manage his illness, Jack spent more time talking to his sisters and brother, by phone, than he had in the previous decade. He wanted a neat ending.

After a few aimless years, and dozens of brutal beatings as a semi-pro boxer, Marshall had followed Jack to college. He earned an advanced degree in chemistry. Afterwards, for over forty years, he'd labored for a multinational corporation. He extracted the natural flavors of foods, distilled their molecules, and injected the illusion of taste into manufactured meat: lean cuisine for an on-the-go America!

Now retired in Florida, Marshall smoked El Producto blunts beside a swimming pool and praised the "good life." On the phone, Jack heard a constant stream of freeway noise roaring close behind him.

Marshall didn't like to reminisce. He wasn't the sentimental type. He stayed quiet when Jack recalled their mother setting steaming plates on the supper table, saying, "Eat, eat so you can grow up and get out of here!"

Jack mused, "The old man—he was a full-bore son of a bitch, wasn't he? But oh, how I miss him." Marshall just grunted.

Sandi and Ellen had each been divorced. Twice. Their kids were distant and bitter. "Fruit of the spoils," Sandi said. "What're you gonna do?"

Whenever Jack asked Ellen how she was getting along, she always said, "Oh, I'm okay, I guess." A raspy sigh. "You know. Sort of sad for no reason."

Second-Hand Book Shop

In the tenth year of his third marriage, Jack believed that, in the late rounds, he just might make a success of it. He was old now. He didn't have *time* to fuck up.

Thea was not a poet but poetry was her business. She ran a literary non-profit. She raised money for readings, libraries, educational outreach. She understood "what Jack was all about," she said. Privately, Jack groused that he *still* didn't get himself.

They moved into a spacious house in the West Dallas suburb of Mesquite. Lawyers and doctors were their neighbors. Thea hired a crew of Spanish women to clean the place. They came once a week. Jack never got used to someone tidying up his messes.

The women knew him more intimately than he knew himself. They straightened his heart pill vials on the bathroom shelves. They picked his gray pubic hair from the trash. They saw precisely how fast he was falling apart.

At the end of the day, each week, he handed them cash. Silently, they boarded buses back to their unseen lives.

He remembered the empty shoes he'd seen in the desert.

At school these days, he encountered fewer black sheep—certainly no groups of students matched the commitment of that first bunch, the Wildcats, so many years ago. Poetry-writing was a popular elective among business majors. They flocked to the class because they thought it would be easy. He told them poetry wasn't a career, it was a vocation; it wasn't about success or failure, it was a matter of losing one's ego to serve a larger vision.

One day, a freshman boy smelling of soap and cologne, the smell of a "Schmooze," wrote a poem about a poetry teacher who stroked an ego he wouldn't acknowledge by publishing poems in obscure magazines. No one read the magazines except other insecure poets. Jack gave him an A.

A young woman who referred to Jack as her mentor, an exchange student from Colombia, explained to him in his office one day that she'd like to arrange a reading tour for him in the barrios of her country. His words would bring poor, suffering people the spiritual encouragement they needed. *Me? What could I possibly offer, from my perch in the well-swept American Dream?* Jack thought.

This girl was not a poet. She was an angel. Ten years ago he would've tried to sleep with her. "You know, poetry makes nothing happen," he said. She stared at him, confused and a little dismayed.

Once or twice a year, he flew to an academic conference or to invited readings at other universities. If he was seated next to a chatty person on the plane, he had to decide whether or not to confess he was a poet. It was tricky, being a poet in America. Usually, if he identified himself, people turned away and said nothing else, gazing through the window at the wing, investing themselves in something solid, something they understood.

Once, his seatmate asked him if he'd like to do a word-puzzle with him, to pass the time. When Jack answered, "I'm a college English teacher," the man stiffened, as if Jack had called him dumb. "I'm a vet. Two tours in Afghanistan," he said, and that settled the question of who should survive the crash, if God brought down the plane.

Late one afternoon, after teaching his final class for the day, Jack stepped into a second-hand book shop. He'd spotted it on a side road on his way home from school. Not much to interest him. Auto repair manuals, celebrity bios, home computer guides. Candidates' campaign talking-points tricked-up as serious policy discussions.

Freud's *Civilization and Its Discontents.* He'd never read the book, but no author had ever picked a truer title.

Poetry filled the back room. Dusty. Flickering fluorescent lights. Clearly, no one wandered in here. In a teetering stack of chapbooks, he found a yellowed copy of *Black Sun Abraxas.* How thin it looked! Fragile. He clutched it to his chest.

Inside the cover, names and dates had been crossed out in ink. At least three times, over thirty years ago, the book had been given as a gift. Now it was discarded. He remembered his days in Harvard Square,

110

sitting in the aisles at Grolier's, thumbing through books. Random pleasures. Astonishing discoveries. He remembered reading to Nancy, later, in bed. Elizabeth Bishop. Robert Lowell.

Her smile. Her warm smell. Her kind, violet eyes.

Poetry had made everything happen.

With care, he placed the book on a shelf and walked away.

Worse than the Very Worst Night

Willa, weary on the phone: "He told me to go screw myself. Again. Then he ran off to stay with his girlfriend."

Jake was twenty now, impossible to console. Well, of course. He was twenty.

Jack remembered when Jake wouldn't stop crying as a baby. Jack carried the boy outside. In the yard, in the moonlight, maybe in some visceral way Jake would understand how everything vanished in darkness, how vast the darkness was. Somehow, Jack thought, Jake's instinctual awareness of his smallness, his unimportance, would correct whatever was not good.

It didn't work then. It wouldn't work now.

"Okay, I'll talk to him," Jack promised Willa.

He found his son's number in his phone's contact list. He wanted to say, "Jake, you're clinging to your girlfriend just to forget who you are, and she's holding on to you for the same reason. Where's that going to get you?" But he had no moral standing in such matters. He knew that.

Why are you and Mom apart? The unspoken question sharpened every sentence Jake tossed his way.

Jack said, "Please. Apologize to your mother."

"Screw you, Dad," Jake said.

Three years later, in the immediate aftermath, Jack was like a tank commander tearing through Iraq: he had a rage to lock onto every beautiful thing and destroy it.

Maybe that's how Jake had felt.

Not just the anger. The helplessness. The sorrow. In addition to everything else—his life-long confusion about why his mother and father were apart, his shock at seeing his childhood home razed for a supermarket—he feared losing Jack a second time.

Of course that was a factor.

Slumped in the chemo ward, hands shaking, Jack scribbled on a thin sheet of paper, "I would've jumped in front of the bullet, I would've / killed for him, but he was the one who took his life / leaving me swirling in mid-air . . . "

111

Obituary

From *The Dallas Morning News*, May 8, 2009: "Jacob Myers, age 23 of Plano, Texas passed away May 6, 2009, leaving us heartbroken . . . Loved by many, Jacob left us too soon . . . "

To-do List

Do nothing.

Temple

His empty shoes screamed at him, sitting beneath the gurgling IV.

He was breaking down, a pile of pick-up sticks.

For years, he had lined the gray walls of his study at home with his paltry achievements: books, honorary degrees, plaques and awards.

As if he was a minor American god, deserving of a temple. Instead of what he was: a loose affiliation of atoms, about to blow apart.

He'd wanted to show the world what he could do. So he preserved what he had done.

The shoes? They weren't at all impressed.

The Worst Night

The kid had made it to dawn. "Jack?"

Jack stirred.

"I should probably go. Thank you. Thank you for—"

"You sure? You can hang a while longer. I can make some more coffee."

"No, it's okay. I'm . . . okay. I think you saved my life."

Jack shook his head.

"No, really . . . if you hadn't brought me here . . . "

"Hey. We're going to get through this. Both of us, all right?"

Tracy nodded.

"So. You're good?"

"Yeah. Gonna get some sleep."

"If you need to talk again later? I'll be in my office this afternoon."

"I'm sorry, you know, about your wife."

"Yeah," Jack said.

"Okay. Again—"

"Hey. Enough. I didn't do a thing."

"You were here. Means the world."

They stood. The morning air was cold. Jack cupped a hand around his student's neck. "Beautiful man," he said. "Remember your unimportance."

Last contacts

Subject: (No subject)
From: Daugherty, Tracy
To: Myers, Jack
Sent: Thursday, April 01, 2009 3:05 PM

Dear Jack: I heard you were having some health problems. I'm very sorry to learn this, and I wanted you to know I'm thinking of you. Distance—in time and space—is a tricky and terrible thing. Too many years slip past and it's all too easy to lose touch. But I keep your books on my desk and often turn to them. You have been, and remain, a touchstone for me and for many, many others. Hang in there. Love, Tracy.

Re: (No subject)
From: Myers, Jack
To: Daugherty, Tracy
Sent: April 02, 2009 8:13 AM

Hey Tracy. Lovely to get your e-mail. I hope you're flourishing out West, teaching and writing well. Yeah, I'm going through lots of chemo and radiation in preparation for a liver transplant. I have this weird kind of terminal cancer. I'm fine except for all the poisoning. But I'm managing to eke out a few new poems. Thanks for your good thoughts, good words, which I send right back at you. Love, Jack.

Subject: (No subject)
From: Daugherty, Tracy
To: Myers, Jack
Sent: Sunday, May 10, 2009 9:07 PM

Dear, dear Jack: My thoughts are with you as you say goodbye to your son. Recalling an old poem of yours, I will fill a great sombrero full of tears. Much love to you, and blessings in this sad time. Tracy

Re: (No subject)
From: Myers, Jack
To: Daugherty, Tracy
Sent: Monday, May 11, 2009 8:57 AM

Thanks, Tracy. Your kindness has always been your signature. Yours, Jack

Before and After

Jack drove into the desert. The golden urn containing Jacob's ashes trembled on the seat beside him. He wasn't sure where to leave his son's traces but he'd know the right locations when he saw them—perhaps a purple mesa where the sun rose behind a swirl of hawks each morning, or an old river gully etching the possible reappearance of water some-day, renewing life in a valley of waste.

Thea and Jack's doctors had cautioned him against making this trip—he'd miss a chemo treatment; he was weak—but he insisted on the importance of ritual and on being alone, one last time, with his boy.

Pumpjacks rusted all around him in thorny mesquite fields. Late in the day, Jack stopped at a Mobil station just outside of Wink. His tires pounded across the compressor hose, releasing a hiss of sadness. It rose then fell in the dry, crackling air. The woozy fumes of premium-grade gas made him want to sleep, sleep and not wake up. Inside the station, behind the cash register, a fat woman stood wearing a round tin button. The button said, "Ask Me about My Make-Over!" Behind her, on a wooden stool, a young lady, perhaps her daughter, sat doing math homework. A large red rash shaped like an egg marred her leg. On a wall poster above her, an ad for a weight loss program—"Before" and "After" photos of a woman in a bathing suit. Looking none too thin, either way. Jack handed the fat woman a wad of cash. She short-changed him by a couple of bills but he didn't have the strength to complain.

In the men's room, he splashed cold water on his face. It tasted of Sulphur. He gazed at the mirror: a gray void. It wasn't a mirror. It was the interior of an empty towel dispenser. Someone had ripped away its white metal cover.

Still accurate, thought Jack. That's me, exactly.

The bed in his motel room that night came with a "Magic Fingers" box. If you slipped two quarters into the box, the bed would vibrate. Jack fished in his pocket for loose change. Then he lay down, fully clothed, gripping the urn on his stomach. For twenty minutes, he endured a minor earthquake.

Staring at the stunted desert plants, he recalled the apple tree he'd climbed as a kid outside his parents' bedroom. One year, a small split appeared in its trunk, a gash in the bark.

Just as anger and sorrow have split me in half, Jack thought.

After that, the tree never bore fruit.

Cell phones didn't work here. Thea must be frantic. "I miss you, darling," Jack whispered into the dark, dead screen.

Nancy and Ben beside him, in the car. No: that was years ago, in a much different world. He must have been dozing at the wheel. Dreaming.

Leave the road. Rest a while.

Maybe he should just turn around. None of the gullies or hills suited Jake. Trailer trucks passed Jack on the highway, careening at perilous speeds. On the radio, Tammy Wynette cried for her cheatin' man. A stubby fellow in a bright orange vest, part of a road crew, waved a plastic flag at Jack. A gentle benediction. Jack wept.

Mystic Whispers

He returned Jake's urn to the fireplace mantel. The cleaning women dusted it once a week.

One day, Thea said she'd made up her mind: When *she* died, she wanted to be cremated.

Jack wasn't sure how to throw himself away. What if some poisonous essence rose from his body when it burned? Did he want "mini-Chernobyl" to be people's last memory of him?

On the other hand, no one in his home town remembered him. Why should he lie with those bastards (he'd outlasted Bill Smithson, at least)? On a tombstone, he could leave a poem, causing graveyard visitors to pause and contemplate the miracle of their lives. But he'd tried to write poems like that while he was (more-or-less) living. The results were mixed.

He remembered drifting off under the anesthetic just before his heart surgery, thinking, *Okay, I'm ready for death*, and hearing, next, "Wake up, it's over."

Would it be like *that*?

He'd tried to make art of the life he'd led, having failed to make an art of living it.

One late afternoon, sitting with him in the chemo ward, holding his hand, Thea glanced out the window at an oak tree's falling leaves. "Trees are like angels," she murmured.

"What?" Jack said.

"Oh, you know. They're rooted in soil but it's like . . . their arms fly in the air. They make food out of light. They give us our air."

Jack smiled, weepy.

His wife squeezed his hand. "Jack."

"Yes, sweetie?"

"Do you . . . do you ever pray?"

He returned her squeeze. "My prayers have been answered," he said. Then—his prayer for her—he let her go.

Obituary

From *The Dallas Morning News*, November 29, 2009: "In addition to his wife Thea and his remaining children, Ben, Seth, and Jessie, Jack is survived by generations of grateful students."

Recently, in a time of grief . . .

. . . I returned to my old teacher's poems, after many years away from them. My teacher's example, his life—with all its flaws and faults, its bravery and sweetness—rose again before me.

Poetry

So I made this story. Now that it's over—what was it?

An empty shoe, screaming. A falling leaf.

If we could find a book crumbling on a library shelf somewhere, a book on literary form, we might find a description of something like this story: an "impure fiction," perhaps. Jack would probably like that. "*All things are impure*," he'd say. "Never trust the word 'kosher.'"

The real story is in Jack's books. Or maybe not. After all, he was a poet.

But, formally speaking, here's what happened: one day, one of his former students, re-reading Jack's poems, remembering what he'd learned, remembering how Jack saved his life one night, extrapolated this modest story from the work, a gesture of gratitude—too little, too late, as most such gestures are.

Like every attentive student, he stole what he needed from his teacher and made up all the rest.

Why do this? Words are strange.

And because, like so much American poetry, the books are out of print. If you're lucky, you might find a copy here and there, available for a nickel or two.

What're you gonna do? It's enough to break your fucking heart.

Valediction

So that was it—the education of Jack Elliott Myers (1941-2009): "[W]e've all spent years in rooms snowing darkness . . . / All I wanted to say, my friends, is / I'm amazed that you're still singing."

AKHMATOVA'S NOTEBOOK

1.

Thirty years ago, late on a Thursday night, I flew into the rainy Willamette Valley in western Oregon to interview for a job. I was met at the airport by a big Russian who had once been the lover of the twentieth century's greatest poet. I too had loved this poet—but only in translation, on the page, as an undistinguished student in a poetics seminar in a college in rural Texas.

The poet's name was Anna Akhmatova. These chant-like syllables were the first sounds out of the Russian's mouth. He stood like a granite block in the airport waiting lounge. He introduced himself as Vladimir Kaminski and said he was a faculty member in the Department of Foreign Languages at Oregon State University. The job I sought was in the English Department but the English chair had sent Kaminski to pick me up because I had mentioned Akhmatova in my application letter along with Czeslaw Milosz, another poet I'd studied. I'd hoped the names would impress prospective employers.

"Our dear Anna," Kaminski said to me as I plucked my bag off the luggage carousel. Weary kids wailed at their mothers by the rental car counter. "I'm quite curious to hear about your study of her."

It was a forty-mile car ride from the airport to the bed and breakfast near the campus where I'd stay through the weekend; the rain was thick, swirling in pearly mist, so the going would be slow. Along the way, Kaminski said, he would tell me how he had studied "our dear Anna." He laughed in such a low, guttural manner I anticipated an uncomfortable trip, and not just because I'd be squeezed into a little Honda next to this capacious man.

When he slipped behind the wheel he handled his bulk with such lightness and grace I couldn't help but be impressed: he seemed to be demonstrating that flesh was an instrument one could learn to play, teasing from it fresh nuances as it aged, and one's skill and familiarity with it increased. His rock-like head, speckled with patches of thin white hair, tilted upwards over the car's sloping dash. His nose was thin: a little triangle of tin foil in the dim, reflected lights of the parking lot. His profile reminded me of old photographs of Franklin D. Roosevelt, smug and laughing faced with the world's economic disasters, or of Batman's arch-enemy, the Penguin, in the comic books I'd read as a kid.

He wore brown khaki pants, a forest-green pullover sweater—"wore" doesn't quite get it. His body *tolerated* his clothing, like a dog accepting a leash for the outdoor adventure it allowed. In the next few days, I would

119

learn that layered informality was OSU's faculty style. The university had once been an ag college and was struggling now, in the late 1980s, to take itself seriously enough to make the necessary moves, with money and new personnel, to become a viable research institution.

I was—maybe—the type of young recruit capable of revitalizing its humanities classes. I was twenty-eight years old, fresh from a Ph.D program in literature at the University of Houston, a credential that would probably have gotten me nowhere had I not lucked out and just published a novel with a reputable New York house. Luck, I call it: of course I'd worked hard; I flatter myself that I had a little talent, and I'd overcome my natural shyness to cultivate my teachers, socially. Subsequently, one of them had used his New York connections to pitch my manuscript—a coming-of-age-story, what else?—to a literary agent. Here's the luck. The agent had grown up in Texas, thirty miles from Midland, my hometown, and retained just enough memory of the taste of dust and the high whistle of the wind to find my story "authentic." He talked an editor into coughing up a modest advance for the novel.

Already, as an object in the world—it had been in stores for three months by the time I landed in Oregon—my book was showing a pronounced physical weakness, like a preemie unable to fill its lungs. It had received one lukewarm review, but that notice had appeared in the Sunday *New York Times*—"Valuable real estate!" my editor had crowed on the phone to me, his cheerfulness much too forced. I suspected, rightly, this would be the last contact we'd ever have. But the review was enough, along with my doctorate, to convince the chair of the Oregon State English Department that I might be a writer.

As I would soon learn, the school didn't really need a writer. It needed a babysitter to keep kids busy in its writing courses, but that's a common story, and one for another day.

That rainy Thursday night, Kaminski curled the car along a road so dark I thought I understood for the first time the concept of "black holes," voids in space that could *eat light*. The road was doing that right in front of me. Bursts of mist rushed the headlights. Kaminski cracked the driver's side window to keep the windshield from fogging up and a sharp scent of mint pierced my nose. I must have startled in my seat because Kaminski laughed. "Yes. Even now, in deepest February, these fields remain fertile. The Pastures of Plenty." As he spoke, he tapped his heavy gold wedding band on the steering wheel, as if pacing out the rhythms of his words. "Each year, the smell of new life erupts again, it seems, before winter ever gets a firm grip on the valley. We're located fifty miles from the Pacific Ocean on one side and fifty miles from the Cascade Mountain Range on the other. You'd be hard-pressed to find a more beautiful spot in the country."

I nodded. All I could see was rain-spatter and roiling white puffs emerging out of the darkness. And then, just ahead, maybe fifty yards in the distance, to my left, a horse made of light galloped through an open field. I squinted to focus: yes, the delicate red outline of a pony, a warm pulse, its mane a series of vertical slashes, the tail a glowing whip. Kaminski laughed at me again. "A whole new way of seeing out here. Keep looking. You'll find others." And I did: a blue colt nosing grass near a rotting wooden barn, a pair of prancing yellow stallions. The animals' electric curves cast burning haloes in the mist—circles of color undulating up and down the valley. "Last year, the state commissioned an artist from Portland to manufacture several neon figures and place them in fields here and there. There's a lot of public support for the arts in Oregon," Kaminski said. "How's that for a sales pitch?"

We'd reached the south edge of the town of Corvallis, the home of the Oregon State campus—an auto wrecking lot, a stockyard, a 7-Eleven store, a boarded-up tavern and several trailer houses. I realized, with relief, that Kaminski had not mentioned Akhmatova again. The truth was, I'd exaggerated my knowledge of her work in my application letter. I'd read a handful of her poems in translation. I'd read a five-page biography of her in a literary encyclopedia. A few months back, a teacher of mine had advised me that my chances of landing an academic position would improve if I indicated an interest in "feminist studies," so I listed Akhmatova as a "major" influence on my writing. I said I'd drafted a short story based on her life—this much was true—and that I was imagining a fictionalized version of her struggles with Stalin as the core of my second novel. Already, I knew this would never happen. The task was beyond me.

Suddenly, flashing red lights illuminated Kaminski's back windshield, making each raindrop on the glass a bright bead of blood. For a disorienting moment I wondered if we'd been overtaken by a neon horse.

A cop had pulled us over.

"I'll be candid with you," Kaminski said to me, lowering his window as the patrolman approached the car. "The one down side to living in Corvallis is the constant harassment you'll get from local law enforcement. You'd think we were living in Leningrad!" He added, "They don't have enough to do," before turning to greet the officer: "What can I do for you?"

"Evening, sir," the policeman said, tipping his hat, no more mature than the students I'd expect to teach here. His face was a quilt of acne. "Tell me, do you know what the speed limit is along this stretch of highway?"

"Yes, I assumed it was forty-five," Kaminski said confidently, pointing through the front windshield at a speed limit sign not twenty yards ahead of us.

121

"Right, well . . . " The cop glanced at the sign, clearly flustered: he'd confused the road or the speed. He slipped his ticket-book back into his pocket. "Well, yessir, you're quite right. Quite right. You have a good evening, sir." He tipped his hat again and returned to his car.

"Incompetent," Kaminski muttered. "Coming from a world-class city like Houston, you're liable to find this a toy town. But that can have its charms. Don't judge it too quickly."

"Before moving to Houston, I went to school in small towns in West Texas," I said. "I know, and appreciate, the kind of charm you're talking about."

"You're going to have a long day tomorrow—meetings with the chair and the dean, an informal sit-down with some of our students, and then your afternoon presentation. I have an itinerary for you, but . . . are you too tired for a nightcap before I drop you at the B and B?"

I was bushed, but it seemed impolitic to turn him down. A senior faculty member . . . he was one of the people I'd have to impress, or at least get along with, if I wanted to work here. "Sure," I said.

"Good. I want to hear all about you and our dear Anna."

Tommy's 4th Street Grill was attached to a split-level motel on the main street into town from the airport—just a notch above the kinds of shady places offering "Hourly Rates." Who could have believed this grimy setting would begin an unlikely story? Four or five couples, all elderly, and all seriously alcoholic, judging from their sagging, red looks, sat in the bar lounge's murky blue light, beneath hand-lettered signs on the walls for chicken fried steaks and goat-meat tacos. Kaminski led us to a booth in the darkest corner of the room. Was this the sales pitch's opposite—the grim challenge to be surmounted hereabouts? Now that you've heard the good, take a look at the bad, weigh it all carefully? I couldn't imagine why he'd brought me here.

"You'll want a local IPA," he said. "Some of the best beer in the country —brewed right here in the valley."

Again to my relief, he didn't start right in on "our dear Anna." He seemed genuinely interested in my life's particulars. I'd been told by my teachers that it wasn't appropriate for a hiring committee to get too personal, and I was coached not to answer any questions that seemed too intimate. *Was* Kaminski on the hiring committee? He wasn't in the English Department. *Were* his questions inappropriate, or was he just being friendly? Was it okay to sit in this bar with him? I was too new at the dance to read the signals or to strategize a smart response.

I told him about Patty—how we planned to marry in the spring once my job-picture clarified. How she was seven years older than I was, much more mature and settled in her life, a long-time instructor at the

University of Houston, teaching English as a second language. Still, she was willing to move anywhere in the country, wherever my prospects took me.

"And why is that?" Kaminski wanted to know.

Perhaps it was the beer and the exhaustion, or my confusion about the circumstances, but I thought Kaminski's tone implied I'd suggested something unsavory about Patty—meekness or opportunism or weakness of character. I hastened to dispel any such notions. "She loves me," I said, smiling. "Plus—on the practical side—she can't get tenure in her field. We're hoping I can land a more secure, higher-paying job. You know, it's tough for academic couples."

"Tough for couples, period," Kaminski breathed into his glass.

I told him I'd met Patty three years ago at a department picnic—I'd glimpsed her face across a bare meadow in a park and thought she had the nicest smile I'd ever seen.

I didn't tell him I'd had second thoughts, lately, about getting married.

Nor did I mention Sarah. Or how Sarah had left me, quitting school and fleeing Houston, six months before a friend introduced me to Patty. I didn't explain how Sarah had recently returned to the city. Three years, not a word from her, and now she was back. I didn't tell Kaminski I'd met with Sarah three times since her return—all in public, all on the beaches at Galveston . . . still, the meetings were a secret from Patty. I didn't tell him how Sarah pleaded with me to call off my wedding plans and move in with her—or to at least give my decision a little more time. Nor how, in spite of her pleas, she confessed to me that she was pregnant with another man's baby.

I didn't tell Kaminski the reason I was so exhausted had less to do with the stress of a job search and the plane flight than with the things I wasn't about to tell him.

He raised his almost-empty glass to me. "Congratulations," he said. "I hope you have a splendid wedding." And then he ordered us another round.

It was getting close to midnight. My first meeting would be at eight a.m. By now, I was certain that Kaminski was putting me through some kind of test—gauging my professional mettle based on my personal reactions to things. But how would I pass the test? By matching him drink for drink? Or by asserting my independence and insisting it was time for him to drop me at my B and B?

I thought a broad show of checking my watch would indicate responsible awareness without insulting him or necessarily revealing weakness. All it did was prompt him to assure me not to worry. I'd have no trouble getting into the bed and breakfast at this late hour.

The proprietress would be asleep, it's true. But she had left the front door code with him and she knew my schedule tomorrow. My room would be ready and breakfast would be waiting in the morning. He ordered us a third round of beers.

Wasn't his wife worried about *him*?

By this point, we were well into a discussion of "our dear Anna." Kaminski had started it, asking quietly, "So. You love Akhmatova?"

The Rolling Stones' "Wild Horses" played softly through a jukebox speaker. One of the elderly drinkers by the door removed his dentures and set them on the table next to his basket of fries.

"I love her work, yes."

"But do you love *her*?"

"Well, her work, as I've encountered it . . . you know, mostly in the Kunitz and Hayward translations . . . " I feared my stumbling had revealed what a fraud I'd been in my application letter, but Kaminski was after something different. With his open palm he slapped his chest. "I loved her," he said, lowering his head in a way that forced me to lean close. "*Her*. Do you understand me? That magnificent woman."

In my mind, I had a sudden, frantic picture of him chasing her around a table. "You knew her?"

"Oh yes. In Petersburg. 1940. Of course, it was called Leningrad, but those of us who loved the city kept its old name locked in our hearts. Pushkin's city, as Anna thought of it so warmly. Her son, Lev, had just been jailed again to stop her from writing."

"I'm envious," I said. "I mean, of your time with her."

"Yes, well, the days were hard. Make no mistake about that. Brutal, even. Anna was skin and bones. Living on cold tea and stale cabbage. But still regal. Still a beauty. She put no words on paper for fear they'd be circulated, confiscated. She didn't want to endanger Lev any further. So she would recite her poems in a hoarse whisper, right into my ear. The opening lines of 'Requiem.'" He leaned back in the padded red leather booth. "'Such grief might make the mountains stoop, / reverse the waters where they flow, / but cannot burst these ponderous bolts / that block us from these prison cells . . . '"

He'd quoted the Kunitz translation, I noticed, just for me. Did I believe this man?

"Then she would tell me, 'Forget it now. Go. Pretend you never saw me.'"

"Did you—"

"We were lovers for six months," he said, self-satisfied, "and then I immigrated to England. As you know, Anna would never think of leaving. She was determined to be a martyr." He shook his head.

"You think she made the wrong decision?"

"Certainly, in terms of her personal happiness. Obviously, not with regard to the posthumous value of her poetry." He took a sip of his beer. "*You're* an artist."

Was he mocking me now?

"What do you think, young man? Is it worth sacrificing your happiness, your well-being, for your writing?"

"Well, I—I mean—"

"That's why I ask, 'Do you love her?' If you love her, you must love her example."

He *was* a believer in tests.

"Let me show you something." He reached into the inner pocket of his suit jacket and produced two small notebooks, one ancient-looking with a cracked black leather cover, the other more modern, made simply of heavy paper. "This is a little project of mine. You might be interested in taking a look at it over the weekend, while you're here."

Another challenge—as if performing tomorrow on too many beers and too little sleep wasn't enough? He was a minor tyrant, Kaminski. I was about to make another show of checking my watch when he opened the black notebook: crabbed Russian lettering in heavy ink, faded on stiff, yellowed pages. "Our dear Anna," he said.

"This was *her* notebook?"

He nodded. "Entrusted to me for safe-keeping."

I was about to say, "I thought she didn't write anything down," but he riffled the pages of the second notebook.

"Off and on for many years now—not as part of my professional work, but as a personal labor of love—I've been slowly translating passages of this into English. I'm not sure it has any worth. These were Anna's hasty scribbles. Of course, she's become quite famous since her death, so *anything* of hers would stir public interest, but . . . these were her intimate thoughts. I feel somewhat protective of her." He urged the notebooks on me. "Hang on to them for the next day or so. Look them over. Let me know what you think. Maybe you can help me figure out what to do with them."

How could he seriously trust me, an inexperienced job candidate, a stranger he might never see again after this weekend, with something so valuable? Surely this was another set-up? "I . . . you know, I can't read Russian," I admitted.

"Let me know if the English sounds to you like the Anna you've encountered. And indulge yourself . . . touch the pages that Anna touched. Enjoy the experience. It's a rare privilege, yes?

"Yes, indeed. Thank you."

"Now, excuse me, I'm going to make a phone call. How about another round?"

125

"No, I—"

"Yes, I think one more. I'll be right back."

Again with consummate grace, he slid his bulk out of the narrow space and headed for the wall phone by the bathrooms in the rear of the bar, pausing to order two more IPAs from the bartender. I had promised to call Patty once I'd settled into my room but it was too late to phone her now. She was two hours ahead. I sat, trying to focus my vision on the small, arched letters in the brittle notebook. I held the pages to my nose, hoping to catch the essence of poet.

And then the poet walked in the door.

When Akhmatova died in 1966, she was puffy and gray. For many years she had suffered heart disease and scads of ravages brought on by the filthy, unheated flats she dwelled in, always on the move, the tainted water she'd ingested, the intermittent, poorly-balanced meals she'd managed to scrounge. Stalin kept her from publishing and from earning a living because he feared the power of her language to rouse her countrymen into being alive. The authorities had murdered her husband and repeatedly arrested her son. The last photographs of her show a woman still defiant but softened by hardship, weakened by depression, bloated in her limbs, a tottering grandmother.

But the woman who walked into Tommy's 4th Street Grill was a manifestation of the young poet, the seductive and scandalous beauty of St. Petersburg, distinguished by her haunted stare. One glimpse of her face, and the word "sadness" could have no meaning for you other than "those large, brown eyes." They seemed erotically naked because of the thin, black bangs trembling just above them, a veil lifted to reveal what it shouldn't. The strong chin, the high cheekbones formed pale, perfect geometric planes straight out of a Modigliani painting. The nose—a little boomerang of flesh that should have been slightly repulsive but was, instead, mesmerizing in its uniqueness. She wore a simple black dress, a delicate shroud.

I'd had just enough experience with "feminist studies" to know I was guilty of a loud and outrageous "male gaze."

Kaminski crossed the bar and kissed her small right ear. "I just tried to call you, to see where you were."

"I'm sorry I'm late," she mumbled. "I had to finish a paper."

They stood side by side, arms casually touching. Instantly, I knew they were sleeping together. She wore no wedding ring. She was a good forty years younger than he was. I wondered if their affair, and the need to keep it secret, accounted for Kaminski's attraction to Tommy's dark corners and the adjacent motel. "Jeremy, this is Bridget Beresford," he said to me. "Jeremy Allman."

"Hello," the woman said. An unidentifiable accent—barely detectible, but there.

"Bridget is a senior in the English Department, and quite a fine young poet." He studied my face— to see, I believed, if I'd noticed the uncanny resemblance to "our dear Anna." I nodded and smiled. "She'll be one of your escorts as the department puts you through your paces tomorrow. You'll meet him just after breakfast to take him over to campus, yes?"

"That's right," Bridget said. Shyly, she avoided my gaze.

Kaminski brought our beers to the table and a glass of white wine for Bridget. The three of us sat silently for the next twenty minutes, Kaminski staring openly at Bridget as if she were an apparition oblivious of our presence. She stayed focused on her hands, wrapped delicately around the stem of her glass. I felt very much like a third wheel, and awkwardly memorized every inch of the goat-meat poster.

Finally, Kaminski rose to pay our tab. "Bright and early tomorrow, Jeremy."

"Yes."

"I'll come by around 7:30," Bridget said, still just barely looking at me.

"Thank you." I tucked the two notebooks into my coat pocket.

"Okay, I'll run you by the B and B," Kaminski said. Bridget remained in the bar. I presumed she'd wait for his return. And then what? Would they get a room? Was this behavior—sophisticated? sleazy?—the exception or the rule in small-town academia?

It was just a short, six-block drive through the center of town, but on the way, two police cruisers passed us, moving slowly. Either Kaminski was right, and the cops had little to do in Corvallis, or he was a magnet for them. The place *was* beginning to feel like my impression, from the little reading I'd done, of war-time Leningrad.

2.

The bed and breakfast was in an old, three-story Arts and Craft house perched on the northern edge of the town's central park, next to a former chapel that appeared to be modeled on the farmhouse in Grant Wood's *American Gothic*, turned now into a quaint little arts center. I couldn't tell much about the B and B in the dark: mullioned windows, gabled eaves. The night's persistent rain had become a slushy snow. Kaminski said, with apologies, he'd not see me into the house, as the going might be a little slippery for him. I was sure he couldn't wait to turn the car around and get back to the bar. He gave me the front door code and a copy of my itinerary. I pulled my bag from the back seat, thanked him for picking me up and welcoming me to town. I patted my coat pocket. "I'll take good care of the notebooks. Thank you."

"Yes," he said. "We must cherish our poets."

His words conjured for me a picture of slender Bridget in her sleek, dark shroud, sitting, demure and alone, back at Tommy's among the goat meat and the loose dentures while Keith Richards growled inside the jukebox.

I carefully climbed the wooden porch steps and managed the door code in the dark. On a small round table in the vestibule, a hand-written note beneath a lamp (a single red rose painted on the lamp's silk shade) invited me to make myself at home, to take the room at the top of the stairs on the second landing, and to expect breakfast at a quarter to seven.

In the front parlor, at the bottom of the staircase, an air-brushed black and white photograph of Ronald Reagan hung on an otherwise empty wall. Beneath the gilded frame was the typed caption, "Our Current U. S. President." Perhaps the lady of the house gets a lot of students here as guests, I thought, trying not to find the picture and the label as strange as they seemed. Perhaps she's compelled to dispense civics lessons.

My room was a high-ceilinged triangle, with a single window opening onto the park. Below, bare shrubs shivered in chilly lamplight, surrounded by hearty green patches of things staunchly refusing to die. The gray wallpaper's pink, printed daises spun around the room—I was dizzy-drunk, not terribly so, but enough so I couldn't lie down and close my eyes right away. It was nearly two o'clock. The bar would be closing. Kaminski would be sneaking into the slick night with the ghost of his poet. Except she wasn't a ghost.

I flung my bag onto the bed, popped it open, and laid the suit, shirt, and tie I'd wear tomorrow for my interviews and presentation across the back of a big, stuffed chair. I pulled a snapshot of Patty from my wallet and propped it against a table lamp by the bed. That lovely smile of hers—special because, in the mild downward curl at the ends of her mouth, the smile made room for doubt: "Should I really be smiling?" Her light blue eyes lent a cloudy look to that uncertain glimmer, and made the effort to smile seem doubly brave.

I imagined Patty asleep on our bed in Houston. We shared the bottom floor of a duplex in Houston's Montrose neighborhood, a semi-seedy area of the city starting to gentrify. Six months ago, the day after one of my secret meetings with Sarah, long talks in which we both seemed incapable of decisive comment—she about why she had not stayed with me in the past, me about why I could not come to her in the present—Houston was hit by a hurricane. High winds popped windows out of downtown skyscrapers, and in Montrose venerable oak trees toppled onto cars. Our duplex was battered by broken limbs, flying through bursts of rain packed with pebbles. The pine doors of the two-car garage out back flipped madly up and down, as light as matchbook covers. Patty and I cuddled inside one of her grandmother's old quilts, watching the methodical destruction of our yard. I felt narcissistically guilty (a new sensation in my young life—or a sensation I was newly aware of), certain I'd invoked this punishment through my duplicity with Sarah.

The following morning, the wind was still, the sun shone, and people stepped tentatively out of their houses, tip-toeing through street debris as if walking in the world for the very first time. In spite of all the damage to buildings and cars, the day felt magical, a new beginning, notwithstanding the fact that we had no control of it. I hugged Patty close, everywhere we went.

Now she slept alone in our bed. The thought of her there, isolated in the dark while I sat in a strange room thousands of miles away watching snow drift into a tiny park, made me cry. I was still a little drunk.

I unpacked the rest of my clothes, pulling from the depths of my bag an envelope packet containing extra copies of my curriculum vita, notes for my talk, sample writing exercises to hand out to students—and two recent letters from Sarah. When she'd returned to Houston, she'd left several loose ends in Washington, D. C. That's where she'd spent the past three years after quitting school. Following our last furtive meeting, just a month ago now, she'd flown back to Georgetown to close up the apartment she'd been living in, box a few items to ship to Texas, and finish a couple of projects she'd started at work before submitting her resignation. She'd been a publicity rep for the National Endowment for the Arts. In our first reunion in Galveston, she explained to me that conservative organizations constantly pressured Congress to eliminate

129

the NEA's funding. They claimed government had no business supporting the arts: arts grants were "welfare for the cultural elite." It had been Sarah's job to push back on these efforts through press releases and lobbying meetings with congressional interns. Recently, the controversy over "Piss Christ" had heated up. The artist Andres Serrano, supported by an NEA grant, had displayed a photograph in a gallery of a plastic crucifix immersed in a beautiful golden liquid, an arrestingly gorgeous image, capturing the shimmering, halo-like aura associated with religious ecstasy. The trouble was, that golden liquid was urine. Senators Al D'Amato of New York and Jessie Helms, from North Carolina, alerted to this outrage by their evangelical constituents, tried to pass a law legislating decency standards, severely restricting the NEA. Arts groups praised Serrano's work as a brilliant and ambiguous meditation on beauty, on religion's place in society; conservative Christians condemned it as a vulgar blasphemy; and debates over censorship swarmed around the senators' proposed legislation. Before leaving D. C., Sarah had worked several overtime hours drafting press releases on the topic, and she owed her boss two or three more documents before her resignation became official. Since returning to Washington—and right before I flew to Oregon—she'd sent me a couple of letters. I'd only had time to read through each of them once. I'd brought them to pore over.

Sitting on my bed now while heavy snow tapped the window, I unfolded the first page of the first letter:

Since my short time away, Washington seems to have become more and more authoritarian. Everywhere I go now—shopping malls, cafés, bars—businesses have installed television screens, playing either sports to keep us distracted, or cable news shows: sparkling capped teeth chattering away, telling us what to think, what to listen to, what to read. It's wearying!

Well. Of course, none of that is what's really on my mind. I want to be frank with you, Jeremy: I've seen the man I was seeing here, the one whose child I'm carrying. Talking to him was part of my unfinished business. We've agreed I'll abort the baby. Neither of us is ready to be a parent, and I'm trying to move on. But he's pressing me to stay here, and to try again with him.

I love you. I made a mistake. Several mistakes. But I don't know where things stand with us. If you really love Patty, then . . .

Maybe you could define desire. Maybe we could define it together. My thought: it's inevitable, but not worth acting on if you love someone else.

As you love Patty.

Maybe I should never write you again. Maybe you should never write me. Maybe you could write me once and say I can't write you for a long while (if ever).

Sometimes I think it's just impossible—resolution, I mean. Between us. And then I think: It's going to be a good year. Things are beginning (for you, especially). Just before I came here from Houston, I noticed tulips blooming in the courtyard of my Houston apartment. Tulips, and birds in the mud.

I refolded the yellow notepaper and placed it back in the envelope. I sniffed the envelope and then licked the inside flap where Sarah had run her tongue to seal it. I remembered Kaminski imploring me to touch the pages that Anna Akhmatova had touched. *Maybe you could define desire.* Certainly, distance did not seem to diminish it. Nor lack of knowledge.

Even a bad translation communicates *something*, I thought.

What the hell did *that* mean? What was going through my head? Boozy, my brain was full of nonsense. Water, I thought. Drink some water. In the bathroom, I filled a glass from the tap. Then I returned to the bed and picked up the newer notebook, the one containing Kaminski's translations of the poet's "hasty scribbles."

I read: `Who can refuse to live her own life?`

And: `Women whisper that they bleed beneath their skirts. In Petersburg the men, in a hurry, won't listen. Instead they hear a clamor of crows, the bell of the gray cathedral. Irritable, quiet, I pass through their rooms, dreams replacing dreams all night.`

I drained the glass, drew some more water from the tap. My head was no longer spinning. I turned a page.

`A drayman in an oak wagon offers me a ride to the square. On cloudy days, not much light, I still look young.`

`"Where are you going?" he says.`

`"To the prison."`

`"What for?"`

`"My son," I explain.`

`"Arrested?"`

`"For the third time."`

`"What's he done?"`

`I've made him nervous. "His mother's a poet."`

`"Is that so?" He flicks the reins. His horses shiver. "Maybe I know you."`

`"I don't think so."`

`Outside the prison, women in black shawls stand one behind the other. "Come to the tavern with me," says the drayman, trying to be cheerful. He pats the wagon's seat. "You can sit here under the feather blanket while I buy you a beer."`

I thank him for the ride.

"I'd like to hear a poem."

I smile, shake my head, then take my place in line. The walls are scratched and gouged. The woman in front of me, grieving, waiting hopelessly for someone inside, turns and asks me, "Can you put this into words?"

I tell her, "I can."

A few light taps on the pane made me turn to the window. Silver flakes, dark flakes. The moon was attempting to show through the clouds, but it wouldn't succeed.

3.

Snowdrifts as massive as German shepherds reflected pink-and-orange dawn-light in the park. I'd not slept more than an hour all night. As I stood rubbing my eyes at the window, I saw a fellow wearing a wool cap and white parka rise like a snowman from a blue mound near one of the big, bare shrubs, pick up a sleeping bag and brush it off, check a trash can, and stumble down the street. Apparently, even here, among the Pastures of Plenty, homelessness was a problem.

As a desert kid, growing up in West Texas, and now as a city-dweller in Houston, I wasn't used to pastoral calm. *Bucolic*, I said to myself, savoring the word's odd bumps. *Bucoli-land*. The place *looked* like a college town, small in scale. It seemed all the more "academic" to me swept by snow, a quaint-village image I'd always associated with austere Ivy League campuses.

I showered and shaved. As I brushed my teeth at the old-fashioned, stand-alone sink, I had a brief memory of Sarah, early one morning, years ago, holding her toothbrush next to her nose, squinting, unable to see without her contacts. I slid into my suit: gray herring-bone with a blue Arrow shirt and a red tie imprinted with tiny pictures of Michelangelo's David, a gift from Patty, from an Italian student of hers. I took a chance that Patty would be up and made a collect call on the bedside telephone. "I was so worried about you!" she cried.

I told her the Kaminski saga, leaving out Bridget Beresford's dramatic appearance in the bar. I wasn't sure why I kept quiet about her—I think I feared that, in describing the young woman, I'd reveal how incredibly attractive I'd found her, and this was one more dollop of guilt I couldn't carry around Patty.

"What do you think of the place?" she asked.

"I haven't seen much of it yet. I'll have a fuller report this evening."

"Don't forget to ask about their ESL programs."

"I won't."

"I'd take any position, even an entry-level one." This made me feel guilty, too, though she hadn't intended it to.

She was nervous because, later today, she had to meet her supervisor to discuss a student complaint. A week earlier, she'd given her upper-level students a writing assignment. One member of the class, a young man from Nicaragua, had written about Eugene Hasenfus, the American pilot whose cargo plane had been shot down months ago over a Nicaraguan jungle. Found on board the plane were weapons, and in

Hasenfus's pocket, according to newspaper reports, the private phone number of Vice President George H. W. Bush. Still, as Patty's student pointed out, President Reagan continued to insist there was "no U. S. involvement" in the wars in Central America. The young man had read his paper aloud to the class. One of his classmates, a Japanese boy, the son of a diplomat, went immediately to Patty's supervisor to complain about the "inappropriate politicization" of what was supposed to be an English language course. Patty told her boss the assignment had been a free-write—students could choose any topic they wanted. She was not promoting political agendas. The supervisor scheduled an official meeting and said they'd have to talk more about it.

As Patty enumerated her worries, I imagined her sitting on the edge of our bed wearing her Dr. Seuss pajamas: a flannel blouse and pants featuring Horton, the Grinch, the Cat in the Hat. Me, here, in my scratchy suit—we couldn't have been farther apart.

"I just hope I can make her understand," she said of her supervisor. Slim chance, I thought. I'd never cared for her boss, a dour, Texas-matron type who could never fathom someone as smart and well-traveled as Patty. Patty had taught English all over the world as a young woman just starting her career: Spain, Portugal, Mexico, France. She'd once told me she'd never felt at home anywhere (her parents had been Christian missionaries, always keeping the family on the move), but maybe for that reason she seemed to me to fully belong, wherever she went. Her manners were impeccable, always putting people at ease. She often referred to a Seder she'd attended with a Jewish friend of hers in college. "When they got to the part about Elijah, raised his cup and opened the door to let him in, I got goosebumps," Patty said. "I don't know. I must have identified with him—they called him the 'eternal wanderer,' this outsider who nevertheless always appears when people gather, at meals and when children are born."

That last bit—it didn't sound like her. One of the things she revealed to me, early, was her serious commitment to teaching. She wasn't a domestic-type. She didn't want children. In fact, she'd had her tubes tied. I didn't yet know where I stood on the kid question, but—and I had never admitted this to Patty—it bothered me that she'd closed off the option.

"You'd make a terrific father," Sarah liked to tell me. Powerfully seductive words. When she returned from Washington pregnant, and I touched her belly on the beach in Galveston (she wasn't showing), I couldn't help but think, "This should have been mine."

"Well, good luck. I'll be thinking about you," I told Patty now on the phone.

"You, too."

"I'll need it. I'm exhausted. And a little hungover."

Patty laughed. "The challenge'll keep you on your toes."

"I love you, my dear."

"Love you, too."

I'd heard no sounds in the house and tried to keep quiet as I went downstairs. Every step groaned beneath my feet. At the bottom, I nodded hello to our current U. S. President. In the dining room, a lovely space with a big picture window overlooking an ocean of blue snow in the yard, a large table was prepared with three place settings. No one was about. A bowl of sliced oranges and cut strawberries sat next to a basket of fluffy croissants. All I wanted was gallons of coffee to fuel me for the day.

A wiry woman in an apron, quick and tough-looking, bustled through a swinging door from the kitchen. She reminded me of Bonnie Parker, the Depression-era gun moll, whose picture I'd seen in Texas history books. She carried a tray heaped with platters of bacon and scrambled eggs. Before she even introduced herself, she said, "I haven't read your novel."

"That's okay," I said, startled. "Few people have."

"Bob thinks it's solid."

"Bob?"

"Fields."

She meant the English Department Chair. I understood, right away, this lady had her finger on everyone's pulse in town. "Well, I'm flattered," I said.

"I think you've got the inside track on the job if you don't blow it today."

"Okay."

"I've got two other guests. They'll be down shortly to join you for breakfast, but you can go ahead and get started. I'm Irene."

"Thank you, Irene. This looks lovely."

As swiftly as she'd appeared she vanished back into the kitchen.

I took a slice of bacon and a pinch of watery eggs. A few minutes later, two burly men trundled into the room: burr haircuts, jeans, plaid Pendleton shirts. I said hello. Both made some sort of grunting noise in return. My presence seemed to upset them. They plunged into the food. In low voices, they talked sales figures, marketing strategies—somehow, they were involved in selling washing machines. They kept glancing at me, warily, as if I were a spy sent by their competitors to steal their trade secrets. Finally, I said, "Hey, it's okay, you guys, if you need to talk business, don't mind me. I'll be out of here soon." After that, they exuded even more coiled hostility.

I retreated to my room, gathered the materials I'd need for the day. I was about to place Akhmatova's notebook and Kaminski's translations in a drawer in the bedside bureau, when an image came to me of the nosy gun moll sorting through my possessions. She was clearly a snoop, Irene—up-to-the minute on the English Department's job search, probably perfectly aware of how much every family in the county spent on toilet paper, tampons, and booze. I realized—the consequence of absorbing the strangeness of a new place—I didn't quite trust anyone in Corvallis.

I slipped the notebooks into the inner pocket of my suit coat.

At the bottom of the stairs, Irene, sans apron, wearing what appeared to be a gunnysack, said to me, "Of course, you've got some awfully big shoes to fill. My daughter used to babysit Bern's kids when they were little and his family lived over on 31st Street. God help you if you ever disturbed him while he was writing."

It took me a moment to realize she was talking about the great short story writer and novelist Bernard Malamud, who'd taught here in the 1950s, in the university's cow college days, composing his first books in relative obscurity before moving on to praise and international fame.

"Philip Roth came to visit him, once, back when Roth was a nobody and Bern was just making a name for himself," Irene said. "Roth stayed in this house—I think, maybe, in the same room you're in. I don't remember."

I've slept in Philip Roth's bed! I thought. Well, I'm hardly alone . . .

"He hadn't published much yet, but I remember Roth impressed Bern with his work habits," Irene told me. "Bern sat there in the dining room, over breakfast with the younger man, and asked him how he managed to kick out so many pages of fiction. 'Psychoanalysis and laxatives,' Roth said."

I laughed. Irene stared at me, grim. Who was I to make light of my elders' wisdom?

"So, anyway, who knows?" she said. "Maybe if you get the job here, this place'll be step one to the Pulitzer, just like it was for Bern."

I laughed again. "I can't even conceive—"

"Ah, fake humility! Why do writers pull that shit? It was just the same with Bern. I knew that, underneath all that methodical quiet, he was ruthlessly ambitious."

What else did you know about him? I wanted to ask. I'm sure no secrets escaped your itchy tentacles.

We had an awkward few moments in the vestibule before being rescued by the door knocker. Irene opened the door—an avalanche of chill air—and what little breath hadn't been snatched by the shock of the cold fled my body at the sight of Akhmatova's face. In the daylight, Bridget's resemblance to the poet was even greater, more exact, than it had been in the dank misery that was Tommy's 4th Street Grill. How

136

many noses like this can there be in the world, I thought—a little ocarina, an earthen flute, vibrating, no doubt, with sacred music? Or it was a pale, white root in the valley's rich loam. She'd pulled her hair up into not-quite-a-bun; a dark tendril wisped around her neck. She wore black pearls over a red-and-yellow kimono blouse, just visible beneath her heavy fur coat.

"Are you ready?" she asked me. That accent again.

"Ready as I'll ever be."

She couldn't have gotten much more sleep than I had but she looked fresh and energetic. I felt awful, assuming she had a secretive relationship with Kaminski. Was I projecting onto her my furtive dealings with Sarah and Patty? But I'd been a witness to her secret, just hours earlier, hadn't I?

I turned to Irene. "Thank you for breakfast."

She sent me off with, "Lose the fake humility."

"Vee kept you out much too late last night—Vladimir, I mean," Bridget said as we moved gingerly down the icy porch. "He shouldn't have done that, but he was enjoying your company."

"And I his." I hesitated a full five seconds before adding, "And yours as well."

She smiled.

The Honda was parked in the drive. I'd assumed it was Kaminski's car. It was hers? Or had he lent it to her for the day? Was he home with his wife? Teaching classes?

"I'll take you to Moreland Hall, where the English Department is located and where most of the literature and writing classes are taught. Your first meeting will be with the chair."

"I appreciate your time. You must be very busy. It's near the start of the new term, isn't it?"

"Yes. But I'm aware nothing's more important than hiring new faculty—preparing the future, Vee says."

And reckoning with the past.

She fumbled with the Honda's gear-shift, knocking loose a little notebook sitting between the seats. I bent to retrieve it and noticed thin Russian scrawls marking the pages. "You write Russian?" I said.

"I'm taking a class from Vee. I should warn you—"

"Yes?"

"Over and over today, you'll hear talk of Ken Kesey and Raymond Carver"—two of Oregon's literary lights—"but you're going to be overwhelmed by our *local* hero, Bernard Malamud."

"I know. It's already started."

She smiled. "He's the shadow in which every person here with the slightest writerly ambitions has to live."

137

"Even poets?"

"Even poets."

"What's your work like?"

"Not very good."

"Fake humility."

She shrugged—a gesture which seemed to me, under the circumstances, supremely confident and ravishingly seductive.

She turned a corner and pointed to a nondescript brick house. "That's where he lived. The Great Man."

I studied the boring front door, the undistinguished windows. I imagined Malamud waking, early in the morning, padding barefooted into his second-floor study to write his delicate stories about sad losers and well-intentioned naifs, pounding fists against a world so evil, it seemed magical in its wicked genius. (Forgotten, on a side table in his study, the student themes he was supposed to have graded the night before.) I imagined the groggy wails of his children, just being wakened for school, the sighs of his wife as she prepared the coffee pot and fried several eggs for breakfast, trying vainly not to disturb him.

The life of a writer!

"The Malamud Room," on the second floor of Moreland Hall, appeared to be a former storage closet. It had been turned into a shrine —presumably after someone in the university's fund-raising arm told the department it might secure donations from the Malamud family if it formally recognized the genius the rest of the country had lionized long ago.

Bridget deposited me there to wait for the English Department Chair.

"Once you're done with your morning meetings, I'll come back to take you to a luncheon with a few of the junior faculty members," she said.

I felt bereft once I realized she was leaving.

"Do you have everything you need?"

Could you stay and hold my hand?

"I'm fine. You've been very kind. Thank you."

Alone in the tiny room, I examined the display, in a glass case, celebrating Malamud's relationship with the Oregon State English Department (called, in the 1950s, "Lower Division Studies"). There were the humble job letters he'd written, a New York Jew, an intellectual, a literary man, so desperate for a monthly paycheck to feed his family he was willing to accept a menial position (to take *anything*, like Patty), even if it meant moving West to what was, in those days, more of a pioneer outpost than an educational institution. There were the galley sheets from his earliest publications in serious journals, *Commentary, Harper's*

Bazaar, Partisan Review, New World Writing. There were the thumbnail histories, unable to gloss over his humiliation at not being allowed to teach literature because he didn't have a Ph.D. He'd been forced to teach composition—courses in which members of the department squared off in rages over the proper uses of "shall" and "will," a cycle of meaningless triviality. The glass case held reminders that, when he'd arrived here at the height of McCarthyism, if he had any doubts about propriety, he need only review the short careers of a young poet named Lester Eugene Lundahl, fired for marching with OSU students against the Korean War, or of science professor Ralph Spitzer, fired after being accused by the provost of communist leanings. To fit here, Malamud would have to shut his mouth and take up golf.

The life of a writer.

I found it so dispiriting, I retreated to a monstrous black couch at the other end of the room. I should have skimmed the talk-notes in my packet, but my hand went instead to Kaminski's translations of Akhmatova's notebook. *Gravitas*, I thought. A reminder of literature's essential place in human evolution. *That's* what I needed before being sucked into this dizzying day.

I opened the notebook, looking for consolation.

Dry snow, candlelight mirrored in a stranger's dining room window. First course (served in silver dishes by a dour maid): roast duck with apricots, cranberries, a light Gewürtztraminer. Next, mushrooms in lobster sauce, cream gravy, Jarlsberg cheese. Coffee and chocolate for dessert.

Afterwards we sit by the fire. The rug is soft and warm.

"I could treat you to meals like this every night," says my host. He ships vegetables and fruits around the world, acres and acres of foodstuffs.

"And what would I have to do to earn them?"

He laughs. "Nothing. Enjoy yourself."

I shake my head. "I did enjoy this evening. I'm glad you invited me."

I'd seen him at the market earlier this week. I couldn't afford to purchase anything. He was supervising a dozen crates of Jonathan apples unloaded from a Dutch steamer. He offered me a bite.

"I'm not the first to ask you," he says now.

"I'm comfortable living by myself. Choosing my friends."

"And your lovers? There must be several men."

I smile.

"Poor bastards."

"I don't lie to them."

"Food's going to get scarcer in the coming months—the army will need it. I can help . . . " he says.

"Thank you, no."

"Tell me then."

"What?"

"How do men kiss you?" He lifts my chin. "Tell me how you kiss."

So. Even the twentieth century's greatest poet had her tawdry affairs? Unless . . .

I could imagine Kaminski's titillation, reading such a passage—especially if it had been written for him by a comely young student hoping to snag his attention. Was that possible? The creative response to a class assignment? A little something for teacher to translate?

I turned a page.

In the bars, men sat at my table and swore they loved me. We discussed art about women, women as artists. One night Mikhail, a painter friend of mine, said, "Feminine beauty is an imperative." He couldn't afford oils; I often gave him lipstick to mark his large canvases. "It tugs at my hand when I pick up the brush."

"Romantic nonsense."

"No no," said another. "It's the serenity I'm interested—"

I slapped the table, spilling beer. "Listen to you. All of you. Have you ever really seen a woman?"

"We've offended poor Anna."

"Here, have another glass," the men said.

"You don't even begin to know—" I pulled a cigarette from a pack and leaned toward a white candle stuck in a bottle's mouth.

"A toast to Anna," Mikhail teased. "A magnificent, fearsome woman."

"Listen to me—" I said.

"To Beauty."

"To Art."

"And to bed."

And what of Bridget's looks? She *had* to know she resembled the poet with whom Kaminski had been obsessed for decades, whether or not he had actually known Akhmatova. Did Bridget cultivate that appearance, work on it every morning in front of the mirror to get the eyes just right, the sad smile, the tilt of the head? Did Kaminski coach her? Criticize her if she acted just a little too "American"? What was it, then, between them?

I opened the other notebook, the one Kaminski said Akhmatova had given him for safe-keeping. It *did* appear authentically old, the pages

140

flaking at the edges, coarse as cardboard, the ink a nearly translucent, robin's-egg blue.

A big man burst into the room, kinky-haired, bearded, blond. He looked around. "The instructors were supposed to have a meeting in here . . . maybe I've got the wrong room." His eyes lingered on me. "Who are you?" he said: an unfriendly challenge. "Do I know you?"

"I'm Jeremy Allman. Job candidate in creative writing."

"Oh." He wheeled toward the door. Then he stopped. An almost comic double-take. "*Oh.*" He turned, put his hands on his hips, and looked me over. "I thought your novel was shit," he said.

My heartbeat quickened, a little skip of happiness. Someone had read my novel!

"I mean, how many dust storms do you *need* in a story?"

"I don't know. What does E. M. Forster say? Precisely three, unless you're Tolstoy, in which case you can get away with as many as you please?"

He didn't appreciate my attempt at a joke. "Have you ever done anything besides go to school?" he said. "Have you ever had a *job*?"

Was he on the hiring committee? Something told me no. "I made pizzas at a Pizza Inn. I could never get the anchovy smell off my hands. Worked as a cashier in a bookstore. Mostly, we sold astrology pamphlets to wealthy widows."

"Ha! How can you be a writer—how can you have anything to write about—if basically all you've ever done is go to school? I was a firefighter!"

I didn't know what to say to this. "Congratulations."

"Every summer. I kept this whole fucking state from exploding!"

"Um . . . thank you?"

He plopped into an orange leather chair next to the Malamud display. The dead writer looked down on us, wryly, from the cover of an old *Saturday Evening Post*. "Listen. I'm a senior instructor here. They're about to fire us all and bring in grad students to teach our classes. It's a cost-cutting move for them. Get the cheapest labor possible —experience and pedagogical principles be damned."

"I see," I said.

"If you were here, what would you do about it?"

"Do?"

"Fuck. Another diplomat. You're just like them. Timid. Toe the line. You'll fit right into their little ditch." He popped up to leave. In the doorway, he turned "They were going to fire me, anyway, you know. I'm the only one who'll tell the goddam truth around here."

"Okay," I said.

"The writing classes—they're fucking jokes. Crammed with students. There's no way you can give them the individual attention they need." He

141

wagged a finger at me. "Last year, I had the governor's daughter in my class. She couldn't spell her own name, and she damn sure wasn't going to learn to do it here. I wrote an op ed piece about that for the *Oregonian*, and let me tell you—" A bitter laugh. "They didn't like that one bit, here in Moreland Hall! So maybe you'll get my old office. I'm sure you'll be welcomed." If the floor were made of dirt instead of Latex carpeting, I think he would have spat at my feet. I thought he was going to spit at me, anyway. He swaggered down the hall, clearly pleased, on some level, with his martyrdom.

Welcome to OSU.

Robert Fields, the department chair, led me into his spacious office in the eastern corner of the building's first floor. This was in the days before mass shootings in public schools had become run-of-the-mill in America, but after my encounter upstairs in the Malamud Room, I remember thinking, "This man is trapped back here." If an angry student or faculty member came after him, he'd have no exit. I made a mental note: if you get the job here and decide to take it, buy a can of mace and keep it in your pocket.

Fields's first words: "I'm sorry about Kaminski. If I'd known, I wouldn't have sent him to come get you last night. Seems he's having a dispute with his department . . . I guess it's a mess . . . anyway, anyway, I don't really know the man. Met him at a few faculty meetings . . . seemed nice enough . . . and I thought, you know, the Akhmatova connection . . . we've already invited him and his wife to the dinner tonight, and it would be awkward to un-invite him, so . . . but there'll be plenty of other people there, you know, so you'll be all right." He took a breath as if coming to consciousness and realizing he shouldn't have told me all this. "How *was* your evening with him?"

"It was great," I said.

He invited me to sit in a wooden chair across a round plastic table stacked with copies of the *PMLA* and the *Chronicles of Higher Education*. He was a Milton scholar. Two dozen copies of *Paradise Lost* lined his bookshelves, a pointed message (I thought) repeated in case I didn't get it. He crossed his legs—khaki pants, pullover sweater—and spent five minutes breaking down the salary range and the teaching load (the former too low, the latter too high). And then we talked football for half an hour. In addition to being Department Chair, he was the university's representative to the NCAA. "The Beavers—it's an embarrassing mascot, but you'll learn to live with it—they haven't had a winning season in twenty years, but we're quite proud of our boys. They're good kids in the classroom, and the coaches are happy to work with us to get them the grades they need."

This sounded ominous.

Fields hurled himself back in his black leather chair. He crossed his hands on his belly. "I wanted to be a Jesuit priest," he said dreamily. His eyes went glassy for a moment and he stared around the room as if not entirely sure where he was. I imagined him thinking, *So how the hell did I wind up here?*

But no. That's what *I* was beginning to think.

"So. Bern's second coming, eh?" He grinned at me.

"There was only one Malamud," I said.

"Indeed, indeed. I arrived here right after he went back East, but the stories about him were still fresh. In his day, the English Department was situated in an old World War II-era Quonset hut. They were all over the campus then. It's said he'd write in his office all morning and all afternoon, between classes, leaving explicit instructions with the department secretary that no one was to disturb him. At noon, his wife would come slip his lunch to him through the window on a little tray and leave without saying a word. I heard he kept an egg-timer on his desk—a miniature hourglass. When students or colleagues came to see him during Office Hours, he'd keep a close eye on the sand inside the timer. Colleagues got five minutes, students two." Fields laughed. "Of course, these days we expect more . . . shall we say *citizenship* . . . from department members? None of this 'writer-cloistered-in-the-attic' stuff."

"Of course," I said.

"I'm sure you've achieved the proper balance. Life and art," he said. *Notice is served.*

"I try."

He rose and pulled Malamud's novel, *A New Life*, from his shelf. "You know this book?"

"I'm a big fan of his stories, but that one I haven't cracked yet. I've been told I have to read it if I come here."

Fields nodded. "His roman á clef. All about the campus and the town. He published it the year he moved away. He hurt a lot of people's feelings. Several of the characters are recognizably based on people who were still here when I arrived, and the portraits . . . well, they're not always flattering." I'd heard the book was a fierce satire of small-town pettiness, Western isolationism, political backwardness, and intellectual vacuity. Already, especially after my run-in with the agitated fellow upstairs, I was thinking, *I'll write a sequel*: The Same Old Life.

Fields patted the book. "I guess sometimes writers are pretty squirrelly, eh?" Another warning? He handed me the novel. "Take it for the weekend. Maybe you'll get a chance to skim it. Learn a little something about the place."

My informal meeting with the students was scheduled for the Malamud Room. After leaving Fields's office, I ducked into the second floor men's room to splash cold water on my face. It woke me up a little. I'd barely managed to keep my eyes open toward the end of my session with the chair. I stepped into a stall, closed the door, and set *A New Life* on the floor at my feet. I slapped my face to get the blood flowing. Automatically, I reached into my coat for Akhmatova's notebook. Fanned the pages. The smell of the past. Earth. Grounding. Then I opened Kaminski's translation.

A priest stops me outside the prison. "Good woman, come pray with me."

"I'm not a good woman," I tell him. "Besides, there's no one to hear."

Five or six rabbis also wait outside the gates.

"Of course there is. We each have an angel—"

I laugh "I'm a descendant of Eve, Father. Read your Bible." I lace my boots up tight.

"No forgiveness for those who won't seek it!" he calls after me.

That woke me up. No twenty-year-old Oregon State student had written this.

Lev is thin. Black bread and sugarless tea. I appeal to the authorities on behalf of my son, but my voice, in chorus with dozens of other women, is indecipherable.

I've been a bad mother. When Nikolay—may he rest in peace—first proposed marriage (he was cocky as a prince), I told him I hadn't the patience for courtship; I wanted to sit by the Neva, reading Hamlet.

"So you want to be a poet," he said. "What are you going to write?"

"I don't know. Whatever interests me."

"Pretty odes on wind chimes and cats?"

"Of course not. Why are you being so hateful?" I turned toward the river and opened my book.

He shook my shoulder. "Have you ever heard rifle fire? A young soldier moaning and clutching his guts in a field? My God, Anna, what do you know of the world?"

"Enough to tell you no," I said. "Leave me alone. Go be a man."

The following day he took a holiday train to France with six other young army recruits. Three weeks later I heard he'd swallowed a vial of strychnine. For nearly a day he lay unconscious in the Bois de Bologne before a young couple stumbled upon him. Three times he threatened suicide in sloppy attempts to persuade me, twice I refused to marry him

144

But it turned out he was right.

A witness to one's time. What else is a poet but that?

When Lev was born (October, mild and warm) I discovered how little I possessed of the simple love by which people live day to day. Working for each other, eating together under the same roof. Nikolay spent half the year hunting in Abyssinia. I read my poems, shouting over drunks, in bars.

Our son grew up in his grandmother's house, eighty kilometers east of here. I didn't even visit.

I got up, cupped more water to my face. From the brief biography I'd read about Akhmatova, I remembered she had cherished, as a girl, an old myth about the city of Kitezh. Elders said the city had been saved from the Tartars by prayer. It was lifted straight into heaven beyond a row of gentle hills. On days when the fish were still and all the mud had settled to the bottom, you could see its reflection in a lake. Each man had a wagon. Their wives raised many, many children.

But then, as an adult, Akhmatova heard a different story. Kitezh had never been saved. It was just a city of brides. Their husbands had gone to war. The Tartars invaded, raped and murdered all the women. Left only bones.

What you saw in the lake—it was either a reflection of the sacred city from above, or the damned city itself, its rotting remains drowned near the bottom of the earth. Which was it? How could you tell? The decision was yours, but if you felt mysteriously drawn to live in the city of Kitezh, to occupy the land of poetic myth, as Akhmatova did and never ceased doing (even when her devotion threatened her son), it was not a decision without consequence.

Bern's wry smile, on the cover of the *Saturday Evening Post*, seemed to have faded since I'd seen him last, an hour ago. Six or seven sleepy students, all in khakis and pullover sweaters, boys and girls both, sat on the floor beside the display case, leaving me a spot on the brutal couch. They looked like undeveloped children. Nothing approaching Bridget Beresford's womanly maturity.

I thought of saying, "Psychoanalysis and laxatives," and promptly leaving the room. The best advice they'd ever get in school. Instead, I opened the session by asking them what they liked best about their current writing classes and what they'd like to see changed. They agreed that the reading assignments were too numerous and there was too much emphasis on "craft." Creative writing was supposed to be *creative*, right? Instead, it was deadened by rules.

I asked them who they liked to read. Stephen King: the clear favorite.

145

What about Alice Munro? Toni Morrison? Flannery O'Connor? William Trevor?

Dutifully, they wrote down the names and said they'd check them out.

Ken Kesey? Raymond Carver?

Shrugs.

Had anyone here read the resident spirit, Mr. Malamud, sitting quietly in his glass case?

They turned to look at the round face beaming from the *Post* as if they'd never noticed him. I suppose they hadn't.

What was the most important lesson they'd learned from their previous writing teachers?

"Avoid clichés," said one incurious boy, ripping open a Milky Way candy bar.

By now—sensing energy leaking from the conversation—I was feeling contrary, even confrontational. "Clichés are lovable," I said. "It's not our job as writers to avoid clichés" (I thought again of Bridget . . . *tragic poets, dressed in black . . .*).

They stared at me as though I'd addressed them in Cossack.

"Clichés become clichés because there's truth in them. *Some* truth worth repeating. It's our job to re-see them, re-energize them, freshen them up, dig into their deeper meanings." I had intended to hand the students a series of exercises, writing prompts, for them to take back to their dorm rooms or apartments. Instead, I said, "Let's try something together. Someone give me a cliché."

"'And they lived happily ever after.'"

"Good," I said. "Now, get a piece of paper and write that sentence at the top—'And they lived happily ever after.' Below that, block off two columns. Now, imagine a couple. You can make these people up or base the details on your own lives or on anyone you know. Fiction draws from all sources. In Column A, sketch out a scenario in which your fictional couple lives happily ever after. List, say, four requirements for their contentment. Then, in Column B, list exactly the *opposite* of those requirements—not as negatives. As *positives*, even though they counter-act the first set of felicities. You see where I'm going, right? A good story doesn't avoid the cliché of 'living happily'—it *complicates* the notion by admitting the contradictions and ambiguities at the heart of our romantic ideals. It muddies matters by suggesting many things can be true at once."

And Jeremy and Patty lived happily ever after in Corvallis, teaching hard each day, writing, enjoying a plain brick house empty of the noisy laughter of children.

And Jeremy and Sarah lived happily ever after in Houston . . . or Washington . . . with a passel of lively kids, spending their days passionately crusading for the arts.

No, I thought, watching the students scribble intently under the stoic gaze of the ignored old writer. That's not right. You're breaking the rules of your own exercise. You're breaking the goddam rules.

4.

All morning, the snow had continued to fall. The campus quad—designed by the Olmstead brothers, I'd heard—looked like one of those liquid-filled globes you'd shake to make a tiny world shimmer. It looked too perfect to be real (my youth at the time, combined with longings I could barely define, contributed to the splendid illusion, I'm sure; years later, when I was a senior member of the Oregon State faculty, a young architect I met informed me that the Olmsteads had vociferously proclaimed, "It is obvious that boundaries and topography very materially limit the possibilities of forming a fully satisfactory college here").

No matter. To the degree that I was already leery of campus politics and administrative structures, I was equally as smitten by the physical beauty of the place, agape at the perpetual fertility, the natural bounty. This impression was reinforced by the reappearance of Bridget Beresford, who'd come to take me to lunch. Her cheeks, slapped by the cold, were dark red, as though she'd just received/endured a dozen kisses.

"I'll take you across the quad to the Memorial Union, where you'll meet with junior faculty," she said.

"Of course you'll be joining us?"

"I'm afraid not. I have a class."

"Oh! I'm disappointed." I was pleased to see her blush. Emboldened by that unexpected response, I added, "When will I get a chance to hear about your experiences here? I talked to other students, earlier, about their impressions of the place, but I'd be most interested to hear what it's like for you."

"I don't know . . . I'm not . . . "

"We *must* talk. You're an English major. A poet. Your perspective is crucial."

"Hardly. It doesn't—"

I smiled. "Don't you want to prepare the future?"

She burst into tears.

"Bridget! Bridget, my god, what—"

"The future!"She laughed harshly. But then she recovered herself with impressive speed. She wiped her cheeks, stiffened her back. "We're here," she said, and indicated a door to a café inside the Union. "I'll leave you to it."

"Bridget, I'm sorry. If I said anything—"

She hurried away.

I was greeted inside by a slew of assistant professors, ordering coleslaw, tofu, and garden salads—all in order to maintain (I assumed) good appearances. I was certain that once they'd earned job security they'd indulge themselves with burgers and fries.

I joined them in the marinated tofu.

The group consisted of medievalists, a Shakespearian, an eco-critic. No writers (though writing was a grudging part of what they all had to do—grudging more for some than others). I learned that instructors, like the kinky-haired man, whose name, I was told, was Barry Greiner, currently taught all the creative writing courses. In the past, however, on occasion, special hires had been made—efforts to jump-start interest in the curriculum by bringing in a Writer-in-Residence.

"*Rotter*-in-Residence," a skinny prof muttered at the end of the table. I hadn't caught his name. His specialty? *Assholery*, I decided.

"The title was more grandiose than the position," the Shakespearian, a handsome, dark-haired woman, explained. "They were low-paid instructors, all the same."

One of them, a "neurasthenic" poet with a "fondness for young men—which was quite frowned upon back then, as you can imagine . . . " ("*And* now," added the skinny prof.) "He was arrested one night over on the coast, walking naked into the ocean chanting William Blake's ecstatic lyrics. I think that's the last time the department took a chance on an 'official' poet."

"*All* creative writers are crazy," Skinny Boy said. The table fell silent.

I broke the ice again, asking about the university's English as a second language program. "Quite robust," said Ms. Shakespeare. "We're on the Pacific Rim here, you know, so we have quite a few international students on campus. Lots of Asians." She took a piece of paper from her purse and wrote down the director's name for me. "And we're particularly favored by Middle Eastern students—the OSU Agricultural School has established some partnerships with the Yemeni government through USAID, helping them improve crop yields. That sort of thing." It's astonishing to contemplate now: this was fourteen years before 9-11, before U. S. distrust of Muslims became so hysterical, and long before Yemen's tragic civil war kept Americans from traveling there. Too perfect, indeed.

The word "international" spurred Skinny Boy to mention a current campus controversy. Apparently, Richard Rodriguez, a Mexican-American intellectual who had recently made a name for himself as a PBS commentator and as the author of a book on assimilation, had been invited by the Foreign Language Department to speak in Corvallis. Several students had protested his upcoming appearance. They demanded the invitation be rescinded. Rodriguez had upset many people by arguing that Mexicans who wished to make a life in this country should turn away from their native languages and traditions, learn

149

English, buy suits, and fully assimilate. "No, no, no, his position is hardly that extreme," said one of the medievalists. "You've made a hash of his argument."

"Well, *whatever* he's arguing, it's hardly politically correct," said Lady Bard.

"But you'd be violating his right to free speech": Skinny Boy.

"When has speech ever been free? I mean, *really*?"

"You're saying we just pay it lip service?"

"I'm saying don't be so naïve."

This silenced the table once more. I piped up, meekly, "I met a very interesting fellow from the Foreign Language Department last night. Vladimir Kaminski? He picked me up at the airport."

"Kaminski!" Skinny Boy laughed. "Now, *there's* a piece of work." He asked the others, "Have you ever served on a committee with that guy?" He rolled his eyes.

"I had his granddaughter in a class last year," said the youngest medievalist. "Nice girl. Quiet."

"Yes, I've had her, too, in a *Hamlet* course. She's a good student. I thought she was off on some international study abroad this winter, but I saw her in town just the other day. Something must have happened."

Kaminski had a granddaughter?

The luncheon ended in yet another prolonged silence, and then the Shakespearian said I'd have an hour and half to myself, to rest and collect my thoughts before the final sprint this afternoon: a meeting with the dean, my formal presentation, and a Q and A with the English Department faculty. She'd walk me to the library and set me up in a private study room, where I could look over the notes for my talk, if I wished. She'd come get me when it was time to meet the dean. I took this to mean I wouldn't see Bridget again, and I slumped a little. Or maybe it was just post-lunch torpor.

We set out across the quad, in snow drifting up to our knees.

The study room was like a closet with a table and a chair. Quiet. It was on the library's sixth floor (Philosophy: Kierkegaard and Hegel). No other souls appeared to be using the building. The students were skipping studies, out romping, engaging in snowball fights. I heard their distant laughter in the quad.

I had a powerful thirst, but didn't see a water fountain anywhere on the floor.

So Kaminski had a granddaughter! I flashed on the Honda. The family auto? Had I misunderstood their body language together? Their intimacy—*blood*, not lust?

I dozed in my chair. Woke and dozed and woke again. Lunch and lack of sleep lulled me into a half-waking reverie: partly in dream, partly in overactive imagination, I entertained the possibility that Kaminski's love affair with Anna Akhmatova in St. Petersburg had produced a child, Bridget's mother, erased from the history books and biographies. Akhmatova could never bring herself to speak of her because the child had been lost to her when Kaminski left for England and then America. Bridget—perhaps she had been born in the English countryside. Yorkshire, say; maybe that accounted for her accent. At some point, she sailed to the West Coast of America with her grandfather.

Exhausted, drifting, I imagined receiving a job offer from Oregon State, of walking away from Patty and Sarah, from the pain of measuring love, looking past illusions, determining future consequences. I'd move to the Pastures of Plenty and marry the granddaughter of Anna Akhmatova.

New Year's Eve. Snow tapping the windowpanes. She had been trying to read *Fear and Trembling*—a manuscript in poorly-translated Russian, smuggled into Petersburg and passed among her friends—but the cold stew she'd eaten for supper and the half-bottle of vodka Pasternak left with her on his last visit had made her sleepy. She dozed and woke. Laughter from the revelers in the street below prompted a half-dream, a visitation: old friends from her youth (most of them dead now) tramping up the wooden staircase outside her flat, wearing New Year's costumes, the way they used to do in the Wandering Dog and the other bars in town, back when they all danced, carefree, until dawn, exchanging lovers like changes of clothes. Oblivious of the rumbles of war and revolution, they laughed and challenged Hell to open wide for them.

Here was a harlequin, at the bottom of the landing, a single mascara-teardrop dabbed near the corner of his eye (beneath the face-paint, she thought she recognized a boy she'd been in love with, a young would-be poet who'd loved another girl and committed suicide beneath her window). There, the harlot for whom the boy had died, dressed only as herself with pearls and a feather boa. And here, slouching in her open doorframe, sneering, hissing, "Let me in. You know you've been waiting for me. Where can I meet you where we won't be seen?" the devil, skinny, beet-red with fleshy horns. Who was he, really? Nikolay, resurrected, the scar from the executioner's bullet still marring his forehead underneath the smeary greasepaint? Or was it one of her former teachers—an old man who'd taught her dactyls and cunnilingus?

"Anna. Please. Let me in."

She startled. This voice she wasn't dreaming. She blew out the nearly-melted candle on the table.

"Anna!"

She recognized Kaminski's urgent whisper. Quickly, she checked to see if the baby was still asleep beneath the cotton quilt on the bed—a dark-haired girl with Anna's brown eyes—and then she opened the door. The wet conditions outside had loosened his thick, black hair: moist strands plastered his rocky forehead. When he embraced her, sluices of snow fell from the shoulders of his coat onto her thin white shawl. Even through the heavy padding of his clothing, she felt his thinness, the curves of his ribs.

As she knew he would, he implored her once more to travel with him to England. "The only things waiting for you here are tuberculosis and starvation. The revolution is devouring its children! And you won't escape being caught up in it, even worse than before. You're too well-known."

"It's true," she said. "Only the dead can smile. They're at rest."

"Oh, enough, Anna! Enough! I'm asking you to come with me as an ordinary woman. As my wife. As the mother of our child."

She stared at the candle's remains.

"But no." He swept his arm around the room. Its spare furnishings. His voice had made the baby stir. Faint whimpers underneath the quilt. "*This* is what you choose! Mildewed clothes hanging above a stove that won't light half the time. Scraps of wallpaper peeling to the floor. A cupboard drawer that won't shut because it's stuffed with biscuits you're saving for your son, your son stuck in a dreary prison clear across the country . . ."

"Don't you talk about my Lev."

In the street below her window, a pair of drayman's horses shat in dirty snow. Nothing Kaminski was saying had any substance next to those dark, steaming piles, she thought: the natural frankness of daily life here. Light from the streetlamps glowed red across the horse's backs. In this moment, Anna felt as rooted as the heavy animals to the filthy streets of Petersburg.

"Anna, things are just beginning for me. Don't you see that? I can get a job teaching. We can start a new life. I can take care of us." He turned to the infant. "All of us. Anna. I can be a terrific father. I know I can."

She shook her head.

"Damn you. Your stubbornness is misplaced, you know. It's all very well to die for one's country—"

"Dying *for* one's country is easy. Dying *with* it is another matter entirely."

Kaminski picked up the baby and held her to his chest. Quietly, he said,"It's going to be a good year, Anna. Just this morning, in spite of the snow, I saw tulips blooming in the downstairs courtyard. And birds. Birds playing in the mud."

5.

"She's famous. Why doesn't she say something on our behalf?"

"It's because of her fame that her son is in jail."

"She's no better than the rest of us."

The women's hushed voices echo beneath the pine-wood ceiling. Lev lies, in a half-stupor, on the cold cell floor. I cup my palms beneath the spigot in the courtyard, run quickly back into the prison, but by the time my hands reach his lips there's nothing left to drink. "Lev, Lev . . . "

Fame is so much water.

Today I can't afford both dinner and a beer. I buy a squash, hurry home and toss it in a pot on the stove. Start some tea.

Early in the morning the men arrived . . .

They came at dawn . . .

At dawn they came . . .

While the kettle whistles I write this sentence, tear it apart, make it again, slightly new.

———————

Polonius, to Hamlet: "What do you read, my lord?"

"Words words words."

"I have the utmost admiration for—and not the least understanding of—how you fiction writers manufacture details here, there, to create whole scenes out of nothing. Malamud, of course, was the absolute master."

"Of course," I said.

"And we are eager, here at Oregon State, to extend his fantastic legacy."

Yes, well, in his memory, you certainly offered him a fantastic, I mean just a super storage closet, I thought.

And for the rest of the hour the dean talked football.

Twenty minutes remained before my job talk. I glanced at my notes. Then I returned to Akhmatova's story. I read that every time she entertained foreign visitors in her apartment—Isaiah Berlin, Alfred Weller—the government punished her. Exhausted, in a delirium one night, she wrote, I solemnly renounce my hoard / of earthly goods . . .

*

I had entitled my job talk "Magpiety" after a poem I loved by Czeslaw Milosz. He was a Nobel laureate—along with "our dear Anna," a contender for "Greatest Poet of the Twentieth Century." Born in what is now Lithuania, he saw, in the Second World War, Russian soldiers watch passively through binoculars as the Polish Resistance was slaughtered by troops under Hitler's command. In his prose works, he denounced Stalinism more eloquently than anyone besides Akhmatova (he did so directly; she did it with simple, heartbreaking scenes of daily life). In his lifetime, Milosz witnessed enough human folly under the tattered banners of nationalism and tribal unity to say, with stern conviction, "Language is the only homeland."

I began my talk with his poem:

> *I walked through oak forests . . .*
> *A magpie was screeching and I said . . . I shall never achieve*
> *a magpie's heart . . . flight*
> *that always renews just when coming down.*

My theme was inspiration—how to inspire young writers. The English Department faculty sat crammed into a tiny seminar room. My mouth was dry; they'd forgotten to get me a cup of water. The old-fashioned wall radiators (what did *that* say about the department budget?) clanked and rattled as I spoke. Clearing my throat, coughing once or twice, I analyzed Milosz's opening lines: "Drawn by something bright and shiny on the ground, the bird comes down, but it doesn't stop moving," I said. "At the instant it plucks what it wants, it is starting to soar again. It is not thinking, it is not calculating, it is not worrying about how this fresh piece of treasure will mix with previous cast-offs grabbed by the bird. The creature is operating on pure energy, not the hurry of anxiety but the motion of excitement generated by the inspiring object. The bird is ascending: the word 'mag-piety' implies heavenly movement. There is something sacred in this stealing!"

In the back row, Barry Greiner stuck two fingers in his mouth and mimed retching. So. I knew where I stood with him. The rest of the faculty—including the medievalists, the Shakespearian, and Skinny Boy —appeared to be dozing. I was fully awake for the first time all day.

"In Milosz's poem we hear a sense of regret, of lost opportunity: 'I shall never achieve   . . . / a magpie's heart.' The poet seems to have missed some crucial chance. We only get one life, one turn on a two-lane road, one moment to pluck that shiny object from the ground, and then that moment is gone." Naturally, thirty years after the fact, I recognize that my talk was centered on something far different than what I thought it meant. "Perhaps *this* is the sacred quality in the magpie's act of thievery: the recognition that this glimmering object, this beautiful thing that has caught your eye, that has *inspired* you, will not be here later to grace this spot. If you don't take it now, it will be lost to you, and maybe lost to others. Perhaps the *plucking* is not greed but a deep thirst for the world's abundance, knowing this abundance can't last. That's as good a definition of inspiration as any—a profound reverence for this moment, this moment that you breathe into your lungs before you're forced to exhale."

I reached behind the podium for water that wasn't there.

Looking over my sleepy audience, I concluded, "By its very nature, I think, writing is elegiac. A song to what's passing away, an attempt to capture, as permanently as possible in words, that which will soon be lost in the fullness of time: feelings, thoughts, events, people, places, things. Is elegy, then, our major source of inspiration? Is it *why* we pluck and hoard?"

I didn't tell my listeners I'd once met Milosz. At the time, I was a new graduate student at the University of Houston (about a year before I met Patty), and he'd been invited to campus to read. I was sent to retrieve him at the airport the night he arrived. The freeway traffic was heavy; it would take us at least an hour and half to get back into the city. An hour and a half for me to try to engage this grand figure who knew so much more than I did, who had seen so much more of the world than I could imagine. He had witnessed some of the twentieth century's most tumultuous moments. He was internationally famous, a Great Man, and on top of everything else, his English was stiff. It would be a long drive.

After about thirty minutes of silence, he said he hadn't eaten on the plane. He was hungry. I-45 didn't offer many five-star restaurants, the only establishments worthy of a Great Man. Frantically, I wondered where to take him. Just then, Milosz spotted a yellow Denny's sign. "I like very much Denny's!" he said. So I wound up eating a rubbery hamburger in a dirty plastic booth with one of the greatest poets of the twentieth century—and he loved every minute of it. He was charmed, I remember, by a scene through the window, across the busy freeway: spotted roans running wildly through an overgrown field.

During the Q and A after my talk, no one mentioned Milosz. Poetry wasn't a topic of interest. My possible new colleagues wanted to know my teaching strategies. "How would you handle a writing workshop of forty students?" someone asked. I wouldn't, I wanted to say. "If you were asked to teach an introductory literature course featuring Dante, Hemingway, and Bob Dylan—there really is a textbook including all these fellows—how would you approach it?" I wouldn't. No fucking way.

One of the medievalists, a severe young woman who had not removed her heavy fur coat in spite of the broiling radiator, raised her hand. (Possibly she *wasn't* "severe"—maybe I've just cast her that way in memory.) "I noticed in your application letter . . . you say you've written a short story based on the life of Anna Akhmatova. Isn't it inappropriate for a male writer to appropriate the voice, the story, of a female, since females have traditionally been silenced by males? Furthermore, this is a woman quite capable of speaking for herself—and she has. Isn't there a problem of *cultural* appropriation, as well?"

Hey, I've positioned myself as a feminist, I thought. Goddammit! Why won't you let me be a feminist? Before I could say anything, she went on.

"Finally, the novel itself—as an aesthetic form, I mean. It's rather problematic, isn't it? This is the age of collaboration—as we've learned from the *success* of collaboration, studying women's traditional roles. The whole idea of the single-author-great-man, the genius . . . isn't it passé? Even dangerous?"

Yes, I almost said. Once more, exhaustion overtook me. Yes, yes. You've got me there. You should put me on a plane back to Texas right now. Instead, I said . . . I don't remember what I said. Some jargon-laced bullshit that seemed to satisfy the group or at least fill the time without too much embarrassment until we could all leave the room.

6.

"Well, that went rather splendidly, I think," the Shakespearian said.

So: she's an *actress*, too.

She led me to her frosty car. She'd drop me back at the B and B for forty-five minutes and then Robert Fields would retrieve me for dinner. The dinner would be held at a faculty member's home, just a short walk from the bed and breakfast.

In the car, the woman said, "It doesn't often snow like this in the valley. This is pretty special. You're lucky your plane got in before it began. I suppose there's some chance you might be delayed on Sunday, but the forecast is for clearing. I think you'll get out of here okay."

No, I don't think I'll get out of here okay.

Irene greeted me in the vestibule. She still wore her gunnysack. "Your president is speaking," she said. "You'll want to come hear him."

On the television in the living room, Ronald Reagan, his aged face resembling a sagging pancake, was saying, "America has been blessed to have the service and spirit of Bill Casey. He consistently sustained a vision of the public good, and fidelity to the values that make our nation great."

Casey had just resigned as the director of the Central Intelligence Agency, Irene informed me. "The poor man is very ill, you know. Brain tumor."

"First and foremost, Bill Casey brought to the Central Intelligence Agency a keen sense of history, a deep understanding of the geopolitical forces at work in the twentieth century," Reagan said. "He saw firsthand what pride and morale mean to those on the front lines of freedom."

Two months earlier Casey had suffered two seizures and been hospitalized in Washington, just a day before he was scheduled to testify before a U. S. Senate panel about the CIA's role in illegal arms sales to Iran. That's enough to make any man sick, I thought. It was an uncharitable sentiment, and I didn't dare mention it to Irene, whose love of Ronald Reagan was obviously deep and abiding. I decided it was best not to know the reasons for this: there was no need to invite such a serious level of involvement with my hostess. I doubted I'd see her again after Sunday.

I happened to know that William Casey's hospital was just around the corner from Sarah's former office in D. C.—the office she was cleaning out, even now. This was a detail so random, so meaningless, no fiction writer would ever go near it.

157

"Excuse me, Irene, I only have about forty minutes before they'll come get me for dinner. I'm going to go upstairs and freshen up real quick."

"I hear you tried your best to blow it, every step of the way today, but you didn't succeed," she said.

"I'm sorry?"

"They're willing to forgive an awful lot because you're young and understandably nervous."

She knew more than the damn provost! I nodded and turned toward the staircase. The washing machine salesmen pushed past me, out the front door, fiercely debating spin cycles.

Sarah's second letter, sent just a week after she'd mailed me the first one, was written on the back of a Xeroxed map—a circular representation of ancient Greece, showing the mythic Isle of Sirens and the Land of the Lotus Eaters. "The World of Homer, Ninth Century B. C.," said the label: "Homer's poetry reflected geographical concepts of his day and influenced man's mind for centuries." I assumed it was a scrap from a document left lying around the NEA offices.

Two nights ago—three—I dreamed about you [Sarah wrote]. *You were trying to send messages to me in the form of objects. One was sent by your son. Jeremy's son, I thought in my dream. Does Jeremy have a son? I woke convinced that Patty was pregnant. But Patty can't get pregnant—didn't you tell me that? I'm sorry. I shouldn't be writing this.*

Are you happy? Excited about going to visit Oregon?

Jack—man's name, here—is being unbelievably good to me. Something I'm not used to (sorry, again). I've always enjoyed his company but he doesn't understand art and that makes me sad. I think about you. Last night, a friend of mine here—she reads Tarot as a goofy hobby—she sat me down and I asked about you. The final card came up, which signifies the future—it came up the Nine of Swords: nine swords suspended over a weeping woman. Miscarriage, sadness, separation. Tarot's silly stuff, I assure myself. Why does it scare me?

The last time we saw each other, Sarah and I had agreed to meet by the seawall in Galveston. The beaches were fifty miles or so south of Houston—none of our friends were likely to spot us there. We walked for a while, not talking, in the mild salt breeze, past hotels, cafés on piers, gift shops. I ducked into one of the shops and bought her a bobble-head toy: a fat, bald man staring forlornly at his feet. A caption printed on the stand said, "I'll Never Smile Again."

"What are you trying to tell me?" Sarah said, smiling, not-smiling.

"This is me in forty years."

"I don't think I like this."

"Come on. It's cute."

"It *is* sort of cute."

We walked along the high tide's surging rim, up a sandy hill to a beach house under construction, an incomplete skeleton. Multiple rooms—it was going to be a mansion. Sarah's stride had always captivated me: a skitter-slouch, her left shoulder thrust forward like a gunslinger heading out for the final showdown in the streets of Tombstone. She kept her black hair cut short, a pixie-cap, bangs just skirting her eyebrows.

We sat on a grassy cliff-edge, facing away from the sun. Her pregnancy wasn't showing. A blue-and-gold butterfly landed on her sweater, just above her right breast. "Oh my god," Sarah said. "How's that for romantic? Isn't *this* the cliché of the century?"

I held her chilly hand. I tried to warm it. "Clichés are lovable," I said.

I didn't think Patty would be home yet. She had told me she was going out for a drink to unwind with a work-friend after the meeting with her supervisor. I tried the phone anyway, and caught her. "I *did* go out, but didn't feel like staying long," she explained.

"Does that mean the meeting went badly?"

"Not badly. Not well. You know. I don't think we reached a resolution. She believes me, that I don't push politics in the classroom, but she doesn't think I've got enough safeguards in place to prevent sensitive topics from upsetting certain students."

"Especially certain students who are the sons of world-renowned diplomats, and whose fathers might be possible donors to your program?"

"Listen to you. One day on a campus visit, and already you're talking like a future administrator. Yes. It *is* a consideration."

"That woman's a blockhead."

"Jeremy—"

"Through and through."

"I have to work with her, okay?"

"I'm just saying."

"This is not helpful."

"All right. I'm sorry. What's on for the rest of the evening? Pajamas and popcorn?"

"Just sleep, I think. It's been a day. I can't imagine how *you're* holding up."

"Holding, but not *up*, much."

I cheered her a little, giving her the name of OSU's ESL director. Then I told her I'd better go splash my face with some icy Oregon water. "One more ring of fire to pass through. Dinner reception."

I placed *A New Life* and my job packet in a bureau drawer, and tidied up the room. My face in the bathroom mirror could have used Ronald Reagan's volcanic make-up to add some color. Michelangelo's David, marching in repeated patterns across my tie, sagged a little: a triathlete running his last race. *This is not helpful.* I heard Patty's parents whenever she said this. Strict Southern Baptists, they were fearfully impatient with her as a girl, she'd told me once, harsh with all the other poor children they taught in Bible Study sessions. When the kids fidgeted during recitations, or giggled or whispered, her mother and father shouted, in tandem, "This is not helpful!" They'd pound the Good Book to snag everyone's attention again.

In college (she'd gone to Baylor, at her parents' insistence) Patty rebelled. To her teachers, one by one, and then to her mother and father, she declared her agnosticism. When her father threatened to disown her, she found a therapist who, instead of counseling compromise and reconciliation, as she'd anticipated, said the only way to save her psyche was to tell her parents goodbye. (Later, her father used this incident, in public speeches, to denounce the "evils of academia"—the doctor had been university-trained.) Patty called her parents to her therapist's office one day. Standing in front of them, wearing her best Sunday clothes, she said, formally, firmly, "Mother, Father, I bid you farewell."

That's why I knew that if Patty and I had a big break-up, if I were to heed Sarah's call, the tears would be few. Patty would stifle the dramatics. Her pride, her dignity, her innate politeness, her incredible discipline, would spare us both a lengthy ordeal.

I wasn't sure this comforted me.

Bridget's tears, this afternoon, had *certainly* been unpleasant. Could she really have gone to class after that? And what had brought it on? The *future*.

Indeed.

I lay on the bed, still fully suited, thinking of Patty, considering Bridget. Ten minutes, I promised myself. No sleep. I'll just rest my eyes.

Her days, these days, were exactly like her nights. A series of non-meetings. Admissions of nothing. The roomer below was afraid to meet her on the stairs.

She was certain they were reading her mail. Clearly, the latest letter from Kaminski had been unsealed and hastily re-taped.

This one from America.

You wouldn't know our girl. Or yes—I think you would. She looks just like you. Her maturity, her demeanor . . . how swiftly she has grown! You'd be proud, Anna.

160

Too painful. She set the letter aside, picked up another. A request for a visit from a Western diplomat stationed in Russia: Mr. Alfred Weller, First Secretary in the British Embassy in Moscow. "I humbly ask for this meeting out of admiration for your work."

As the candle began to gutter, she reached again for Kaminski's letter:

I worry, though, Anna. She's restless. As though she's never quite at home. It's more than an attitude. Almost an aura—self-exile? Out of it comes a remarkable empathy for others. Especially for peers of hers who have arrived here from different parts of the world. Our rainy western valley attracts quite a few international students. Already, she has told me she thinks she might like to teach languages. Perhaps English, so others can learn to fit in. She is quite fluent in English, naturally, though I don't let her forget her basic Russian.

The night Mr. Weller arrived—a heavy snow just beginning to fall— he settled uncomfortably into her armchair Pillows stretched across the floor.

"I'm afraid I have only boiled potatoes to offer you," Anna told him.

"No, no, nothing for me. Thank you."

"Your letter said you'd just returned from Paris?"

"Yes. I have news of some of your friends." His Russian was awkward. She stopped him and asked him to repeat. "Aleksander Halpern, Pasternak, Shileyko—they're all doing well. Modigliani has become quite famous since he died."

"Really! When I knew him he'd dig and dig in his pockets and never make the price of a drink." They laughed. Mr. Weller watched her closely. His eyes were small. He hadn't much hair.

"They're very concerned about you, your friends. Every day we hear more rumors out of Germany. War seems inevitable."

The tenant below noisily unlocked his door. They glanced at the walls.

"Would I be any safer in Paris?"

"At least you'd be among friends. You could publish." He stared appreciatively at her ankles.

"I couldn't leave Petersburg now. Old habits and all. I can hardly bring myself to say its new name. Leningrad. Cold and official."

"Do you have any recent work I can take to your colleagues in Europe?" asked Mr. Weller. "They're eager to see what you're doing."

She lighted another candle. "As a matter of fact, I've finally gained traction on a long poem. I've been working on it for quite some time. It's dedicated to the women who wait with me outside the prison."

"Yes. I heard about your son. I'm sorry."

161

She glanced at the page—at the few lines she'd committed to paper for the first time in over a year. It wasn't about her son. Truthfully, she hadn't thought of Lev in days. "Do you find me attractive, Mr. Weller?"

He tugged at the bottom of his coat. "Naturally," he said softly. "Don't."

Of course [Kaminski had written], *it's a long way off, Anna, but my biggest worry? That she'll fall in love someday and leave me, as all daughters leave their fathers. Some dreamy boy drawn to teaching . . . a boy who wants to be a writer or a poet, God help us all! And then what? She'll move to France, maybe. Or the English countryside. She'll have a daughter of her own, and the cycle will start again . . .*

Anna read Mr. Weller the first lines of her poem:

At dawn they came to take you away.
You were my dead, I walked behind.
In the dark room the children cried,
the holy candle gasped for air.

She asked him, "Can you follow the meaning?"

"Yes," he said.

"These words, these little scribbles, Mr. Weller, are all that matter to me. More than your admiration. More than the prison. Or my son."

"You don't really mean that."

She sat. "Sometimes . . . I do . . . yes. I do. "

"Your escort is here!" Irene called to me from the bottom of the stairs.

"Yes . . . thanks . . . I'm coming!"

I rubbed my face. Snow was falling now on every part of the dark central park beneath my window, on the treeless path near the little gazebo where brass bands played in the summer, on the barren thorns fronting the icy street where Robert Fields and I would walk to dinner.

7.

"Your generation—you've gotten over Joyce, I take it?"

The professor who asked me this, a handsome, middle-aged man with a fondness for single malt Scotch (he was on his third glass since I'd arrived, and I'd been there maybe twenty minutes) stood on the living room rug, a garish red-and-black affair, next to a cozy brick fireplace. A dozen other people circled the room, sipping golden cocktails. Some I'd met during the day, some I was introduced to for the first time. The house was an old Victorian with a late-addition California ranch-style kitchen.

I accepted a glass of cabernet from my host and turned back to the Scotch man. "How do you mean?" I asked.

"Well, *my* generation—we took one look at *Portrait*, *Ulysses*, and *Finnegans Wake* and thought, 'Hell and damn, what's the point of writing novels anymore? Joyce has done everything you can do with the form.' And he had. The number of unwritten novels by my despondent peers . . . well, they'd fill whole libraries."

"I think that, just as writers choose their influences, they also pick their problems," I said. "Which to tackle, which to ignore, given one's individual strengths and weaknesses. It's no insult to Mr. Joyce, whom I greatly admire, to say I don't choose to see him as a problem."

"I don't know if that's a wise answer, Mr. Allman, but it *sounds* wise, I'll give you that."

A goatish fellow who'd been introduced to me as an emeritus prof was sitting on a couch, saying to Robert Fields, "I miss the old days when literary arguments were *literally* arguments, complete with fisticuffs! Norman Mailer and Gore Vidal. William Buckley and Gore Vidal." He pondered, staring into his lager. "Maybe I just miss Gore Vidal."

The resignation of the CIA director was a hot topic, as were the on-going Iran-Contra hearings and impromptu diagnoses of Ronald Reagan's mental health. A sociologist whose specialty was "Human Sexuality" moved through the house asking women what kind of birth control they used, "solely in the interests of research." I overheard the feminist who'd nailed me in the Q and A tell a small group milling near the crudities, "We shouldn't kid ourselves. *America* is the Evil Empire."

An avuncular older man leaned over a celery tray. "Old news," he said. "Where have you been since Vietnam?"

"Or the Trail of Tears?" someone interjected.

The front door flew open with a puff of snow and in walked Kaminski, a tall wool cap on his head, its fur ear-flaps, each the size of a small cat, smothering three-quarters of his face. A heavily scarved woman followed him into the room. Conversations eased for three or four seconds and then resumed, accompanied by the background noise of Kaminski disrobing: Burberry coat, lighter coat, button-up sweater, pullover sweater, fleece. The woman—his wife?—removed her coat and scarves and handed them to our hostess. She was tall and slender with dark, angular features, rather like a garden trellis. Auburn hair. Quite a bit younger than Kaminski. Late thirties, perhaps.

And healthily pregnant.

Kaminski nodded hello to me. Our hostess clapped her hands and announced that dinner was served. "I thought, as we eat, we could all discuss a piece I read in this week's *New Yorker*," she said, apparently not trusting us to continue our small talk. She summarized an article none of us had seen about Arctic oil-drilling. Fortunately, the discussion petered-out quickly. I don't remember what the dinner was, other than cold beets and boiled potatoes. I remember not eating much of it. I fielded informal questions about Larry McMurtry—did I agree he was the best writer Texas had ever produced?; Southern Gothicism—didn't I agree it was overrated?; dust storms—why so many in my novel?

Over dessert, Robert Fields informed me I had the day free tomorrow —he was sure I would welcome this news. I could rest, catch up on my work from home, right? On Sunday afternoon, late, the valley shuttle would come get me for the forty-minute drive to the airport. Word was, the weather would clear. I had the distinct impression he was happy to be rid of me—Irene's assurances notwithstanding. He told me the department had two more candidates to fly in and evaluate, and then the hiring committee would meet in early March to make its decision. I could expect to hear from him then.

Some people left immediately, others lingered over pie and cake, still others poured after-dinner cordials. I was given a small glass of amaretto and invited to sit on the couch near the fire. Kaminski's wife—her name was Teresa—sat by me. Her perfume smelled like spring roses. "Vladimir is impressed that you know Akhmatova's work so well. She's always been a special interest of his."

"Yes. It's nice to meet someone with a shared passion," I said. I congratulated her on her pregnancy.

She blushed. "My first—though Vladimir has a grown daughter from an earlier marriage."

"Oh? Does she live here in town?"

"No, she's in Idaho. *Her* daughter is here, though—at the moment. College student. She was going to study in France this term, but . . . she's restless. Young, you know? Lacking direction right now."

I learned that Teresa had grown up in Utah, the child of Mormons.

"It was a very sheltered upbringing." She spoke softly. "It was hard for me, but as an adult, I turned away from my parents' beliefs. I guess I grew tired of the restrictions. I imagine—I might be wrong about this—maybe you faced something similar in Texas. From a distance, Texas has always seemed to me . . . I don't know . . . insular? The way it sees itself. Like a place apart."

"You're right. My fiancée—" The word sounded strange to me. "She had an experience like yours. Her folks were fundamentalists—very common there—and she struggled to find her own way."

Teresa smiled. "Well. I was lucky to meet Vladimir. He's a big personality, as you've seen. His uninhibited guidance was a great help in pushing me forward, out of the dark ages and into the modern world, as he puts it."

Three or four others joined us, sitting on the floor, toasting my visit, praising the greatness of Malamud.

"Malamud, eh? Do you know his most enduring achievement? It was to accurately depict this community as sluggish and dull, and the university as a mediocre institution mired in oppressive academic politics," Kaminski bellowed, elbowing into the group, next to the fire, balancing a plate of chocolate cake and a full brandy snifter. He was colossally drunk. I took a good look at him for the first time all evening. He appeared to have been put through the wringer much worse than I had, and not just because of our late night together. He was used to nights like that. "You want to know Oregon's *greatest* writer?" Kaminski said to me.

"Jesus, Kaminski," someone said.

"William Pierce."

"Who?" I said.

"Former physics professor. He interviewed for a job here just as Malamud was leaving in '61. Lucky for Bern. Pierce rejected Einstein's ideas because Einstein was a Jew. Late at night, in our esteemed campus library, Pierce worked on a novel called *The Turner Diaries*. Ever hear of it?"

His colleagues groaned. "Kaminski," one said. "Give it a rest."

"I don't know it," I said. "*The Turner Diaries*?"

"Set in the not-too-distant future. During a U. S. race war. Nowadays, nationwide, white supremacist groups have adopted Pierce's book as their Bible. A blueprint for far-right revolution." He drained his brandy. "I'll wager that William Pierce is more widely-read, and more powerfully influential than Bernard Malamud will ever be."

"You're full of shit, Kaminski," said a young prof, also well into his cups.

Kaminski grinned. He spread his arms. "William Pierce: The final word on literature's legacy in America."

Of course I didn't believe him. Not that night, anyway. Eight years later, when Timothy McVeigh blew up the Murrah building in Oklahoma City, a highway patrolman found a copy of *The Turner Diaries* in his car. I heard Kaminski, in my head, say, "I told you so." The novel's central chapter concerned the annihilation of a federal building, using ammonium nitrate fertilizer.

"Vladimir, Vladimir, please, let's go. It's late," Teresa said, tugging his sleeve.

"I haven't finished my cake! I knew Bill Pierce," Kaminski said. He swayed above me, spilling lemon icing on my legs. "I was here in '64, right before he left town. The election that year came down to Johnson and Goldwater. I ran into Bill on the quad one day and asked him what he thought of the candidates. 'I'd give two hundred dollars apiece to see both those sons of bitches kicking at the end of a rope,' he said." Kaminski laughed. His bitterness had doubled in twenty-four hours.

One by one, the guests left. Teresa pulled his sleeve. I remembered Bridget touching his arm, the night before. No, I thought. That girl is not his granddaughter. Not his granddaughter. Not at all.

"It's been a long day," I said. I thanked my host and hostess.

"I'll walk you back over," Kaminski said.

"That's okay. I know my way by now."

"I hear you've got nothing on tap for tomorrow. Come for a late brunch, or an early dinner—whatever. 3:00?" He turned to check with Teresa. Before she could answer, he said, "Yes. 3:00. We'll barbecue or something."

"Vladimir, it's snowing!" Teresa said.

"What the hell!" He patted my shoulder. "You've still got those notebooks of mine, so . . . 3:00, okay? I'll come get you."

166

8.

I walk in a field of factory ash with only my shawl and a hairful of snow. My books have been burned in the square.

This morning Lev's face is bruised, his lips are chapped and torn. "What did they do to you?"

A dry cough. "Stop it, Mother."

"Don't strain. Quietly."

He lifts his face toward mine. "They put a bag on my head. A bag of water. When they kicked me, my nose and throat filled till I thought I would drown. I couldn't stop choking."

I stroke his sweating back.

"Who was it?" he says.

"What are you talking about?"

"In your apartment?"

"When?"

"'If she insists on entertaining foreign men in her apartment,' they said . . ."

He closes his eyes. His long black hair comes off in scrappy patches on my hands.

Mr. Weller requests another chat. On the phone I tell him no: "Since your last visit, they tortured my son. The Party's asked me to write a poem praising Stalin."

"I'm sorry I caused you so much trouble." According to international reports, he says, the Germans are murdering hundreds of thousands of Jews.

"Why the Jews?"

He doesn't know.

Not, not mine: it's somebody else's wound.
I could never have borne it. So take the thing
that happened, hide it, stick it in the ground.
Whisk the lamps away . . .

In the early morning, carrying the notebooks, I walked through hummocks of snow to the little river, ice-blue and burbling, on the eastern perimeter of downtown Corvallis. I sat on a frosty bench, the puffs of

167

my breath like steam from a speeding train. I slid my fingers across Akhmatova's stiff pages, absorbed in Kaminski's translations.

This evening I can't see the lake: no moon. But I know where it is. I can hear it. I can sense the city of Kitezh.

The news from Paris is bad. Men say that all of Europe may fall to the German attack. Russia, too, perhaps. My friends urge me to join them—next month they're sailing to America—but "someone," I write Shileyko, "has to be a witness."

Bats echo in the hills. I walk back to town. Two soldiers with rifles on their shoulders leave a house by a darkened side door. Someone's crying in the kitchen; I duck down the street A young woman carrying a child in a burlap sack sniffs around the empty market stall where I'm hiding from the men. Rotten peach halves. Scattered apples. She scrubs the dirt, hands a grapefruit rind to her baby.

"No," the child protests.

"Eat, eat."

Fresh graves and bread crusts end another day of commerce.

Lev will be released in ten days. The prison official smiles at me. "No more guests?"

"No," I say.

"The Party, I understand, was quite pleased with your tribute."

A young wife, waiting for news of her own, squeezes my hand. Across the room, other women—tired mothers—glare at me.

I stop by the market. Cabbage is all I can afford and still have the price of a drink. Tucking the small head under my arm I treat myself to a beer in a tavern not far from where the Wandering Dog once stood.

When the Dog burned down, the poets and writers of Petersburg scattered, each like Lear without his kingdom. Cigarettes, candles, amorous dancing—the fire was an accident, police said.

"Bohemians," they called us. "Pimps and whores."

Most of my friends stayed silent, then, or quietly left. I sat by the Neva and wondered what people would say about our city? Flat, white buildings, haphazard construction, the squalor of the market. Increasing numbers of soldiers on the streets.

In the apartment now, still holding the cabbage, I fluff my pillow, straighten the Modigliani in its cracked brown frame. My eyes, as he painted them on the canvas, have faded a bit. With a towel I dust the table before setting the cabbage down.

From my window I see draymen returning from the fields, milk cans clattering, empty, in their wagons. Children menace each other with

168

sticks. A couple of soldiers pass in the street. "Keep me company tonight?" one yells up at me. His friend laughs and bumps into two old women, knocking the frailer one to the ground. She spits. The soldier scolds: "Watch where you're going. Crazy old bitch!"

The world will never want us. I know this. I swear—I'm going to tell everyone.

I closed the paper cover, watched lazy flakes in the sky.

In the light of day, with a better night's sleep, with the stress of interviewing over, I could see Kaminski a bit more clearly, I thought: a loud, undisciplined man, careless with others, apparently an adulterer, occasionally unprofessional (Fields had mentioned a "dispute" with his department), but—I believed—not a particularly strategic thinker, not, in the most devious sense, a dissembler. From me, he had made no attempt to hide his affection for Bridget. That didn't mean he trusted me. It meant I didn't figure in his world. There was no reason for discretion.

I didn't think he would lie to me about his relations with Anna Akhmatova. No need to. I was not someone he had to impress. Why had he lent me the notebooks? Unwise, perhaps, risky, but I credited it to a puppyish, impulsive form of collegiality. I liked a poet he liked. That was enough for an enthusiast, a voluptuary, like Kaminski.

Nothing suggested the old notebook was not authentic. On the river bank, I remembered Akhmatova's poem, "Lot's Wife." *Who will grieve for this woman?* Akhmatova cherished the creature "who suffered death because she chose to turn," to look back, to reassess the life she had abandoned. *Does she not seem / . . . insignificant . . . ? / Yet in my heart I will never deny her.*

The need to look back . . . certainly, I was feeling it strongly. I was on the verge of leaving the life I had known. Whether my new life would begin in Corvallis or somewhere else, I didn't know. Whether it would be with Patty or Sarah . . . sometimes I *believed* I knew. But that was hardly a solid ledge on which to stand.

The water's surface reflected the bare limbs of freezing oaks. Or were the trees stuck *beneath* the river, rotting and black?

On the winding, snowy bank, I recited Akhmatova:

Three things enchanted him:
white peacocks, evensong,
and faded maps of America.
He couldn't stand bawling brats,
or raspberry jam with his tea,
or womanish hysteria.
. . . and he was tied to me.

The poem's pain made me ache for Patty and Sarah. Tears blurred my vision. I had come to a small steel bridge spanning the river. An empty hawk's nest perched in its rust-green girders. Beneath it, on the bank, in what would have been a scraggly mud-plain full of nettles, if not for the snow, half a dozen homeless men huddled in sleeping bags around a spitting fire. The dark figures moving in the cold, among blue-white cattails, assembled as if in a scene from Eastern Europe, in the war, forty years ago.

God's elusiveness builds a city like this.

Weary, heavy, I headed back through town, past Tommy's 4th Street Grill ("Today: Oyster shooters, two for a dollar!"), past a closed movie theater and an empty hardware store. As I neared the B and B, I noticed, sitting on a bench in the park, next to the tiny gazebo, a disconsolate young poet.

"Bridget," I said. She was wearing a black lace shawl over a maroon dress made of some shiny material.

"I came to see you," she said. "The woman in the house said you'd gone for a walk."

I sat, not close, at the other end of the bench. "Yes. It's a beautiful river. Beautiful town."

"I wanted to apologize."

"What for?"

"Yesterday. You didn't need . . . while interviewing . . . well, a hysterical girl dissolving into tears."

"You were hardly hysterical. And I was fine. *Concerned* about you."

"That's kind."

"May I ask . . . what it was about? Everything okay?"

She folded her hands in her lap. Green wool mittens. "A long-standing problem. Of my own making." With her head bowed, her bangs hid her eyes. She was pale but her skin glowed bronze from the cloudy light filtered through naked trees, reflected from the snow.

"You and Kaminski?" I said. Behind us, a slushy clump dropped from the crook of an oak. "I'm sorry . . . not my business," I said. "But the other night, well, it seemed clear that . . . "

She nodded. "I don't want you to be . . . I mean, you don't need to get drawn into my silly little drama. And frankly I'm ashamed to talk about it. I really just wanted to say I was sorry, I hope it's been a good visit for you otherwise, and—"

"Bridget, please don't worry about what I need. Right now, I'd like very much to sit and talk with you, okay? If you'll forgive my presumption, I think you *need* to talk. But for god's sake, can we go someplace warm?"

She smiled—more openly. We walked a few blocks to a downtown coffee shop. The espresso machine steamed the windows. Bridget huddled in her shawl like a frostbite victim unable warm up. At first, I steered us into background chat. Where was she from, what had brought her to Corvallis? She spoke in a rush—long bottled-up. Her mother was American, she said, her father from Brisbane (accounting for the accent). He worked for a pharmaceutical company. When she was three, the family moved to Nigeria for her daddy's business. She lived in Lagos until she was nearly fourteen. The return to the States as an adolescent was extremely difficult, she said. She felt she had fallen off a cliff at school. She was socially awkward. She feared her friends' pets—"Dogs were generally wild and dangerous in Lagos"—and grew more and more timid, increasingly silent. Writing poetry in the privacy of her room was her one solace.

"Why Oregon State?" I asked.

"My family lived in Portland. I tried the University of Oregon first— it's the state's humanities school. I mean, it's far more established than OSU, better funded—"

"Yes, I've been briefed," I said. "I understand that if I come here, there'll be a lot of program-building. So you went to U of O?"

"I was immediately intimidated. The students there were so much better-read than I was. They knew poets I'd never heard of. John Donne, Andrew Marvell . . . anyway, I stopped writing altogether the year I was there. I felt horrible about myself. So I transferred here, determined to avoid all but the required English classes. I didn't know what I was doing. My advisor said I had to take a foreign language. I couldn't have known that in Vee's introductory Russian course, I'd rediscover poetry."

She stared at her coffee.

"He gave you Akhmatova?"

She nodded.

"Turned you *into* Akhmatova?"

"When he showed me her picture, I had to admit . . . the resemblance . . ."

"Can I ask—?"

"What?"

"Is he on the level? About her?"

"Who? Akhmatova?"

"He told me they were lovers."

"I believe him."

"Okay."

"He's a remarkable man. I know, physically, he's . . . well, obviously he's a mess." She blushed. "And he can come across as boorish, but really he's . . . "

"You don't have to explain anything."

"And now he's in trouble because of me."

"I heard. A 'dispute' with his department?"

171

"It's not a dispute. He's *had* disputes."

"Like what?"

"Over the school's anti-Semitism ..."

"*Is* it anti-Semitic?"

"The institution doesn't honor Jewish holidays. He's convinced campus culture has always been racist. No. They want to fire him for sexual harassment." Her fingers shook on her saucer. "I knew I wasn't the first ... I mean, he hasn't made a habit of, you know, seducing ... anyway, anyway, I wasn't the first. So okay. He never pretended I was. Apparently, a girl from one of his classes years ago ... when she heard about me, she wrote a letter to the chair. Jealousy? Revenge? Unfinished business? I don't know. But now he's been summoned by Affirmative Action, there's an official investigation ..." Tears brightened her face.

I reached for her hand.

"I just wanted to be his Anna," she said.

"I know."

"I'm sorry. I guess I *did* need to talk to someone."

"It's okay."

"I think you felt safe. You're not part of all this."

"And I'll be leaving." *And because—it can't be helped—you're Anna for me, too. Our dear poet.*

"I'll *also* be going away," she said.

"What do you mean?"

"Quitting school."

"Bridget."

"Now that it's all out in the open... and oh my god ... my god, his poor wife! That poor woman, expecting a child. I've been so selfish. I can't believe myself. You must think I'm terrible. Maybe if I leave, he can—"

"No. Believe me. He'll do whatever he does, but it shouldn't affect *your* plans. Quitting school? You don't want to do that. Bridget."

Déjà vu. Shit, I thought. My head spun. The caffeine. The cold. But no. This was about unfinished mansions on the beach. A blue-and-gold butterfly perched on a breast.

"Don't leave. It's a mistake," I said. "As hard as it is here—" It was no concern of mine. I didn't have full information. And yet I was pleading as passionately as I'd pleaded years before. "You can work it out." I almost said *we.*

In parting, I made her promise to meet me the following day for coffee before I had to go to the airport.

I had an hour before Kaminski was set to pick me up. It would be a dreadful afternoon. How could I look at Teresa, now that Bridget had confirmed for me she was sleeping with the man? Did Teresa know? Would Kaminski worry about me—afraid I'd give away what I'd seen the other night in that godawful bar? If so, he wouldn't have invited me to his house, would he?

The bed and breakfast was quiet. The salesmen had checked out. Irene was not about. This was my last chance to sit with the notebooks.

"Did you love my father?" Lev slouches over cabbage and boiled potatoes. His second day home—too weak, until this evening, to speak.

"I felt sorry for him. Would you like another potato?"

"Yes. Why? What made him so pathetic?"

"He wasn't pathetic. I never thought that. It's just that he wanted—what? To be a great man, I suppose. First as a writer, then as a husband, a hunter, a soldier. He used to tell me, 'I was born for these things.' He'd say, 'You and I, Anna, we'll live to see the True Twentieth Century.' He thought it would be a period of triumph. I knew better."

"Was he really a traitor?"

I stack our plates on the counter. "He was killed because of his poetry."

"That must have increased its value."

"His spare style, the Bolsheviks said, 'betrayed our rich Russian culture.'"

"And you?" The color has returned to Lev's cheeks. His back still aches. "Don't you want to be great? A great writer?"

"Yes."

"So I should feel sorry for you?"

"People's judgments are beyond my control. Your father couldn't accept that."

"I suppose I've helped your career."

"What do you mean?"

"Jail. Your loneliness. Your terrible suffering—all that."

"Hush."

"I'm sure you've written about it."

"No."

"Then you will. It's too good to pass up, eh And who knows—a poem here, a poem there, perhaps I'll wind up in prison again."

"I'm sorry, Lev. I never intended my work to affect your life this way."

"But it has, hasn't it? Maybe I should get myself killed. Then you'd surely be great. The Great Akhmatova." He stands, painfully. "Where was she until I wound up in jail?"

"You knew where I was. You could have come to me."

He tosses his cup onto the pile of dirty plates. The cathedral bell rings once, twice, twice again.

———————

A small steamer's anchored in the river. On board, dozens of young soldiers, crisp in their belts and boots; crates of fruit. Women clutch rosaries near the now-empty market, whisper prayers, wave at the boys as they pull away in the boat.

"I hear that your son is home again."

I nod to the woman beside me.

"Thank God. You're very fortunate."

"Yes," I say. "I am."

———————

This evening, a bright full moon. It's clear to me: what we see in the lake is not a reflection of Kitezh, but the city itself. Marble columns, cobbled streets, fish rounding corners, quick as light.

The True Twentieth Century: I've finally lived to see it. I drop my shawl on the bank, remove my shoes and skirt. The water is cold. Pinnacles, vaulting, an Ogee arch. Stained glass, crockets engraved with ball flower designs. Rotting wood. Straight ahead, a white gate: is this the way in?

Yes, voices whisper. Or maybe it's the water swishing. Louder now, yes: Closer, come a little closer . . . join us   . . .

Here I am. My lungs ache. No, I think. Closer, Anna, come this way . . .

No. My place is with the dying, not the dead.

I surface, catch my breath. My skirt, a purple patch, waves to me from the shore.

———————

In town, merchants fold their awnings. I shiver, shake back my short wet hair. A light goes out in a window. This is how the world ends. Acquiescent. Peaceful. No help needed from us. I sit by the Neva and laugh. All my pretty fools, my lovely foolish home . . . I've forgiven everyone.

9.

The Kaminskis owned a small clapboard house set back from a winding road in the town's southern hills, and down an unpaved drive, nestled among Douglas firs and pine trees. It overlooked a section of a country club's golf course, part of the back nine. Kaminski seemed none the worse for wear after his debauch the night before. And the night before that. He wore a gabardine suit and bulky black shoes. They reminded me of preachers' shoes—the Baptist preachers back in Texas whose sermons my mother made me hear as a kid. The sermons were punctuated by the *thock-thock* of the shoes' big heels on the church's wooden stage. God's footsteps.

Kaminski, hunched and stony, looked like a minor gargoyle atop a Gothic cathedral.

On our way to his house in the Honda, I noticed three different police cruisers turning corners as we passed. They weren't following us, precisely, but the sheer numbers seemed excessive for such a small town. Kaminski *had* told me cops didn't have enough to do in Corvallis, but I wondered: did they know he was being investigated for sexual harassment on campus? Had the police been engaged to keep an eye on him? No. That was ridiculous. I was being paranoid. Too much Stalin; CIA and secret wars; too much *twentieth century*.

Maybe, as the Kaminskis' marriage soured (had it soured?), grimmer incidents had occurred. Domestic abuse? Once again, my imagination was running away with me.

He ushered me into a living room simple and plain. Watercolors, also simple and plain, adorned the walls, portraits of the house in each of the four seasons. They were signed, in tiny lettering, "Teresa." Their blue and gray colors matched the large hooked rug beneath a glass coffee table in the center of the room stacked with academic journals.

Kaminski picked a box of matches off the table and lighted the kindling set neatly inside the fireplace. He checked the flue and put the fire screen in place. Teresa popped her head around the kitchen doorway to say hello and to ask if I'd like a drink. She was drying her hands on a yellow dish towel.

"Water would be fine," I said.

"Oh, come now." Kaminski patted me, hard, on the back.

We joined Teresa in the kitchen—a bright oval room whose picture window overlooked a grove of maple trees sloping downhill toward a brown creek that must have drained into the river downtown. Sure enough, on the back deck, Kaminski had prepared a gas barbecue grill, in spite of the snow piled high against the railings.

Underneath an apron, Teresa wore a maternity dress busy with brown and red checks. "I know he'd like an IPA," she told me, smiling. "You might as well stop resisting."

I laughed. "Well, if I'm forced."

Kaminski stunned me by raising his bottle in a toast. "To our newest colleague."

"I think you're premature."

"No, no. I have a good sense of these things."

"I don't think I performed all that well, to tell you the truth."

"Doesn't matter. What matters is, you fit here. I can see it. Others will, too."

"Based on what?"

"*Gravitas.* A little untested, it's true." He laughed gently. "But it's there."

On the blue-tiled counter, beneath a row of copper pots and pans hanging from large silver wall hooks, there was a small, framed picture of a chubby woman with abundant black hair. She was holding a red-faced little girl. "Your daughter?" I asked.

"Yes, with our granddaughter when she was younger."

"Teresa told me your granddaughter lives here in town."

Kaminski sighed. "Do you plan to have children, Jeremy? You and this woman you're about to marry?"

I didn't like the way he said it: as though he knew my judgment was impaired when it came to this wedding. I pictured Sarah sitting on the beach in Galveston. My hand on her belly, through her sweater, just beneath the butterfly resting on her breast.

Patty had her tubes tied. I didn't tell Kaminski this. "We may."

"Take my word for it. They're a trial and a tribulation, children." He sighed again.

"Vladimir!" Teresa mock-scolded him. She rubbed her round belly. I had a powerful urge to reach out and touch her there. I tightened my grip, both hands, on my beer bottle.

"Anna knew. She and Lev were always at odds. Darlene, *my* sweet daughter, has been living for the past ten years with a group of . . . I don't know what to call them . . . back-to-nature enthusiasts, the last of the nation's hippies . . . in northern Idaho," Kaminski said. "Naturally, with an upbringing like that—which is to say, no upbringing at all—our grand-daughter, Lisa, has never had direction. She enrolls in classes for a while, drops out, enrolls again, decides to study abroad, comes back after less than a month, enrolls, drops out . . . you see? Trials. Tribulations."

"And what kind of upbringing did Darlene have? A father who never left his study, constantly poring over Russian literature?" Teresa said.

She must have intended this as a gentle jibe, a not-so-serious nudge in the ribs, but it sounded extremely bitter.

"And what do you know about it, my dear? You weren't yet in the picture, were you?" Kaminski answered, equally harshly.

Then they smiled at each other. She returned to arranging raw vegetables on a tray, he turned to his foaming IPA.

There was a war in this house.

A little too cheerily, I thought, Teresa narrated for me how she had met Kaminski in Portland, where she'd landed after breaking with her parents and leaving Utah. He was giving a lecture at a community college she was thinking of attending: a talk on Ukraine, its history, its geopolitical importance, tips for those who might travel there. "Such a charmer," Teresa recalled. "He couldn't stand still. He had to pace as he talked, but he needed to stay near the microphone, which was attached to the podium. So he simply picked up the podium and dragged that heavy thing around the room as he prowled!" This drew a faint smile from Kaminski. Teresa laughed. "I'd never seen such energy or heard such wit. Afterwards, as the room was emptying, he caught my eye and asked me out for coffee. Charming *and* fast. I'll tell you, I wasn't used to men like that."

"All right, enough of the Tales of Lothario," Kaminski said. He touched my elbow. "Come on. Before I put the chicken on the grill, let me show you the study I never leave."

We crossed the living room, past the fireplace, and ducked through a low doorway next to one of Teresa's watercolors: the house in autumn, looking cold and forgotten.

Dozens of volumes of Akhmatova's poetry in Russian lined his floor-to-ceiling shelves, along with English translations by Kunitz and Hayward, D. M. Thomas, Lyn Coffin, and Judith Hemschemeyer: *Evening*, *Rosary*, *White Flock*, *Poem without a Hero*. Multiple biographies. 8 X 10 reproductions of famous photographs, framed behind glass, had been tucked among the books: Akhmatova wrapped in black, appearing furtive and harried, her youthful face just beginning to break, scoured by deprivation, almost trembling even in the still picture; and here, the Mother of Russia—Akhmatova right before she died—her skin hardened to stone, crazed with cracks and seams, all except for that strange bump of a nose, which alone seemed to have softened with age. The fat of her neck overflowed the tight collar of white pearls she'd chosen—surely she was choking. Her gray hair wisped back in waves, faint traces of ripples left in clay at the bottom of a creek bed. Innocent, jaded, young and old: how could all of these be the same woman?

Kaminski tapped the top of his Cherrywood desk. "Here is where the great work gets done." He laughed. "You know Pushkin's description of writing?"

177

"No."

" 'A mass of . . . at three o'clock I . . . ' Oh, I forget the exact quote. Essentially, he recounts how boring his daily ritual is."

I pulled the notebooks from my jacket pocket and set them on the desk. "Boring, I don't know. Tedious, I can imagine. But important. I think you should try to publish these translations. Surely they're of immense value?"

He rubbed his stubbled chin. "But do they add anything to our understanding of her? After all, most of this raw material eventually found its way into the poetry one way or another."

"The raw before it's refined . . . that must tell us *something.*"

"Spoken like a scholar." He smiled.

"Everything she wrote about—personal decadence, the threats to freedom—it's still relevant to our time."

"But who in America will heed it? Except impotent academics?"

"Well. Anyway," I said. "I'm flattered you'd ask my opinion of it. Thank you for letting me read it. Letting me rest my hand where Akhmatova's hand once moved."

He ran his fingers over the books. A sound like snow on glass. "Jeremy, we haven't had a chance, since the other night, to talk about your impressions of Bridget," he said. Charming and fast? Oh, indeed.

What could I say to him? Should I reveal what I knew? Did he already know the extent of my knowledge? Hadn't he *wanted* me to witness his affair?

I said the only thing that *could* be said, or so it seemed to me then. "She's Anna."

He fell heavily into his padded desk chair and whisked his hand miserably over his face. "Yes. She's Anna." Immediately, improbably, this old Russian and I, strangers three days before, were plunged into an intense and awkward intimacy. "I'm that worst of clichés—a methodical and boring old man, mired in his work, looking to youth for revitalization," he admitted. "And this *particular* youth struck me with such force. As if she was a reincarnation. But of course that isn't fair to her. I have to let her go. But I can't."

"She told me she's leaving."

He nodded. "I've tried and tried to convince her to stay. Assured her things will change. That we can still be friends, that I can help her, still, with her poems . . . ah well, apparently it's all too late."

"You're in danger of losing your job?"

He didn't even blink. He spoke to me as if I'd been here for a decade and knew all the facts about him. I think, now, it was a strange form of narcissism, an assumption that his business should be everyone's business, and we should drop everything immediately to care for him. In

178

years to come, I was to meet many such men in academia. "Hard to say," he said. "The process is in motion, but . . . my peers are going to judge *me*?" He laughed. "That's rich. Around here, it's very much a case of 'He who is without sin . . .'"

"You're about to have a child," I said. "A new beginning? New life? A chance to start over?"

"Are you trying to sound wise beyond your years?"

I smiled.

"You know, I had a fantasy, when Fields showed me your application letter and I saw your attraction to Anna. Before you even got here, I imagined you as the decent young man you've turned out to be. I imagined you hitting it off with Bridget, getting the job here, settling down with her and keeping her in town so I could at least still work with her from time to time on her writing."

"And we'd all live happily ever after?"

"Something like that."

"I'm getting married," I said. Maybe. "And I doubt I'll get the job here."

"As I said." He spread his small hands. "A fantasy. Even an old man will indulge in romantic silliness when he's desperate as all hell."

The sad honesty on display in his room of books vanished at dinner, to be replaced by an almost insufferable pedantry. "Our dear Anna has never gotten her due," he said, filling his glass from a bottle of Bordeaux. "She's famous, yes. Revered by certain younger poets. But still, generally, academia celebrates the men first. Pasternak, Mayakovsky, Blok."

"But *your* work has changed that," Teresa said with a self-effacing smile. Her manner had stiffened. Could she have overheard us in the study?

"*My* work! Obscure critical articles in journals no one ever sees."

"You know you're proud of what you've done. It's unbecoming of you, dear, to denigrate yourself."

"Not myself. This stultifying profession of ours!" He reached across the table, past a bowl of green beans, to pat my arm. "I'm sorry, Jeremy, but you may as well know, if you don't already. The path you're setting out on is filled with mighty pitfalls."

"Like *any* other path?"

"Well. It's good there are young upstarts coming into the ranks. It's a young man's game, really. I've done what I can do to advance Anna's reputation in the West."

"The notebook," I said. "Don't forget."

"And you. This novel you're proposing, based on Anna's life . . ."

I shrugged.

"Don't *you* start," Teresa said to me. "*One* self-deprecating man at this table is plenty."

"You need to go to Russia. Do firsthand research," Kaminski told me. "Learn the language—or a little of it, at least, so you can feel Anna's rhythms. Maybe that would be the way for me to cap my career. Go with you to Petersburg." I couldn't tell if he was kidding. "Show you the places Anna lived—though most of them are long gone, of course. Ramshackle hovels to begin with. I could tour you through important sites, mentioned in the poems, describe for you how she looked—"

"Oh, he knows what she looks like, doesn't he?"Teresa said. Very carefully, she folded her cloth napkin. She placed it firmly on the table. "We all know what she looks like."

It was as though the sliding glass door leading to the deck had flung itself open, letting in the cold.

Kaminski took a magnificently slow sip of his wine. He glowered at his wife. He said, "Perhaps we should—"

"Perhaps we should've. A long time ago," Teresa said. Her mouth began to tremble.

"What do you mean by that?"

She rose and left the room.

"The pregnancy," Kaminski said quickly, glancing away, trying to explain what had just happened.

He set our dishes in the sink, poured us each a small glass of cognac, but the energy and wit his wife had praised him for had departed with her. She didn't reappear. Kaminski and I sat in the living room watching the fire die, concluding our astonishing get-together with pleasantries, meaningless good wishes for the future, promises that, if everything worked out, my new wife and I would invite the Kaminskis and their baby for dinner—our first guests in our new house in town, in the fall, just before classes started.

Kaminski's last word with me arrived the following morning, before I even got out of bed. When I came downstairs for breakfast, Irene, under Ronald Reagan's stare, handed me an envelope with my name on it. "Someone slipped this under the front door," she explained. I opened it. It was from Kaminski. A single sheet of light blue paper.

Pushkin: "I wake at seven o'clock; I drink coffee, and I lie around until three o'clock. Not long ago I got into a writing vein and I've written a mass of stuff. At three o'clock I mount my horse, at five I take a bath, and then I dine on potatoes and buckwheat porridge. I read until nine o'clock. There's my day for you. And they're all just the same."

10.

I've tried and tried to convince her to stay.

Kaminski's helplessness, as he'd sat in his study explaining his situation to me, was doubly painful to witness because it echoed so precisely my experience with Sarah just over three years earlier.

She'd left me, but it wasn't really *me* she was fleeing when she broke the lease on her Houston apartment, sold her furniture and her car, and flew away—to Washington, as it turned out, though I didn't know this at the time. She had a cousin there who put her up, and she wound up staying. Silent, "doing penance," was how she framed it three years later when she called me out of the blue and asked was it true I was getting married? Could we meet, somewhere we wouldn't be seen, maybe in Galveston? Could we talk?

"Please. I'm asking you to stay," I'd said to her on our last night together before she'd left school, left town.

"After I've hurt you this way?"

"We *all* have a lot to sort out. You're hurting, too. I understand that."

We were lying in my bed, teary, after a failed attempt to make love. Glaringly—grossly—on my desk, near the bed, the multi-page contract for my first novel. It had arrived that morning from the publisher. Sarah had congratulated me on it when she'd first showed up. Instead of being gracious, I'd said, "I saw his car parked in front of your house last night."

"What do you do? Do you drive around spying on me?"

"Yes."

Sarah bowed her head. "He came by to ask me not to leave. But I've decided. It's best for us all."

"He" was the writing teacher with New York connections who'd helped me get my novel to the publisher. I'd deliberately arranged the contract on my desk so Sarah would see it. I wanted it to pierce her: *I know what this is—it's like fucking blood money, isn't it? It's how he hopes to buy me off so he can have you.*

In fact, I would never entirely lose the suspicion that it wasn't just "luck" that got my book into print. It was a sad attempt to clean up a mess. This is why, in later years, I all but disowned that novel, though it did, I suppose, help me get the job at Oregon State.

Why Sarah and I went ahead and tried to make love that night, knowing it could only end in disaster, I'm not sure. One last feverish attempt to touch. We lay in bed, weeping together, she urging me not to blame the teacher, he was a great man but a flawed man, a lonely man,

I shouldn't turn away from him—he could aid my career. I bemoaned the fact that I'd introduced her to him at a party one night. I'd heard of his reputation for sleeping with students; I should have known where *that* would lead . . .

"Please. I'm asking you to stay."

Silently, she dressed, pulled her shawl across her shoulders, and left.

Three months later, no word from Sarah, I sat in a bar with the teacher. He'd invited me out after class—a class I'd nearly dropped because I didn't want anything more to do with him. But I was nearing graduation. I'd be entering the job market soon. I'd need a letter of recommendation. I opted for practicality rather than principle—an option Sarah never got.

We ordered a couple of beers and he toasted the upcoming publication of my book. He said he was proud of me. "Of course, you realize it doesn't change anything. You're still the same old wretch you always were. Tomorrow morning, you'll have to get up and sit at your writing desk just as you always have." Then he said he wanted to thank me. He'd learned I'd quashed vicious rumors floating around school about him, and about Sarah's departure.

"I didn't do it for you," I said.

"I know. I tried and tried to convince her to stay. For *your* sake," he said. I didn't believe *that* one. "The worst of it is . . . I fucked up the teaching."

Four months later, I met Patty at the picnic in the park.

The night before she left, Sarah told me she'd said to the teacher, "I *have* to leave. I have to, because this—what we're doing here together— it isn't fair to others. To Jeremy. Or your wife."

"My dear," he'd replied. "When is anything *ever* fair to the others?"

11.

On Sunday morning, I packed my bag and left it sitting by the door to my room at the B and B. The airport shuttle would come for me around mid-afternoon. Piles of snow remained at the bases of trees, among bushes and shrubs, but no new precipitation had fallen and the streets had been cleared. From the window of my room I saw heavy bulbs of mist curl around the gazebo in the park, and obscure the stained-glass windows of the arts center next door.

I still had Robert Fields's copy of Malamud's *A New Life*. I decided I'd leave it on the bureau with a note to Irene, asking her to return it. I opened the book and read:

The sight of the expectant earth raised a hunger in his throat. He yearned for the return of spring . . . He was now dead set against the destruction of unlived time. As he walked he enjoyed surprises of landscape: the variety of green, yellow, brown, and black fields, compositions with distant trees, the poetry of perspective.

It seemed that Malamud had found *some* grace in Oregon.

Downstairs, in the dining room, I poured myself a cup of coffee from a big silver pot. After handing me the envelope from Kaminski, with the Pushkin quote inside, Irene advised me, "Now, when they offer you the job, don't leap at the first salary figure they toss out. They'll try to lowball you." Underneath a red and yellow apron, she wore gray sweatpants and a brown wool sweater.

"I don't think they're going to offer me the job, Irene. They've got two more candidates to consider."

She waved her hand dismissively. "And when you get here, *buy*. The housing market's good right now, but it's going to get tighter in the years ahead. More expensive. The city's planning process is overregulated and archaic. It scares away builders. A shortage is coming, mark my words."

Time would prove her right (and I *didn't* buy when I should have).

I called Patty, to remind her I'd be arriving in Houston late that night. She wasn't home. I left a message on our machine: "Can't wait to see you. Love you very much."

Bridget arrived at ten, wrapped in a black fur coat. We walked past Tommy's and an abandoned lumber yard to the same coffee shop we'd gone to the day before. It was cold inside the shop and I kept my heavy jacket on.

183

Bridget blew on her steaming cocoa. "Have you gotten all your questions answered?" she asked. "About the university, the department, the job?"

"Yes. But when it comes to *you* . . . I wonder if you know what you're doing." My presumption shocked her. "It's okay. I'm safe, remember? Hours from now, I'll be gone and you'll never see me again. So tell me. What is it, *exactly*, that makes you think you have to leave?"

She spread her hands. She'd kept her green mittens on. "Isn't it obvious?"

"No. Not to me," I said.

"It's—"

"You feel you're being unfair to Kaminski's wife? 'That poor woman,' you called her."

"Well, yes. Absolutely."

"So why must you be the one to leave? Why not him?"

She looked at me, her brown eyes uncannily like those of the hunted poet haunting Kaminski's dreams. And my dreams too . . . from this snowy weekend forward.

"He has a wife and a family. A house. He's lived here for decades. He's—"

"Nearing the end of his career. Any day now, perhaps, if the department rules against him. You're just beginning, *whatever* path you choose. And quitting school is not the way to prepare. Bridget, he was—forgive me—the *adult* in this situation. It's not up to you to atone for his weakness."

"I was weak, too. And why are you being so cruel to him? He was nothing but nice to you."

"He was, yes. And I'm grateful. I don't mean to be judgmental. Of anyone. I'm just . . . please. I'm asking you to stay. For *your* sake. Don't let guilt or shame or plain old lousy feeling cloud your thinking. Nothing about this is as dire as you believe it is. Time will pass. Things will get better. I know that's hackneyed, but . . . "

"Maybe that's the worst of it, in a way. How selfish I'm being. Selfish and little. I know that nothing I'm going through is anywhere near as horrible as . . . "

"Anna Akhmatova's life?"

"Well . . ."

I tried my best Bogey on her. "The problems of three little people don't amount to a hill of beans in this crazy world. Someday you'll understand." She was too young to know the reference. I waved my hand: *doesn't matter*. "Kaminski thought I should go to Russia to research a novel. Maybe not a bad idea."

"I've thought . . . someday I'd like to go to Russia, too."

184

Right here, right now, then, a new story could begin, I remember thinking. Depending on what either of us says in the next few seconds . . .

I also thought: In Petersburg, they'd take one look at you, my dear, and faint.

Neither of us said a thing. We finished our drinks. She seemed excessively shy all the sudden.

"Thank you for meeting me," I told her. "I hope you'll think about what I've said. It really is none of my business, but I'd hate to see you quit school, Bridget. Put yourself first, here, okay?"

She smiled weakly. I was no better now at changing women's minds than I had ever been.

In the snowdrifts in the park, outside the B and B, I hugged her gingerly. "You took fine care of me. I appreciate it," I said.

"I'm glad to have had the chance to meet you. I'll look forward to reading your novel."

I laughed. "I don't think you'll like it much. The prose is . . . well . . . pretty dusty. But you keep writing. I'll look for your name in the magazines."

She shook her head.

"Don't do that," I said. "Be good to yourself."

She walked away. White clouds of snow stirred at her feet. *We don't know how to say goodbye*, I thought: one of the first Akhmatova poems I'd known. *We wander on, shoulder to shoulder. / Already the sun is going down; / you're moody, I am your shadow.*

I turned toward the bed and breakfast. *. . . let's sit . . . / on the trampled snow, sighing to each other. / That stick in your hand is tracing mansions / in which we shall always be together.*

185

12.

These pages could have reflected another story. I had one other campus interview that winter, at Southern Illinois University in Carbondale. I could have recounted that experience instead of my weekend in Oregon, but in truth, nothing intriguing happened to me in Illinois. If it had, I might have accepted the university's offer and begun a much different life.

There was one similarity between Oregon State and Southern Illinois: SIU also had a resident literary spirit, a novelist named John Gardner. He'd died on a wooded back road at the age of forty-nine in a motorcycle accident. At one point in his life, he'd crossed paths with Raymond Carver, fresh out of Oregon, and become Carver's teacher. He helped Carver get into print. All weekend, in Carbondale, faculty members told me, "If you come here, you could be the next John Gardner," as if I could aspire to nothing higher in this world (a *New York Times* book reviewer had once described Gardner's appearance—long white hair, pot belly, leather jacket—as that of a "pregnant woman trying to pass for a Hell's Angel"). He was known to me for writing a book called *On Moral Fiction*, in which he'd argued that all contemporary American writers were spiritually anemic, "tinny, commercial, and immoral." (He called Bernard Malamud an "enormously serious writer" who nevertheless kept "blowing it" in his work, whatever that meant.) "The present scarcity of first-rate fiction does not follow from a sickness of society but the other way around," he wrote. "Real art creates myths a society can live instead of die by, and clearly our society is in need of such myths." However tempted I might be to agree with that statement, my enthusiasm was always trampled by Gardner's tone—scolding, self-serving, implying that all writers who failed to meet his moral standard deserved to be silenced.

That winter, after my campus interviews, whenever I thought of *On Moral Fiction*—its hectoring, authoritarian approach—I remembered Kaminski in his Honda, harassed by the flashing red lights of the cop car: "You'd think we were living in Leningrad!"

I could have written about many other people, aside from Patty and Sarah, who affected my life that winter—foremost among them, my parents, both dead now after long illnesses. Without question, they were the most important influences on my life, and my grief for them is boundless. But they are not central to this story.

I could write, yet, of my many happy years of marriage to a woman named Melanie, whose daughter Haley, three years old when I met her mother in Corvallis, would be the child I ended up raising (I never fathered a biological child—bad luck, and then, in late middle-age, prostate surgery). I have cherished no one in my life more than Melanie and Haley—but they deserve a narrative of their own, rather than cameos in this one.

This one—this ragged, snowy tale—ends on a wet road in western Oregon. On the airport shuttle, that late Sunday afternoon, I felt certain I would never return to the Willamette Valley. As the bus passed through Corvallis and then onto the highway, I said goodbye to the university, to Tommy's 4th Street Grill, to the steel bridge and the homeless encampment beneath it, with its eerie echoes of Eastern Europe. I could not have known that, energized by the notebooks Kaminski had shown me, I would return to Houston and kick out, in the space of two days, a revision of my short story based on Akhmatova's life. "Akhmatova's Notebook," I called it, and within two weeks, I had sold it to a prominent national magazine, only because I had sent them the manuscript when they were desperately short of material for their next issue. At the last minute, they had killed a lengthy story they'd scheduled to run, a piece about Bill Casey and Iran-Contra—fact-checkers had discovered cracks in the reporting. Lucky me.

I could not have known that Robert Fields was about to offer the OSU job to another candidate when I phoned him to update my vita. The prominent national magazine impressed him. He postponed the call to the other candidate, convened a hasty meeting of the hiring committee, and by a four to three vote, I got the nod.

By that point (I'd learn much later, from my new colleagues), Bridget had already left town, for destinations no one I talked to ever knew. Apparently, she did not look back. She never returned.

Broken, Kaminski resigned rather than wait to be fired. He died of a heart attack a scant four months later, just as Fourth of July fireworks were exploding in cloudy skies over Corvallis, above its beautiful river. Teresa and her brand new baby moved to Portland. When I started teaching in the fall, the Kaminskis' clapboard house was fresh on the market, and I could have bought it for a nice price, if I'd been wise enough to listen to Irene.

Akhmatova's funeral, held in St. Nicholas's Cathedral in Leningrad in March 1966, was thronged with citizens from all social walks, with photographers, writers, and film cameramen, people whose faces reflected a palpable longing, observers recalled—a longing marking them all as "Akhmatova's orphans." The twentieth century's children. Teresa buried Kaminski privately, I was told, in an unmarked grave in a rarely-visited lot just north of Corvallis.

I could not have known—though I should have—that Patty and I would never settle the kid question. In time, she might have overcome her resistance and agreed to adopt a child if I'd pressed my wishes strongly enough. But I dithered, unwilling to commit to fatherhood until I'd firmly launched my career.

I could not have known how persuasive Sarah's friend, Jack, in Washington, would be, in spite of her initial reservations about him.

These dear old friends from my youth, who were most of what I knew, then, about American life as the century neared its end.

Four years have passed now since I last saw Patty, in the lobby bar of the Portland hotel she checked into as she passed through the Pacific Northwest, on her way to an ESL conference in British Columbia. We had kept in regular touch through e-mail, though nearly two decades had passed since we'd sat face to face. The night we met in the bar, I had just retired after over twenty-five years in the trenches, teaching at Oregon State.

One of my last official duties had been to testify in a faculty hearing, attended by local law enforcement, on the matter of Barry Greiner's mental state: did I consider him to be a serious threat to himself or to others? Every few weeks, for three decades, anyone who had ever passed through the OSU English Department had received harassing e-mails from him. He insisted that a massive injustice had been committed in the 1980s, when "real" writers like him had been replaced (without due cause) by "false prophets." These "academic poseurs, creative writers," he said, had permanently damaged the capacity of higher education to "inform," in any meaningful sense, the tax-paying citizens of Oregon.

We should all be silenced, he said.

"No," I answered when asked if I thought he posed an imminent threat. Leave the poor bastard alone. Maybe I was thinking of Kaminski. Greiner had pissed me off. But I'd heard through friends of friends in Corvallis that he'd lost an eye to cancer, his lungs were weak because of all the smoke he'd inhaled as a firefighter. Since being dismissed by OSU, all those years ago, he'd had no health insurance.

My poor foolish town. I've forgiven everyone.

That night in the Portland hotel, Patty raised her glass in a toast. "To the future," she said. We were old. How could this silver-haired woman with painfully stooped shoulders be the spry young girl I'd married, briefly, in the 1980s? By now, she'd married and divorced again, and was starting over using an on-line dating service catering to "mature" clients.

She was co-writing her fifth textbook with a colleague. I had just published my tenth novel, the story of a Northwest conservationist inspired to save an endangered flock of birds. The novel's theme was Paradise Lost—how far we'd fallen, in the present, from the great figures of the past. The predictable theme of the disgruntled old man.

Patty and I reminisced with genuine fondness about the eight months we'd spent together in Corvallis, after the move from Houston. Eight months and then, impatient with me and my inability to come to a decision about children, she had driven away, back to Texas. At least, that's how she remembered our marriage.

I recalled, instead, my inattentiveness (without saying anything to her that night in the bar; no point, no point anymore)—my lack of full commitment to her on account of the letters I received each week from Silver Spring, Maryland, where Sarah had moved with Jack.

My sweet pal. I miss you [Sarah had written]. *Think about you a lot. It sounds as though you've been through so many alterations. How's teaching at the university? Does Patty mind if we write? Have you even* told *her we write? What do you do about time? Time alone, I mean. I find I'm frantic if I don't have at least one full day and night a week (weekend, usually) alone. Jack understands—sort of. But I think I make him sad with my insistence. The trouble is, I know he knows that when I'm alone, I'm thinking of you.*

Six months after writing that letter, Sarah married Jack. She suffered two miscarriages before they finally had a daughter together—complications from her abortion. Sarah tells me proudly now, in her generic end-of-the-year Christmas letter sent to all her distant friends, that her daughter works these days for the National Security Agency.

Akhmatova's notebook: Naturally, I wondered what had happened to it after I'd learned of Kaminski's passing. He had not donated his papers to any library or educational institution. I suppose I might have located Teresa in Portland, but I could not picture an encounter with her that would not be unutterably sad.

In the last ten years, several poets of my acquaintance have told me that Akhmatova's world is "too remote now from subsequent generations." Young poets "no longer have much of a feel for her."

The robin's-egg blue of the ink. The letters, beginning to fade.

Our dear Anna. Lost in the city of Kitezh. Heavenly reflection or rotting tomb? Either way, my love, stay and rest. Stay, for your own sweet sake. I'll know where to find you in the future.

That Sunday, the shuttle wound through the valley, past trailer homes and taverns, collapsing barns, hay ricks, cattle pens. The scent of mint. I closed my eyes. It had been a long weekend, an eventful visit. Before falling into a rich and sumptuous slumber—so deep I nearly missed my airport exit—I lifted my lids to catch a fleeting glimpse of horses, impossible, wild animals made of light, as they loped through the valley's tender mist.

NOTES

So Much Straw is a work of fiction. It veers, slightly, from the biographies of John Howard Griffin and Thomas Merton, though it remains largely faithful to the spirit of their friendship. The text makes frequent reference directly, indirectly, and obliquely to the following works:

By John Howard Griffin: *Scattered Shadows*, edited by Robert Bonazzi; *The Devil Rides Outside*; *Land of the High Sky*; *Black Like Me*; *The John Howard Griffin Reader*, edited by Bradford Daniel; *Follow the Ecstasy*, edited by Robert Bonazzi; *The Hermitage Journals*, edited by Conger Beasley, Jr.

By Thomas Merton: *The Seven Storey Mountain*; *The Way of Chuang Tzu*.

By Robert Bonazzi: *Man in the Mirror*.

By Lawrence S. Cunningham: *Thomas Merton and the Monastic Vision*.

The Education of Jack Elliot Myers is a prose poem, part fiction, part biography, part pastiche of the poet's own words. In sum, it is a textual celebration of Jack Myers. It borrows some language from his poems, and the text makes frequent reference directly, indirectly, and obliquely to Jack's work, in the following books:

Black Sun Abraxas (Boston: Halcyone Press, 1970).

The Family War (Fort Collins, Colorado: L'Epervier Press, 1977).

I'm Amazed that You're Still Singing (Berkeley: L'Epervier Press, 1981).

As Long as You're Happy (Saint Paul: Graywolf Press, 1986).

Blindsided (Boston: David R. Godine, 1993).

OneOnOne (Pittsburgh: Autumn House Press, 1999).

The Glowing River (Montpelier, Vermont: Invisible Cities Press, 2001).

Routine Heaven (Huntsville, Texas: Texas Review Press, 2005).

The Memory of Water (Kalamazoo, Michigan: New Issues Press, 2011).

Akhmatova's Notebook is a work of fiction. The notebook entries are invented. They make reference directly, indirectly, and obliquely to translations of Akhmatova's work in the following volumes:

Poems of Akhmatova translated by Stanley Kunitz with Max Hayward (Boston: Houghton Mifflin Company, 1973).

The Complete Poems of Anna Akhmatova translated by Judith Hemschemeyer, edited by Roberta Reeder (Boston: Zephyr Press, 1992).

Anna Akhmatova: The Word That Causes Death's Defeat, Poems of Memory translated by Nancy K. Anderson (New Haven: Yale University Press, 2004).

About the Author

Tracy Daugherty is the author of thirteen books of fiction and eight non-fiction books, including biographies of Donald Barthelme, Joseph Heller, Joan Didon, and Billy Lee Brammer. His biography of Larry McMurtry is forthcoming. His work has been honored by fellowships from the Guggenheim Foundation and the National Endowment for the Arts. He lives in Oregon with his wife, the writer and musician Marjorie Sandor.